Acclaim for SPIT AGAINST THE WIND

'A sympathetic picture of families struggling against poverty and stifled dreams . . . Kath and her group of friends tumble with all the energy and passion of youth. Their adventures are delivered with a wry and addictive humour until life finally dishes out a cruel twist that brings these scallywags up short. It all adds up to a riveting tale that tanks along without missing a beat' *Sunday Express*

'Powerful stuff as you might expect from Smith, a top Scottish journalist . . . A great read and hard to put down' *Glasgow Evening Times*

'Anna Smith's first foray into writing – apart from the small matter of a lifetime in journalism – definitely falls into the rarely-added-to category of modern Scottish classic literature . . . Smith's take on Scottish childhood is vivid, descriptive and colourful . . . She has the rare skill of creating a story that envelops the reader – at times, you will feel you are the fifth kid in Kath's little gang' *Aberdeen Press & Journal*

'A charming and evocative tale about the glories of youth with a bittersweet tang of reality' *The Big Issue*

'In the vein of Frank McCourt . . . An unsentimental reminiscence of a tough and touching childhood where innocence perishes' *Buzz*

'Powerful look at the harsh realities of growing up in a Scots mining village in the 1960s . . . Inspirational and heartbreaking' *Sunday Mail*

'The sights, smells and sounds of childhood are reawakened in this witty and charming tale of innocence . . . The vivid description takes you back to days gone by when heaven was a run on the beach and a sausage supper on the way home. The book leaves you yearning to be ten-years-old once more when life was simple and fantasy could block out the pain' *Belfast News Letter*

SPIT AGAINST THE WIND

Anna Smith

review

First published in 2003
by HEADLINE BOOK PUBLISHING

First published in paperback in 2003
by HEADLINE BOOK PUBLISHING

A REVIEW paperback

10 9 8 7 6 5 4 3 2 1

ISBN 0 7553 0359 8

Typeset in Minion by Palimpsest Book Production Limited,
Polmont, Stirlingshire
Printed and bound in Great Britain by
Mackays of Chatham plc, Chatham, Kent

Papers and cover board used by Headline are natural,
recyclable products made from wood grown in sustainable
forests. The manufacturing processes conform to the
environmental regulations of the country of origin.

HEADLINE BOOK PUBLISHING
A division of Hodder Headline PLC
338 Euston Road
LONDON NW1 3BH
www.reviewbooks.co.uk
www.hodderheadline.com

For my mother and father

'On Pembroke Road look out for my ghost
Dishevelled with shoes untied,
Playing through the railings with little children
Whose children have long since died.'

Patrick Kavanagh, 'If Ever You Go To Dublin Town'

Acknowledgements

I would like to thank the following: my sister Sadie Costello, who was first to read the script and had total faith; my agent Ger Nichol, whose absolute confidence in the novel lifted my spirits on a dreich day in Dingle; Marion Donaldson at Headline for all her help and encouragement; Tom Brown, as well as Joan Burnie, Norma Dewar and Ann Marie Nimmo of the *Daily Record* for their support; friends, Mag McGowan, Eileen O'Rourke and Helen Lennox as well as all the other great friends – not forgetting The Glee Club – who have always been there; the Trustees of the Estate of the late Katherine B. Kavanagh, through the Jonathan Williams Literary Agency. And last but not least my family, who have managed to put up with me all these years.

Chapter One

We could be anyone we wanted to in our dreams. We were cowboys, riding imaginary horses across grassy plains, clearing fences and firing guns from pointed fingers, then falling down clutching wounds that weren't there. We could argue for hours over whose turn it was to be Blue Boy from the High Chaparral and who would be Manolito. We were the family from the Big Valley and I was Barbara Stanwyck, sitting side-saddle on the wall.

We spoke to each other in Yankee drawl, mimicking with near perfection our heroes from TV war films and westerns. We may have fought a war each day, rustled cattle or killed a few bandits. But in our secret little world there were no sad endings, no tears, no concepts.

In the real world there were psychopathic teachers who got some kind of twisted pleasure out of torturing and humiliating you. There were drunken fathers who blotted out squandered lives in smoky, stinking pubs with men just like them who never even glimpsed their day in the sun. And there were mothers who you could hear weeping in the night as they saw themselves growing old in a world of broken promises and disappointment. Oh yes, and there were the shadowy perverts lurking in lots of corners, in the guise of uncles, priests and family friends.

But in our dreams, in the far-flung places we escaped to, nobody could touch us. We were safe and innocent and pure.

1

All of that changed in the summer of '68.

I fell in love as soon as I saw him. I was ten years old. He was eleven. He was digging a hole in the garden with a spade that was too big for his puny body. I watched him from the side of the road, his suntanned neck smooth and brown, soft little hairs wet with sweat in the hot sunny afternoon. He was new. We never had anybody new in our village. Everybody's families had grown up together for generations and seemed to marry each other's children again and again. We hardly ever saw anybody outside of the village, and now I was spellbound by this beautiful skinny kid with his sloppy joe and dirty blue jeans.

He looked up, straight at me, and my heart leapt.

'What you lookin' at?' I could have sworn it was an American accent. I was even more in love now.

'Nothin',' I said, standing my ground. He might have been beautiful but he was in my street and I had lived here for centuries. I stood where I was and kept watching.

To my amazement he pulled out a packet of cigarettes and shoved them towards me.

'Smoke?' he said, wiping his mouth and sticking a cigarette between his lips, just like one of James Cagney's kids from *Angels With Dirty Faces*.

'Naw, I stopped weeks ago,' I said casually, trying to hide my shock.

'Where'ye from? I've not seen you before. Have you just moved in here?' I asked, moving closer to the fence so we were only two feet away from each other.

When he looked up at me he had the bluest eyes I had ever seen, like pictures of the sky you see in calendars or magazines. His hair was soft and the colour of straw. He brushed his fringe away, then drew on the cigarette and blew perfect smoke rings. I was enthralled.

'I'm from America. The States. I just came here with my

mom. My dad was a pilot and got killed and she had to come home. She's got another husband now. He's Polish and he's a asshole. He's not my dad. Shit, I hate this place.' He threw the spade away and spat, glancing at me for reaction.

I could have listened to him all day. It was like having someone from the movies right in your own street. I couldn't wait to tell the boys. This was going to be something. A real American boy would be part of our gang. His accent wasn't exactly Yankee like the way we saw it on the telly, but it was better than ours.

'You want to come and play with us? We've got a gang, well kind of. There's three of us – two boys and me – and we're always hangin' about together. We do loads of stuff.' I was trying to sound casual, but I would have dropped dead there and then if he'd said no.

'Sure ... yeah ... there's nothin' else for me around this shithole anyhow. I hate bein' in the house with that Polack bastard.' He jerked his head in the direction of the house.

'Oh, by the way, my name's Tony, Tony Keenan, after my real dad. What's yours?'

'Kath ... it's short for Kathleen ... Slaven. Everybody calls me Kath.' I felt my face go red as he looked me up and down.

We stared at each other in silence, and his lips moved to the slightest hint of a smile. We were friends. And I knew there and then that I would have done anything for him.

The moment was broken by the sound of a sharp rat-a-tat on the window of his house from the inside. I could see the figure of what must be his 'mom' beckoning him inside. She looked tired. Her hair was in a kind of bouffant and flicking out at the bottom like Millicent Martin, a singer who used to be on the telly on a Sunday night. His mum looked as if she could be quite glamorous. It must have been all that time in America, because nobody around here looked remotely glamorous, apart from the bus conductresses, but everybody knew what kind of dirty women they were, with their short skirts and musty smells.

'I have to go, my dinner's ready. Come for me tonight, in an hour, er ... Kath?' he said, looking over his shoulder as he walked away.

'Yeah,' I said, almost in an American accent.

I was walking on air.

Before I even got to the back door I could hear them shouting. There was always someone shouting or arguing in my house. Nobody ever just talked about happy things or how the day had been. It was always conflict and grunts and everything done and said with some kind of edge to it. Except of course when they were talking to me. I could do no wrong in their eyes. I was the youngest of the family, and arriving late, being six years younger than my older sister and eight years younger than my big brother, I was to be protected at all times. I don't know how they came to that conclusion since I witnessed more fights and tears in that house than anything else. If it wasn't a row over my father being drunk and abusive, it was my mother and my sister Ann Marie bickering over how little freedom she got. She was sixteen, sweet sixteen my dad used to say when he was drunk, and she wanted it all, everything in the world. There was no pleasing her. And if it wasn't them it was my brother Kevin who was eighteen and all the man he would ever be, as he said, who would not be dictated to by a drunken father who spent every penny he got his hands on.

They were all screaming at each other when I put my head in the back door and I could hardly see them for smoke. I choked and started coughing. The place was black. Smoke clung to the walls. Even the holy water font with the Pope's picture in 3D full colour was streaked with black.

'Yer a bastardin' eejit,' Dad was shouting at Ann Marie, who was in tears, her black mascara running down her face. She had left the chip pan on while she was watching *Crossroads* and it was the smoke that wakened Dad, who had been sleeping off the afternoon's drink.

Fortunately Kevin arrived in from work just in time to catch the chip pan as it burst into flames. And being the hero he was, he calmly soaked a towel and smothered the flames, killing the fire, but sending clouds of reek everywhere.

'Right, just calm down. Nobody died . . . It was only a pan of chips, for God's sake,' Kevin was saying, gingerly lifting the chip pan away from the cooker and out of the back door.

'We could have been roasted to death because your head's fulla mince.' Dad's eyes were popping out of his head. His hands were shaking.

Just then the door opened again and in came my mother. She burst into tears straight away.

'Oh Jesus, Mary and Joseph, what's happened? Who's hurted?' Her hands were waving in the air as she spun around the kitchen looking for casualties.

She clutched me to her and I could smell the damp fleshy smell she always had on her when she came back from her work in the frozen chicken factory.

'Are ye all right? Oh my God, we could all have been killed,' she was sobbing.

I always felt like crying when I saw her crying and I had to shut my eyes tight to keep the tears back.

I don't know if she was crying because of the chip pan or if that just gave her an excuse to cry because of the hopelessness of everything around her. I used to lie awake at night and worry about the look in her eye sometimes. She was always so tired from getting up at five in the morning to work in that poxy chicken factory two miles away, where she was on the production line all day freezing to death, her fingers chilled to the bone and her feet raw cold inside the big black wellies she had to wear. Sometimes I used to go down to the main street in the village to meet her coming off her shift and I would watch as she and the rest of the factory workers, mostly women, piled off the bus, puffing their fags and gossiping great guns. The young girls were always having a laugh, but some of the older ones, like my mum, just looked weary and distant as they went their separate ways. But she always cheered up when she saw me, and sometimes she would even kiss me, which left me mortified in case anyone thought I was getting slobbered over. I had to walk fast to keep up with her and she never said much, but I knew she was always wondering what was waiting for her when she got home.

Nothing had turned out the way she had dreamed it would, or the way my dad had promised when they were young. It was just an existence, she said, not a life.

It was hard to imagine my mum and dad as young people like Ann Marie and Kevin when you looked at what they had become. She used to tell me stories about how it was great in the forties when all the young people from the villages around ours would walk for miles to get to a late-night dance in one of the local halls. She said she fell in love with Dad on the dance floor because of the way he looked in her eyes and held her. When he walked her home that night she knew they were meant for each other and that was how they stayed. But now it was all so different.

He drank and preached and ranted. She worked till she almost dropped, and tried to hide the debt and the grinding poverty from us. But we all knew. I could sometimes hear her crying during the night when she was pleading with him to help her and to stop getting drunk and stay in a job for a full month. But she adored him. And when he wasn't arguing with her or insulting her she was putty in his hands. They were the best times, when I heard them in bed laughing and then making noises I didn't understand. But at least they weren't shouting.

*   *   *

Jamie and Dan came round for me and I was out of the house still swallowing my last mouthful of food. I couldn't wait to tell them about the American. I told them he was just like the guys from the movies and that he swore. They couldn't wait to meet him.

We all stood on the steps of Tony's house and I knocked on the door. The boys were waiting with bated breath.

But when the door opened it wasn't Tony, but a big dark-looking man with a mop of black hair and a huge nose. It must be the Polish man, I thought.

'What do you want?' His eyes narrowed and his voice was thick. He was like the bad guy in a lot of the movies I had seen, with his lips drawn back in a scowl and his rasping voice. I hadn't met many real-life foreign people before, except for the missionary priests that came from Africa, where the black babies we paid for at school in class collections were praying for each and every one of us.

The Italians that had the chip shops and cafés in the town were all quite jolly people and spoke with funny Scottish accents mixed with Italian, and most people liked them, even though we called them Tallies.

But this Pole sounded dangerous. He scared me with his gruff voice and his big hands.

'T . . . Tony? Is he coming out?'

He didn't answer but looked all three of us up and down. Then he turned and bellowed in the direction of upstairs.

'Tony? Tony! Geddown here. The's friends here for you . . . c'mon.'

Tony came downstairs looking a little apprehensive, but I was pleased to see his face light up when he saw me. He quickly glanced at Jamie and Dan, who were smiling at the new celebrity.

'Don' be late, ya hear, or it's big trouble for you, boy,' the Pole said, slapping the back of Tony's head a little too hard for my liking. I hated him straight away. He looked like a bully and Tony would have no chance if he ever answered him back.

Tony said nothing and jumped down the stairs to join us. We were out of the gate and into the street. We strode past the tight terraced houses where people sat on the front steps in the early evening sunshine. We were free.

'Asshole,' Tony said, jerking his head in the direction of the house.

I nodded to Jamie and Dan, who smiled approvingly. This guy even swore like an American.

'Kath says your daddy was a pilot, Tony. That right? Was he in the war? Did he get blown up?' Jamie asked as we walked towards the old railway line that led out of the village and into the countryside.

'Yeah, he was a pilot and he was maybe in some war, I'm not sure. But he died just flying a plane and it crashed. That was when my mom came home because her brother used to live here years ago. Then she met that Polack bastard. He came here after the war ... He's no use. He's a tailor with his own shop in town, but he's a bad bastard. He hates me and I hate him.' Tony lit up a cigarette and tossed away the match, aware that Jamie and Dan were gazing at him in awe.

'So what do you do around here for fun?' Tony asked.

We looked at each other, wondering how we could impress him. What could you say to a guy whose dad was a pilot and died in a plane crash and who was an American? We didn't do anything. We never planned anything. We just went out of our houses because we couldn't bear to be in them for any length of time. Outside we were free to make up stories and live out our fantasies.

'We play football,' Dan said. 'And we swim in the burn, and make camps in the woods, and sometimes we steal turnips from the gardens. Oh, and we're altar boys. Do you want to be an altar boy? You have to speak to Father Flynn, but I'm sure he'll let you in.'

'I wanted to be on the altar too,' I said, not wanting to be left out. 'But they don't let girls in. Father Flynn said I could come to some of the altar boy meetings though, if I wanted . . . I might.'

'I don't know much about football, but I could do with a swim. Where's the woods? That's the stuff. An altar boy? Wow, Mom would love that, so would the Polack. He's always praying and sitting with his hands joined, but he's still a no-use bastard,' Tony said.

How we really hated that Polack, we were all thinking. That Polack bastard. For if Tony hated him that was all that mattered. We were all one now, and I could see by the looks of Jamie and Dan that I wasn't the only one who was in love with him.

Chapter Two

S t John Bosco's Roman Catholic school stood at the top of the hill. It had been there for ever as far as I knew, because my dad used to tell stories about his grandad and others from the nearest village walking up to it in all weathers in their bare feet. It was the same with the chapel a few yards away from the school. People used to walk there in their bare feet too, and I was sure they must be in heaven by now if they made that much of an effort to go to mass. There was a story years and years ago, even before my dad was born, that one bad winter, when the village was covered in six feet of snow, a little boy of about seven who got lost in a blizzard was found dead the next day. They found him all stiff and blue in a snowdrift on the hill. People said that on a winter's night if you listened carefully you could hear him crying in the wind. Sometimes in the snow on the way home from school I would stand at the top of the hill and look down into the greyness of the houses in the village all huddled together beneath a blanket of smoke from the coal fires that burned inside them. You could smell the smoke in the air and it felt good imagining everyone inside all warm and cosy. But if I was on my own I didn't ever stand around too long in the snow, just in case I heard the lost boy crying.

Most of the people in the village were Catholics, and my dad told me their grandparents and great-grandparents had come over from Ireland to Lanarkshire on the boat looking for work down the mines and in the ironworks because the Protestants and English were starving them to death in Ireland and burning them from their homes. They came here, he said, for a better life, and I used to think that it must have been disappointing for a lot of people down the years to find out that this was what they crossed the sea for. He said we were Irish as well as Scottish and we had never to forget that, but I couldn't quite understand why he got so excited about it, especially when he was drunk and singing songs about Black and Tan soldiers. It was all too complicated, but as long as you knew what you were you were sound enough.

The Protestants had their own school at the edge of the village, but there weren't so many of them, and we were led to believe their school was smaller because they weren't so important. We even felt sorry for them because they would never go to heaven like us, no matter how good they were. I supposed a lot of them might end up in Limbo like the Catholic babies who died before they were baptized to get rid of the original sin, but they would never be up there with us and God and the angels and saints. I couldn't quite understand that but it was just the way things were. I felt sorry for my Protestant friends, though, who I used to play with in our street, because they just didn't know any better.

I also used to wonder why the teachers just wanted to punch and slap people all day long. Most of them looked ancient and there were one or two it was hard to work out whether they were men or women. They had moustaches and slicked-back hair and they smelled of mothballs and tobacco. I was three months in one class before I learned that the man teaching us was actually a woman.

But nobody terrified us more than Miss Grant. I had seen movies before with people like her in them and they were always in asylums or locked up somewhere. She haunted me in my dreams and made my stomach churn every time she looked at me with her slightly wall eyes under her butterfly glasses. Sometimes when she looked at you you thought it was the person behind, and if you turned around you might just feel the wooden duster hit you on the side of the head. For impertinence.

Tony had been put in our class although he was a year older. Jamie, Dan and me reckoned that it was because he knew more than us and we would learn from him. We used to 'reckon' a lot lately and we used to say 'I guess' a lot, just little Americanisms we were picking up from our new friend.

Tony was only in the class about four days when he got his eyes opened to daily life under the regime of Miss Grant.

She had gone out of the classroom for some reason and we immediately started carrying on. Someone rolled up lots of paper and made a reasonable-size ball which we started throwing around the room and punching like a volleyball. In minutes the whole class was up, diving across desks and hooting with laughter. It was great fun. Tony was brilliant at punching the ball and could jump higher than anybody else.

We were so wrapped up, we didn't even hear Miss Grant come in until she slammed the door shut, nearly shattering the glass. We stopped in our tracks.

'Rrrr . . . right! Quiet!' She was screeching, her mad eyes bulging behind her specs. 'Rrr . . . right! Who started this? Come out, the culprit, and take your punishment, you dirty little vagabond. Come out! Come out!' She strode up and down the front of the class, swaying with rage.

Nobody moved. Everybody stood rooted to the spot because they knew what was coming.

'Hmmm. OK. One by one. You will all get punished until the culprit owns up!'

In a flash she grabbed Marie McCann by the shoulder and pulled her on to the floor. Marie was already in tears. Miss Grant lifted her skirt and her pants and started to slap rapidly, about thirty times. We watched as Marie screamed and her bum went all red. Then Miss Grant tossed her to the side and grabbed Martin McGuire. She pulled up his shorts, exposing the fact that he had no pants on. He was one of nine children, and I guessed there weren't pants for everyone. She started to slap him with the same frenzied motion as she had the girl. Then she grabbed another and another, slapping them then tossing them to the floor. I wished the door would open and another teacher would come in and help us. But then again, I thought, maybe they would join in.

We all stood terrified, waiting our turn. The girl next to me started to whimper and a puddle of water formed between her feet. Still Miss Grant continued with her orgy. She was sweating now and saliva was gathering at the side of her mouth. I wanted to go out and push her to the floor, but I was so scared I couldn't move.

Then out of the corner of my eye, I saw Tony push past me and run out to the floor.

'Stop,' he said. 'It was me. I started it. Leave them alone. It was my fault.' He stood over the huddle of beaten children sobbing on the floor.

His face was ashen. We all breathed a sigh of relief but we couldn't believe what we were seeing. She would kill him.

Miss Grant was crazed. 'Oh, it was you, Mickey Rooney. I might have known. Well, you'll be sorry now, you wee Yankee pagan.' She was almost smiling with delight.

Tony was wearing his blue shorts and she made him turn his back to the class as she pulled them right up at the leg, exposing his left buttock. His head was trapped under his arm as she leaned over him with her full weight. She started slapping him feverishly, longer than the others and harder. She even stopped for a breath and started again. No sound came from Tony. We thought he was maybe dead from shock. Then she seemed to stop, like she was spent or exhausted. She let Tony go and he stumbled, pulling his shorts down.

He limped back towards us. I caught his glance and my eyes filled with tears. His face was red with anger. There was a strange look in his eye, but he said nothing. He never shed a tear. Everybody sat in their seats, well, those who could sit down. Miss Grant sat back in her chair looking like a rabid dog who had just been shot by a tranquillizer dart. She seemed to be drifting away in a different world. The bell rang, and she just looked up and barked, 'Go! Get out!'

We all shuffled out in silence. Everybody walked close to Tony just to touch him. We had a new leader.

There was a place we were not supposed to go to. A dark, secret place that the bigger girls and boys from the junior secondary went to at night, away from the eyes and ears of the village. It was deep in the woods, further than the old steelworks, which was nearly three miles in and much further than we would ever have ventured. It was here, many years ago, when everybody's father in Lanarkshire went down the pits, that the coal was carried by rail across an enormous viaduct to fire up the furnaces for the steel that made the big ships. Or so we were told by teachers and parents.

But we only knew it as Shaggy Island. We weren't quite sure what the Shaggy part meant, but we knew it involved boys and girls and that every time it was mentioned in whispered tones people sniggered behind their hands. For there were a lot of inhabitants of Shaggy Island of an evening, teenagers who used to steal quietly away from the village at nights to smoke and drink and do whatever it was they did.

I often wondered if it was a bit like the Garden of Eden, with people walking around with no clothes on and the kind of funny looks on their faces we saw in the catechism stories about temptation. The very thought of ever going there, just for a look, used to occupy much of our time, and eventually curiosity and temptation overcame us.

I was already feeling guilty by the time I left the house, even though I wasn't sure what I would find at Shaggy Island. I slipped out without saying where I was going while my mother was upstairs and my dad slept on his chair.

Tony, Jamie and Dan were waiting for me by the time I got to Tony's gate. We didn't say much to each other, we just nodded knowingly. This was a mission, a bit like the Man from Uncle, and sometimes special agents like us just had to do things.

It was a warm June evening, the sun slipping lower in the sky, sending a huge orange glow across the fields that stretched ahead of us. One side of the sky was bright red from the chimneys that belched blazing fires from the furnaces inside the steelworks. We jumped the fence into the fields at the edge of the village and on into the countryside, watching for cattle that might be in the mood to chase us.

The grass had just been cut by the farmer and it was flat, hard ground like a racecourse. Some kids who had been there before us had built make-believe fences from grass piled up, and immediately Jamie assumed the voice of a racehorse commentator.

'They're under starter's orders . . . and they're off!'

On cue we all started running, racing against each other with Jamie commentating as we chased across the field.

'And coming up to Beecher's Brook now it's Scobie Breasley on Arkel on the outside from Joe O'Brien on Black Shadow chasing him on the rails. There's only five furlongs to go . . . it's . . .'

We ran and ran, whipping our horses with imaginary sticks and pushing ourselves faster and faster, jumping over the flimsy fences. Tony was like a gazelle, but Jamie was catching

16

up, even though he was still commentating breathlessly.

'And they're at the winning post, it's a photo finish in the Grand National . . . What a sensation . . .' We stopped, panting and laughing, by the big oak tree.

'A photo finish my ass,' said Tony, laughing and wiping the sweat from his head. 'I won.' He danced around with his hands in the air in triumph, saying, 'And here he comes to receive the trophy from Her Majesty the Queen . . . the Grand National winner, Tony Keenan!'

He came up to me and I handed him the trophy, shaking his hand. He bowed.

We quickly got our breath back and all four of us stood looking out at what lay ahead. We had important business to attend to. Shaggy Island was only a short walk away. But we had to be careful that nobody spotted us.

Dan put his hand to his mouth and flicked up his thumb, which was the aerial of his walkie-talkie. 'OK, all systems go.' He murmured into his hand as we all clenched our fists and held them close to our ears, awaiting further instructions.

It was dark in the woods and we kept looking back for a glimpse of the daylight that was getting further and further away. We were all a little scared, hardly breathing, walking softly, almost creeping into the thicket.

'Stop!' Dan said, sniffing the air. 'I can smell smoke . . . we must be nearly there.'

We all stood hushed, our ears pricked. Somewhere in the distance there was the sound of girlish laughter and boys mumbling. We had to be very careful. We followed the sound, darting in and out of trees, watching for snipers.

Further into the woods and down a steep embankment, there it was. Shaggy Island.

It was walled off by branches that had been cut down from trees and piled on top of each other to block the way in. We picked our way around the wall and found a pile of branches so we could ease ourselves up one by one and peep over to see inside.

Jamie was first, standing on Dan's bent-over back and pushed up by Tony and me. He peeked over the wall.

'What d'ya see?' Tony whispered.

Jamie strained his neck. 'A lot of boys in a queue. They're all laughing . . . I don't know.'

'Come down,' Dan said, then we helped him up. 'I can hear a girl, but I can't see her . . . just the guys.' He jumped down. It was Tony's turn.

Whatever he saw he said nothing. He just stared with his eyes wide. He seemed to be there for longer than the other two.

'C'mon, you, let me see,' I demanded. Tony looked at me and jumped down. I was up like a shot.

My eyes scanned the camp from one side to the other. There was smoke coming from a small campfire and jackets and bottles lying scattered around it. Then I saw the crowd of boys in the queue and wondered what they were waiting for as they giggled excitedly. I thought maybe somebody had some drinks or food for them and they were waiting in line. Then suddenly my jaw dropped at the vision before me and I almost fell. As one boy walked away from the queue, the crowd seemed to part momentarily and I saw what looked at first like white breakfast rolls jiggling in mid air against a tree. But when my eyes focused I could see that there were legs attached to them and a pair of trousers at the ankles. What was happening? Was he dancing? Who was he dancing with?

'What is it?' Dan asked. 'What d'ye see, Kath?'

'Sssh . . . wait . . . I think they're dancing.' I was transfixed.

Then the flushed face of a girl I thought I recognized seemed to emerge over the boy's shoulder. Hold on, I knew that face. I knew those auburn curls, that pouting red mouth. It was my sister. Ann Marie. She was smiling and giggling. Her skirt was up. What was she doing? She couldn't be. This couldn't be.

Not Ann Marie. Jesus, I thought. Jesus, Mary and Joseph. My dad'll kill her if he ever finds out.

I don't know how I managed it, but I calmly jumped down and said to the boys, 'Right, I think that's enough now. I think one of them saw me. We'd better get going.'

Tony caught my eye. He knew. He had seen it too. The look said it all.

'Let's go,' I said, and we ran and ran.

We didn't speak until we were out of the darkness of the woods and back across the field. Then, as we slowed down, Dan said, 'What d'ye think they were doing?'

'A line-up,' Jamie said with an air of authority. 'It's that shaggin' thing, with a lot of guys and one lassie. I've heard big Joe Murphy talkin' about it.'

'One lassie?' Dan said. 'I didn't see any lassie.'

I said, 'I think Jamie's right. But we shouldn't have seen that. We'll need to tell it in confession now. Anyway, never mind about it now. We better get home, it's getting dark.'

We walked home almost in silence. Nothing would be the same again now that we had seen what we saw over the wall in Shaggy Island. Our minds were confused. I don't know if Jamie or Dan saw everything and were just being kind by not mentioning it, but I knew that Tony had seen it all. He could see my shame.

By the time we got to our street, the others had gone home and it was only Tony and me who walked together. We didn't speak. There was something more between us now, and we didn't have to say anything.

When we got to Tony's gate we stopped and stood for a moment. The light from the streetlamp shone on my face and I could feel my eyes fill with tears.

He reached out and touched my arm, squeezing it gently. I wished he hadn't done that because now I felt like sobbing. I bit my lip and felt my throat choke.

'It's OK, Kath, it's OK ... Don't worry.' His voice was soft.

Tears spilled out of my eyes. I turned from him and ran all the way home.

I was surprised to find my mum and dad sitting watching telly together with my brother Kevin. They hardly ever sat like that. She was always working about the house and he always seemed to be getting ready to go out or was coming back from the pub to set the tone of the night. But this was good, and I felt happy for a moment, forgetting what had happened earlier.

I kicked my shoes off and had some toast and tea, snuggling up to Kevin on the couch. He was great. He would never have taken part in anything like the stuff we saw. He would kill those guys if he knew. But I wondered what he would think of Ann Marie. She was different from us. She never really had any time for me and she just argued with Kevin all the time. Kevin put his arm around me and I felt safe. As long as he was here I would always be safe, I thought. Even if Mum and Dad were screaming and crying and Ann Marie was doing line-ups at Shaggy Island, everything would be fine as long as I had Kevin.

I went to bed, to the room I shared with Ann Marie, and lay watching the bare lightbulb hanging from the rose. I picked at the wallpaper. I hoped Tony wouldn't think bad of me after what he saw of my sister. I heard the front door open and could hear the muffled arguing of Dad's questioning Ann Marie over where she'd been all evening. Then there was the sound of her footsteps coming up the stairs and I closed my eyes tight, pretending to be asleep.

I heard the rustle of her clothes as she pulled them off and I peeked out of one eye as she sat on her bed taking off her pants and pulling on her nightdress over her head. Her breasts were plump. I dreaded the time I would get them and maybe had to do what she did. Her face was red and her eyes looked as though she had been crying. I didn't know why, but I was filled with sorrow for her. I turned my face to the wall so that she wouldn't hear my sobs. Then in the stillness as I held my breath I could hear her weeping into her pillow.

There were laws to be followed by every one of us. But in their homes, in the little empires they'd built, the men were the only law. They could slap their wives from the house out into the street and no other man would intervene. They could go straight from work to the pub and drink a whole week's wages while wives and children waited at home to be fed, and nobody would dare step in and tell them they were wrong. It was the men who made the rules, and broke them as and when they pleased. No wife would dare embarrass her man in public, and if she did, she would take what was coming to her.

The night it happened to Jamie's mum left all of us angry, confused and scared. We would never forget it.

Jamie's dad Jake was a born loser, I had heard people say. Almost every week, if he had a job, he would go straight to the bookies and gamble all his wages. That in itself wasn't too unusual, and my own dad did it from time to time, as did other people's dads. It was quite acceptable once in a while. But Jake McCabe did it nearly all the time.

The night it happened, we were playing football in the street near where Jamie lived when we heard the commotion. Jamie was the first to stop in his tracks when he heard his mother's screams and his dad shouting.

We all stopped and followed the noise. As we approached, I was horrified to see that Jake had his wife Mary by the hair and he was dragging her out of the gate of their house. She was screaming to leave her alone, her desperate cries filling the night air and making me feel sick with dread. When she saw Jamie running towards them she was pleading with Jake.

The other three McCabe children were out in the street in their pyjamas, bawling for their mum.

'For God's sake leave me! Leave me! Look at the weans! Oh please!' She screamed as he slapped her on the mouth with the back of his hand. Blood spurted from her lip.

Jamie ran towards them. 'Daddy, stop! Stop, Da! You're hurtin' her!' he pleaded, trying to grab his dad's arm.

'Fuck off, you, or you'll get it next!' Jake spat, his eyes blazing and his face wet with sweat.

Curtains twitched in the windows of homes all around the street and one or two people were at their doors, their arms folded, watching the sideshow. But nobody stopped Jake. It was his fight. I was filled with rage at them. Why couldn't they help her? They might as well have been out there holding her down while Jake was punching her.

I ran to my house in the next street and burst in the door to get my dad. He was just in from the pub and looked a bit drunk.

'Quick, Dad, you'll have to come, Jake's killing Mary in the street! Hurry!' I urged breathlessly.

He looked at me gravely and took me by the shoulders to calm me down.

'You sit down where you are, Kath, it's not your business now, nor mine. It's for Jake and Mary. Now sit down and let them get on with it.'

I couldn't understand. I sat down, trying to get my breath back.

My mum came in from the kitchen drying her hands. 'What's happened, Martin? What happened to Jake and Mary?'

It was fairly straightforward in Dad's eyes. Mary had come into the public bar where all the men were, looking for her husband. Jake had been standing at the bar holding court with the lads. He wasn't all that drunk, Dad said, but drunk enough to turn nasty. She demanded him to empty his pockets, chouting that the weans were starving and that there was a procession of debt collectors at their door. Jake stood and took it all, saying nothing. But Dad said his face grew very dark and everybody knew there would be trouble.

Dad said: 'Every man in the bar was shocked to the core by what Mary did. It isn't done. In the public bar, for God's sake. No woman in her right mind would walk into a man's place like that and humiliate her husband.'

Mum was angry.

'It doesn't matter a damn what she did, Martin. She doesn't deserve a beating. You should go out there and stop it.' She went and looked out of the window. 'Look! Half the street's standing watching and no bugger will help the poor woman. I'm going out there,' she said, turning away from the window.

'No you're damn well not,' Dad said, standing in front of Mum with his arms blocking her way. 'Listen, Maggie, it's not our fight. Aye, it's a shame all right, but it's McCabe's business. I knew by the expression on his face as he finished his pint after Mary went out of the pub that she would be in for a right hiding. But it's not our fight. We'll mind ourselves and let them get on with it.'

'Why can't you stop him, Daddy?' I protested.

'Because it's not our fight. Now you behave,' he barked back, giving me that look that told me not to contradict him.

I was distraught. Tony came to the door for me to tell me it had calmed down and that Jake had stopped hitting Mary but he wouldn't let her back into the house. He said she was sitting on the steps crying, with blood on her face. He said Jamie had been pulled into the house by his dad and that he was trying not to cry in front of Tony and Dan.

I slipped out of the house and went with him to see what was going on.

Mary was sitting on the front steps of the house sobbing,

with her head in her hands. Tony and me stood watching her, not knowing what to do. Her mouth was bleeding and she kept wiping it with her hand in between sobs. I took my sweatshirt off and gave it to her to clean her face. She was shivering.

'Away home, hen! Go on, Kath, don't stay here. I'm all right.' She tried to compose herself.

I knew it wasn't my business as my dad said, but I knocked on the door anyway, and shouted through the letterbox.

'Jake! Jake McCabe! Let her in! Let Mary in! Ya big bastard!' I was shocked that I had actually come out with that. So was Tony. The door opened and Jake appeared, still sweating and angry. I backed away.

'Fuck off, you, before I kick your arse up and down the street an' all! Now fuck off!' He slammed the door without so much as a glance at Mary.

Mary sobbed even more. Tony and me backed away. I was distraught. I could hear the children wailing inside and I looked up at the bedroom window where Jamie was standing in tears, half hidden by the curtain.

'C'mon, Kath, let's go home.' Tony pulled me by the arm.

The talk the following day was that Jake wouldn't let Mary in and she sat on the steps all night. He finally opened the door early in the morning and she went back inside. All along the rows of terraced houses on either side of the road, people must have been looking out of their windows from time to time, but they did nothing about it. It made no sense.

We saw Mary the next day with her black eye and her burst lip. She looked at me and tried to smile, but her eyes were sad and swollen.

Jamie came out to play with us and we never mentioned the events of the night before. There were some things we just didn't talk about.

Chapter Three

Today was the day. As soon as I opened my eyes in the morning the normal tiredness and groans of getting out of bed for school were absent. It was the school trip to Ayr and we'd been talking about it and waiting for it for months. It might not have been such a big deal to some of the kids in the class, but to the likes of me and others who hardly ever went on holiday, this was as close as we got. I couldn't wait. It would be Tony's first school trip and he was really excited. The sea at Ayr wouldn't be as big as his ocean in America, but we told him how fantastic it was. We would bring our swimsuits and run into the sea as soon as we got there. It was going to be great.

I could hear the rain battering on the windows of my bedroom, but I didn't give up hope. We'd see. The sun would shine.

Downstairs my dad was making my breakfast, which was always a bad sign. He must have upset Mum before she went to work, either that or he was planning something. He only ever got out of bed to make the breakfast when he was trying to make it up to Mum or else was scheming. His breakfasts were always terrible. He was skimpy with the milk and the cornflakes were almost dry, choking you as you tried to eat them. He never buttered the toast at the edges either, not like the way Mum made it, with lumps of butter melting into the bread. There was no use complaining, though, because he just harped on about how it was when he was fourteen and down the pit with a bottle of water and bread and dripping. So I didn't say anything, just ate the stuff. Soon I would be out of here for a whole day at the seaside.

My duffel bag was all packed up by Mum before she went to work. Everything was there, the swimsuit, the jumper in case it got cold, the sandwiches of poached egg which smelled a bit already, and an apple.

'There's your money on the mantelpiece, Kath,' Dad said, handing me my anorak.

I counted it. There was a ten-shilling note plus a half-crown. My heart sank. Last night when my mum was getting me organized for the trip I knew there were two half-crowns on the mantelpiece. Kevin had given me one and I had saved up one. I had been checking it all night, picking it up, feeling it, smelling it. I never had that kind of money except on a school trip. I knew there was a half-crown missing. Dad couldn't look me in the face. He stood with his hands in his pockets looking shifty.

'Right, c'mon then, you're goin' to be late. What's the matter?' He tried to look innocent. I had seen that look before. I wasn't mad. I felt sorry for him because he knew I knew what he had done.

'Nothin',' I said, trying to sound cheery. 'OK, Dad, that's me. I'll get you and Mum a present . . .' I breezed out of the door.

When I looked back I could see him standing at the window, watching me go down the path and along the road. He looked sad. Like the way he looked when he had promised you something and then made up a story because he couldn't deliver it. He always knew that I knew he was lying, but I pretended to believe him and that was just how it was.

Tony was waiting outside his gate for me and my heart lifted when I saw him. He was beautiful in his light blue jumper and khaki trousers. His mother appeared at the door clutching a brown plastic raincoat and shouting, 'Tony, Tony, you forgot your raincoat,' which obviously he hadn't.

'I don't want it, Mom, it's going to be sunny.' He looked up at the grey sky, the rain slapping his face.

She rushed out anyway and handed it to him, but he defied her, folding it and pushing it into the haversack which he had slung over his shoulder. She walked away shaking her head.

She was a pretty woman, not in the kind of way my mum was, but more in a painted way. No matter when I ever saw her, she always had lipstick on and her cheeks were always red as if someone had pinched them. She was a kind woman and I liked her a lot. When I used to go into the house with Tony, now that we were inseparable, she was always offering me a glass of milk and a biscuit. She fussed over Tony constantly and it was always great when there was just the three of us in the house. But when the Pole was in there was always a feeling that something was about to happen. Whenever he walked through the door she seemed to shrink somehow and look afraid. I could understand it because he was a very gruff man and could barely utter a grunt in my direction. But that didn't bother me, as bullying old men like him were ten a penny around here. I wasn't afraid of him at all and he knew it. I always looked him in the eye when he gave me a mean look and I could see it put him off. I wondered how Tony's mum could ever have married him. He was older than her and was always miserable. Most people I knew who were married didn't talk to each other very much, they just seemed to exist in the house for the children. My mum and dad talked and argued and fought, but sometimes I would see the way he looked at her and his eyes would be soft and I would know that he loved her a lot. But with the Pole and Tony's mum there was none of that. I had overheard my parents talking one night, saying that she had a boyfriend she was involved with after she married the Pole, and that she only married him to give Tony some kind of security. Dad said that the Pole had been too miserable to marry anybody and had been on his own since he came to Scotland and set up his own business as a tailor. My mum said she wouldn't be surprised if Tony's mum had a boyfriend, and no wonder, living with that fat old man. My dad used to laugh because I think he knew who the man was. Men just knew things like that.

By the time we got to the top of the hill we could see the school trip bus revving outside the school gate. The excitement was brilliant. We quickened our step. All the kids from our class and the class above us were on the bus and waving at the parents outside, some of whom were in tears. The rain was coming down in sheets and our hair was soaked by the time we got on the bus. Kids were pulling open windows and stuffing streamers outside which flapped briefly before becoming soggy in the rain and sticking to the wet windows.

The driver in his shirt sleeves banged the horn three or four times and we were off, with Mrs Lannigan, the deputy headmistress, shouting, 'Hip, hip . . .' and us all cheering as loud as we could, 'Hooray!'

The dreaded Miss Grant sat at the front of the bus and only got up to do a roll-call to make sure nobody got lost when we got to Ayr. We sat and answered, 'Here!' in a grudging way when our names were called. We had never forgiven her for that day she went crazy in the class, beating everyone, especially Tony.

Miss Lannigan was more fun. She looked a bit like an old man with her white hair pulled back in and some soft white hairs at the sides of her top lip, but she wasn't bad like Miss Grant. She did slap the kids in her class sometimes and we used to see her belting kids with a leather strap, but she didn't seem as dangerous somehow as Miss Grant.

She was marching up and down the aisle of the bus, organizing a sing-song.

'Right ... We'll start off with Our Lady's favourite hymn, "The Sun Is Shining Brightly", and if we sing it really loud then maybe Our Lady will hear us and make the sun come out, OK? One, two, three ...' She began to conduct us enthusiastically.

We all sang till our hearts felt they would burst. 'The sun is shining brightly, the trees are clothed with green, the beauteous bloom of flowers on every side is seen. The trees are gold and emerald and all the world is gay, for it is the month of Mary, the lovely month of May.'

It was actually the end of June, but how we belted that hymn out. It felt great to sing it. You could see the trees and the flowers and the sun blazing down on the big happy world with Our Lady standing smiling benignly from heaven. Soon it would be sunny. We followed it up with 'Sweet Heart of Jesus', then a medley of songs from *The Sound of Music*. 'My Favourite Things', 'Edelweiss', 'Doh a Deer'. The more we sang, the more Miss Lannigan began to look like Julie Andrews and we were the family Von Trapp off to the mountains to escape the Nazis and win the talent contest along the way.

We sang and sang, but suddenly the air was filled with a familiar stench and one by one we all turned up our noses and the song faded out. All we could hear was the retching of Joanne McGuigan being sick through her hands and on to her skirt. Elizabeth Reilly was sitting next to her and leapt from her seat as Joanne lashed vomit again and again. I looked around the bus, feeling a bit sick myself. Suddenly others started vomiting. The smell was overpowering. Tony was sitting next to me, his face the colour of stone. Dan and Jamie were convulsed with laughter and pretending to be sick over each other. Miss Lannigan slapped them on the back of the head with a flick of her hand.

29

Everybody was grabbing for windows to open, gasping for some clean air.

The driver pulled in to the side of the road and brought up the bucket and sawdust from the front of the bus. He cleaned the place up, his face twisted as if he too was about to be sick.

Finally it settled down and Miss Lannigan assured us we didn't have far to go. We would soon be there. 'Just keep looking out of the window for the water and see who's first to spot it,' she was shouting.

The bus trundled on through the countryside and it felt as though we were going to the end of the earth. We all trained our eyes on the horizon, desperately looking for the sea. But we had only left the school half an hour before and we must have been miles away from the sea. But we all looked anyway, willing it to emerge from nowhere just as we willed the sun to shine. And so it did. Just as we arrived at Ayr, while half the bus was asleep, the sun poked its head out from behind the clouds and suddenly the day was bright and clear and beautiful, just like the hymn. It glistened on the water that stretched for miles and miles. 'See?' Miss Lannigan said proudly. 'I told you Our Lady would make the sun shine.' And we all nodded our heads in total belief. Our Lady could do absolutely anything.

Everybody piled out of the bus, relieved to be breathing some clean fresh air and marvelling at the wet pavements steaming under the sudden blaze of the sun.

Other buses had already arrived carrying schoolkids and old folk on day trips and the seafront was busy with kids darting along the promenade and jumping off the high wall on to the sand. Others made their way to the chip shops and cafés, and the smell made us long for a bag of chips soaked in vinegar and salt. Our packed lunches could never match that, but we wouldn't have dared throw them out.

You could hear the hum of engines from the fairground at the end of the pier and see the lights flashing on the waltzers and dodgems. I loved the shows, and I was always mesmerized by the tough guys who worked the rides, with fags dangling from their lips as they did daring balancing acts on the moving waltzers while they collected money from customers.

A bunch of young kids were standing on the grass watching a Punch and Judy show. They were squealing with laughter as the ugly puppet Punch battered Judy with a stick and then set about the policeman. Tony, Dan and me all looked at each other, then glanced at Jamie, who was biting his lip. I hated Punch and Judy. Whenever I had the measles or something and my temperature was high, I used to see ugly faces like that in my sweaty nightmares.

Some other kids were queuing to get their pictures taken by a photographer who had a tiny monkey on his shoulder. The guy looked shifty and the monkey, dressed in a sailor's suit and hat, jumped all over the place. When it opened its mouth wide I could see that it had no teeth and it didn't seem a very happy way to spend your day if you were a monkey, standing around in Ayr when you should be swinging about in the jungle.

But the most magical sight of all was the waves rolling into the shore, and we couldn't wait to get in there.

'OK now, children, everybody gather round and listen to the rules.' Miss Lannigan shephorded all the children on to the grass at the edge of the car park.

We all stood, shifting around impatiently, desperate to get our swimsuits on and into the sea.

'Right, it's midday now and we all must be back at the bus by three thirty in the afternoon. I don't want anybody going into town unless they ask. There's a mile and a half of beach to play on and there are shows at the pier. I'll be around here and Miss Grant won't be very far away if you need us. So everybody go off and enjoy themselves and don't go into the water out of your depth. Now be careful and . . . just enjoy yourselves.' Miss Lannigan knew she was giving us lots of space to run around unsupervised, but she also knew that nobody would disobey her for fear of the consequences.

Miss Grant stood beside her looking even more miserable and mean than usual. She must have really hated children.

As soon as Miss Lannigan dismissed us we ran to the changing huts at the edge of the beach as though if we didn't hurry the sun would disappear and our day would be ruined. In a flash we were all changed and on to the beach, our milk-white bodies almost transparent in the glare of the sun. We were free. We jumped around and ran up and down, not going anywhere in particular, but just laughing and screeching with joy.

Then everybody looked towards the changing huts and doubled over with hysterical laughter.

Nora Brennan came sidling out, her head down, her face crimson with embarrassment. What was she wearing? It was some kind of adult bathing costume with big, hard breasts that made her look like a midget woman. I burst out laughing at the unbelievable sight, then stopped when I saw her pain. The boys were roaring with laughter. Some of them were rolling around in the sand clutching their stomachs in convulsions.

I ran towards Nora, who was standing at the edge of the changing rooms with tears in her eyes. When I got closer I could see that what she was wearing was in fact a big person's swimsuit, maybe her mother's or her big sister's, but it had the bump shapes at the front like the movie stars wore and it was definitely not for a ten-year-old girl.

'C'mon, Nora, it doesn't matter,' I said. 'The boys are just stupid. Nobody'll notice in ten minutes. C'mon . . . stop crying.' I took her by the arm.

'It's . . . it's . . . my m . . . m . . . mum's swimsuit. I haven't got one. She said I could go in with my vest and pants on, but I wanted a costume. But look, Kath . . .' She put her hands on the bumps. 'It's got big tits and everythin',' she sobbed.

I took her hand and pulled her towards the crowd on the beach. Nora was one of seven children and her dad was in a wheelchair. They were even poorer than most people in the village and got a lot of their clothes from the St Vincent de Paul. I glared at the boys, who were still smirking, but beginning to calm down when they saw Nora's tears.

Joe Reilly, as ever, would not let up though.

'Hey, Nora, you look like Marilyn Monroe wi' yer big diddies.' He burst out laughing and one or two others joined him.

'Look, shut it, you,' I snapped at Joe and looked at Tony, Jamie and Dan for moral support.

'Yeah, c'mon, who cares? Last one in the sea's a horse's ass,' Tony piped up, taking off and giving himself a head start.

Everyone ran after him, including Nora Brennan, her big stiff chest sticking straight out as she raced across the sand.

What a day we were having. We splashed each other and dived into waves of freezing water. Even in the strong sunshine our bodies were turning blue with cold and covered in goosebumps. We shivered, but we stayed in the sea, spitting out mouthfuls of salt water at each other and floating on our backs pretending to have drowned.

Jamie and Dan were picking up baby crabs and chasing the girls with them to hoots of laughter.

Tony and I had a walking race in the sea, collapsing with laughter when the waves knocked us off our feet. He took my hand and pulled me out of the water.

He was so beautiful. The drops of water glistened like tiny beads on his shoulders and his hair was soaked and dripping on to his face. He squinted at me in the sunshine so his pale blue eyes were just like half-moons. I never loved anybody as much in my whole life.

'Will you marry me, Kath?' Tony looked straight at me, his eyes with a funny kind of pleading like he would have died if I had said no. I almost swayed with the shock and excitement.

'Aye. Yeah, course I will . . . but not till we're older.' I tried not to splutter. All I could hear was the sound of the waves and all I could see was Tony's face. There was nobody else in my entire world right at that moment.

'Would you let me kiss you, Kath?' Tony stepped towards me, reaching his hand on to my arm.

'Yeah, yeah . . . OK . . .' I was babbling.

Then it was done. On the lips. In less than a second. His lips brushed mine and he looked into my face and smiled. I could taste the salt. Nothing would ever feel like this again.

'That your first kiss?' Tony said, splashing water on me and diving back.

'No way. I've been kissed lots of times. Lots,' I said, chasing after him, kicking water on him.

'Oh yeah?' he said as he ran off faster than I could catch him, and in a moment we were back with the crowd as if nothing had happened. But it had.

We all spread our towels down on the beach and sat down to have the lunches that had been lovingly packed for us by our mums. Everyone was eyeing each other's sandwiches, asking what they had. The ones who had jam sandwiches, like Nora Brennan, were embarrassed. Others had cheap meat spread and Martin McGuire had butter and sugar, protesting when some people started laughing that it was all he wanted. When I pulled my cold poached egg sandwiches out of the duffel bag the smell filled the air.

'What've you got, Kath? A jar of farts?' Dan said, bursting out laughing, and the others held their noses.

'Ha, ha, very funny.' I tried to sound confident but I was embarrassed at the smell. No matter though, I was half starved and wolfed them down in no time.

We were all lying back feeling the sun burning our faces and the salt water making our skin feel tight. Tony, Dan, Jamie and I were as usual sitting in our own little group. Everything felt great. We were full up from the lunches we had scoffed and we just lay there listening to the waves crashing. Tony was sitting up staring along the beach when suddenly his eyes narrowed as he focused on something.

'O-oh! Look what I see. Payback time, kids.' He got on to his knees and screwed his eyes up, watching a figure in the distance.

We all sat up and looked in the direction he was watching. It was quite far away, past the end of the sand dunes and a long way from where there were any people swimming. But we could make out the figure of a woman in a swimsuit, folding her towel and her clothes in a neat pile on the beach, then limbering up by swinging her arms in big wide circles. There was no mistaking who it was. It was Miss Grant. We all looked at each other and sniggered.

I don't know if the same thought was in everybody's mind, but it was obviously in Tony's because he was the first to mention it. And anyway he was the one who had been humiliated by her. He stood up, with his hands on his hips as if he was addressing his troops. We hung on his every word.

'You know, guys, sometimes bad people just get away with it all the time, and kids like us never got to say nothin' And sometimes a little chance arises when we can give back some of the shit they deal out. Well, today, it's the turn of that fat-assed bitch to get what's comin' to her.' Tony looked each one of us in the eye. We knew what he was thinking, and it was too good, too dangerous and too exciting not to go along with.

This was a major mission, more secret than anything we had ever done before. More perilous than ever, and we would have to swear that no matter what, we would never admit any part of it to anybody, even in the confessional. We were all agreed. We nodded to each other and piled each of our hands one on top of the other. We were special agents and we would never desert or betray each other, no matter how much they tortured us.

We crept along the sand dunes using the slopes and potholes for cover as we snaked our way towards Miss Grant, who we could see walking towards the water. On our bellies we crawled the last few yards so that we were looking down on her little pile of clothes lying wrapped in her towel on the deserted beach. We watched and waited. We had all the time in the world.

'Right,' Tony said, raising himself up on his elbows and whispering to us. 'You three keep your eyes on Grant and make sure if she turns around you shout me and get off your mark. I'll get her stuff and then we'll run like the wind with it until we find a place to dump it.'

'What, really dump it . . . like in a bin or something?' Jamie said, wide-eyed.

'Course, dopey. She's gonna come out of that water and wonder what the hell has happened. She'll get the biggest red face she ever had in her life. Hey, and what's more, she's gonna have to walk back on to the bus with her swimsuit on. Howya like that?' Tony had a determined look on his face.

We all imagined the scene and we loved it, even if it was a little scary.

'OK, I'm off,' Tony whispered, and he was over the hill and crawling along the beach.

Miss Grant was splashing in the sea and swimming out further and further. She was a fearsome swimmer, strong and thrashing her big arms into the waves. She was enjoying herself alone in the water and I wondered why she had to be so bad to everybody all the time. But I couldn't allow myself to feel sorry for her, because she had what was coming to her.

Tony was like some kind of desert hunting animal the way he crept his way across to the clothes and snatched them almost in

one seamless movement. He scarpered a few yards then dived
into the sand dunes for cover. The three of us watched in awe
as he came towards us. What a hero. As he approached us he
waved us to start running and we did. We ran a few hundred
yards past the old bandstand and into the car park of a hotel
where there was a huge dustbin.

'Quick, in here,' I said to Tony, who was running faster than
any of us. As he ran towards the bin with us trailing after him
he dropped a pair of pants and Dan lifted them up and waved
them around giggling. We all collapsed with laughter when we
saw the big hole in the back of them.

'She must fart like thunder ... I knew she was a secret
farter,' Dan giggled, poking his finger through the hole.

We could hardly stand up. Tony was laughing too, but he
had more important things on his mind. He dumped the
clothes into the dustbin, then grabbed the pants off Dan.
He took a match out of his shorts and set fire to the pants
then threw them into the bin. We watched, a bit shocked, as
Miss Grant's clothes went up in smoke. Through the smoke we
could see the smiling faces on the wall of the hotel advertising
Francie and Jose at the Gaiety Theatre. I smiled to myself,
thinking of the funny Glasgow guys with the suits and the
gallus walk.

'Enjoy your swim, Miss Grant,' Tony said as the clothes
caught fire.

It was great, but it was scary as well. Maybe we had gone
too far. We all hoped deep down we would be able to carry
this off and keep it to ourselves. This was our biggest test yet.
This was a rollercoaster. It was like hanging on to the back
of a lorry and not knowing where you would end up. It was
going to be some afternoon.

'Jesus, Tony, what if we get caught? We'll get killed.' Jamie
seemed worried but had the look of devilment in him and was
still smiling.

Tony's eyes narrowed as the smoke billowed out of the bin. He had a wild, angry look in his eye. I remembered it from the day Miss Grant beat him in the class.

'We won't get caught, 'cos we did nothin'. We'll deny it till we die. It's our secret. Stuff her! She's a bad bastard and she deserves it! All of them do, all of the bad bastards who piss our lives up. Stuff them all! Stuff Grant, stuff the Polack, stuff every scumbag bastard who wastes it for us!' Tony's eyes were blazing with a rage that none of us had seen on him before.

'Yeah ... stuff them. Stuff all the bastards! Stuff my da! Stuff them all!' Jamie spat, his eyes red with anger, his mind in the dark place that passed for home.

'Aye, and stuff ... stuff ... Father Flynn! Stuff the bastard!' Dan blurted out, and everybody turned to him, bewildered. He was edgy, angry, his bare chest heaving as he tried to get the words out.

'Father Flynn?' I asked, bemused.

'Aye. He, er, he ... k ... k ... kisses me! He kisses me, the big poof!' Dan's face was tight with anger.

'What?' I said, shocked, dismayed, confused. 'How? Where? How can he kiss you? He's the priest.'

We all stood looking at each other, then looking at Dan. His fists were clenched. There were tears in his eyes. We didn't know what to do, what to say. The silence seemed to go on for ages.

'He ... kisses me. In the sacristy ... sometimes after mass.' Dan faltered, the words barely audible. 'He pulls me on to his knee and kisses my face ... I don't know what to do. Nobody'll ever believe me! You probably think I'm telling lies, but I'm not ... I think he does it to other boys as well, but nobody'll say.' Dan was nearly in tears.

'He touches me I'll punch his lights right out,' Jamie said, raging.

Whatever this was, whatever was being said, we didn't

understand it. How could that happen? It was all confusing. Tony stepped in to bring us back to the mission of the moment.

'Right, listen. We'd better get movin'. We'll talk about this later. Let's get back to the crowd before old farty bum gets out of the sea.'

We ran across the sand dunes, our hearts bursting with excitement. We couldn't wait till the moment when Miss Grant would come out of the sea all refreshed only to find out she had no clothes. We could all picture the scene. But overshadowing all of that was the bewildering image that Dan had just painted. Even the adrenaline rush of what we had just done to Miss Grant could not erase the thought of Father Flynn kissing Dan in the sacristy after mass.

When the heavens opened up, it seemed it would rain for ever. We had just finished buying our presents at the shops and were heading for the beach to pick up our stuff. The rain had started to fall in huge drops, splattering on to us as we gathered our belongings. The sky had grown black and thundery, thick slate-grey clouds gathering in from the sea. Then the rain came in torrents as we made our way back to the bus. People were rushing from everywhere to get shelter in shops and cafés. Suddenly the whole place looked drab and sad.

The monkey man stood at the edge of the car park with the rain running out of him. He swigged from a half-bottle of cheap wine. The monkey sat on his shoulder looking tired and bored, the water dripping off its sailor's hat.

Inside the bus we settled ourselves down, our faces and hair wet from the rain. I sat next to Tony, and Jamie and Dan were in the seat across the aisle from us.

We said nothing, glancing only fleetingly at each other when Miss Lannigan remarked that it was three thirty and Miss Grant still wasn't on the bus. We were the only ones who knew the secret. We even knew that she had been wearing pants with a hole in them. It was magic.

I gazed past Tony and out of the window at the rain lashing down. I wondered if Miss Grant had drowned. I hoped not, or we might be implicated in it. Wherever she was at this moment she must be the angriest she had ever been in her whole life. I felt a smile on my face and I was surprised at how much I was enjoying this. I rubbed the steam away from the window and through the grime and rain I could see the figure shambling towards the bus. I nudged Tony, who looked out too, his face never even flinching. There she was in all her glory. Miss Grant. Soaked to the skin in her bright green swimsuit. Her hair hung around her shoulders like rat's tails and her big rubbery thighs were the colour of raw link sausages. She was barefoot. She almost staggered towards the bus. Tony watched, his face impassive. Dan and Jamie strained their necks for a glimpse, but managed to keep their faces straight. This was the moment we had been waiting for. This was payback time.

Miss Lannigan got to her feet with the stunned look of someone who had witnessed something she could scarcely believe she was seeing. She bounded out of the bus and went towards Miss Grant, who was weeping hysterically. The driver dived out of his seat with his jacket and rushed out to cover Miss Grant's embarrassment. There were shrieks and giggles on the bus, but they came to an abrupt halt when Miss Grant climbed up the stairs and stood before us, dripping wet, her body flushed and blotchy, her butterfly glasses all steamed up. There was such a silence we were all afraid to breathe in case it would give the game away.

'S . . . s . . . some . . . Atchoo!' She tried again to get the words out. 'S . . . some of you did this . . . someone on this bus took my clothes.' Her lip trembled. 'But don't worry . . . I'll find out . . . Oh, and when I find out . . . Atchoo!' Miss

Grant looked like the scariest woman we had ever seen. If her whole face had transformed into a snake or a monster or a dragon breathing fire, nobody would have been surprised. All the children on the bus sat stunned, terrified. They had never seen anything like this before. Tony, Dan, Jamie and me sat staring straight ahead. We never spoke nor dared even look at each other.

Miss Lannigan ushered Miss Grant into her seat, then slowly she began to walk up and down the aisle. Our hearts were in our mouths. We had to hold steady. We had to. Miss Lannigan looked each and every child in the eye.

'If it ever comes to pass, children, that any one of you had even the slightest bit to do with what has happened here today, then there will be a wrath upon you that will surpass all understanding. If anyone on this bus has done this, they will pay. And if they don't pay in this life, then there is not the slightest chance of them ever getting into heaven. You will burn in hell and nobody will give you a drop of water for your roasting tongue. I hope you understand that. Do you?' She looked gravely at everyone.

'Yes, miss,' came the resounding reply from the bus load of innocents. Nobody on the bus believed that anyone in their midst would have been capable of doing such a thing. But each and every one of them wished in their hearts they could have been a part of it.

The bus engine revved and we were on our way home. Tony nudged me.

'We're home and dry ... unlike some people I could mention.' He didn't even smile.

I stifled a laugh. I felt great. The heat of the bus soon warmed us and in minutes we were all drowsing, our eyes heavy. My head seemed to slip on to Tony's shoulder as I dropped off to sleep, and I could feel him slide his hand into mine. I was the happiest I had been in my life.

Chapter Four

As the bus pulled into the village we could see the parents standing waiting at the cenotaph where the statue of the soldier stood as a reminder to everyone of the brave boys from our village who gave their lives during the war. All their names were inscribed proudly at the bottom of it, and the cenotaph was the central meeting place where everyone passed the time of day with each other and gossip was added to and lapped up by one and all.

All the kids strained their eyes to see their mums and dads, eager to get off the bus and tell the big story of the day, of how the trip was fantastic, but even better than that was Miss Grant arriving on the bus soaked to the skin, wearing only her swimsuit.

I could see my mum standing talking to Tony's mum, and Jamie's mum was talking to another group of people. But there was something wrong. Nobody was waving back to us in the normal enthusiastic way. All the mums and dads had grave, dark looks on their faces.

Then, as the bus slowed to a stop, we saw Dan's uncle Brian standing looking through the window to see if he could see Dan. His face was red and his eyes looked as though he had been crying. Dan's mum wasn't in the crowd, and we couldn't work it out. Dan had been laughing and joking with Jamie as he scanned the crowd looking for his mum, but when he saw his uncle Brian, his face fell. Something bad had happened. We all knew it.

When the bus stopped, Miss Lannigan got out first and was told something by one of the mums. She shook her head and put her hand to her mouth. She came back on to the bus and stood in the aisle.

'Dan Lafferty, come out a moment, will you?' she beckoned him.

There was fear and confusion in Dan's eyes as he looked at each of us. We were all scared. He picked up his bag and went to the front of the bus. We watched as he climbed down to the street and was met by his uncle, who put his arm around him and ushered him away from the crowd. Some of the mums burst into tears. We could see Dan looking up at his uncle who was crouching over him, telling him something. Then Dan's face crumpled into tears and his uncle clutched him tightly. We were almost crying watching. It must have been something very bad.

Miss Lannigan came back on to the bus, looking very serious.

'Children,' she began, 'something terrible has happened. Dan Lafferty's dad Tommy has been killed in an accident at the pit. There's two other men dead as well. It's been a terrible tragedy. I want you all to mention Dan in your prayers tonight. This is a very sad and difficult time for him and his family. A terrible time . . .' Her voice trailed off. She was an old teacher and must have seen moments like this before when she had to take children out of the class and tell them someone had died.

We sat stunned, hardly able to take it in. Two hours ago we were laughing and screaming and playing the dirtiest trick we had ever done to anyone. Now Dan's dad had died. What was it all about? Was God punishing us? Was that it? We all felt guilty inside. I could feel tears coming to my eyes. Poor Dan. He was the funniest of all the boys in the class and in some ways the baby. And after what he had told us about

Father Flynn, it wasn't fair that he had to go home now and not have a daddy. Who made all these rules? Dan's dad was the best man in the village. He worked every hour that God sent, my mum said, and all he did was look after his wife and kids. Everybody respected him. He was one of the few people left working in the pit, which was being wound down and would soon be closed for ever. But that would be too late for Tommy.

We all got off the bus, shuffling, sad and shocked. As Tony got to the front, Miss Grant grabbed his wrist and stopped him in his tracks. She still had the driver's jacket on, and a towel wrapped around her waist. But it wasn't big enough to cover her enormous thighs. She had on a pair of black gym shoes that Miss Lannigan used to wear when she was teaching us country dancing. Miss Grant held Tony's wrist there for a moment, not saying anything, but looking him straight in the eye. I knew and Tony knew what she was thinking, but Tony stared straight back at her. She might suspect him, but she could never be sure, and he knew that.

When I got off the bus, my mum came towards me and hugged me. I was already in tears. I couldn't look at Jamie, who was walking with his mum, his chin in his chest. Tony stood on his own while his mum was still talking to people in the crowd. She came across to him and ruffled his hair, then they walked away. He had tears in his eyes.

On the way home we passed the Lafferty house, and there were people coming and going all the time. The blinds were closed to tell the world that someone had died. Dan's mum Theresa would be breaking her heart. She was always carrying on with Tommy. They were like young people, still having a laugh. It was hard to understand how quick your life could change. I kept thinking maybe I would wake up and it had all been a bad dream.

'What happened, Mum?' I asked when I could compose myself.

'Oh Kath, it was awful. Poor Theresa, she's in an awful state. It was the black damp . . . you know, the gas down the pit. They just seemed to walk into a pocket of it and it killed them instantly. You get no warning with it, you know, no warning at all. It's terrible . . . terrible. No way for any man to earn a living . . .' She was shaking her head, her voice trembling.

My dad had worked in the pit for years, but got out of it three years ago. I remembered him coming home with his face still grimy, even though he had had a shower at work. My mum used to look out of the window every day when he left and then her eyes looked sad, because she hated him going down into the darkness, never really knowing if one day he wouldn't come back out. It ruined people, she used to say. It made young lads old before their time, and sucked the life out of decent men. She hated it and so did my dad.

Our house was eerily quiet when we got in. Dad was sitting staring at the empty hearth, his face hard and his mind somewhere else. I could see that he had been drinking. Ann Marie was reading the newspaper and Kevin was making the tea. Nobody was saying much. I sat in the chair opposite Dad, not speaking, just looking at him.

Finally he looked up.

'Ah, Kath, ma wee darlin'. How was the trip?' He was drunker than I'd thought.

'Great . . . great, Daddy. B . . . but . . . Dan's daddy's dead. Terrible, isn't it?' I said.

He shook his head and stared at the hearth again.

'He just would not be told, Tommy Lafferty and the others. They would not listen. I told them that pit was a death trap and it was time it was shut, but no, Tommy would work till he died. Well, he's dead now, and Theresa's a widow and Dan and his brother and sister have no da. A lot of good that did him, working himself to a bastardin' early grave' His voice was angry, but tired and sad.

Kevin came in from the kitchen and gave me a playful punch.

'Where's the presents then?'

'Oh . . . I could only get some pens and an ashtray. There wasn't much.' I turned my bag out on to the floor and produced an ashtray in the shape of a big seashell. It had some kind of poem on it from Rabbie Burns. The lines read: 'O wad some power the giftie gie us, to see ourslels as ithers see us.'

'What does that mean, Kevin?' I asked.

'Oh . . . it's some very wise words, that we should all take to our hearts, Kath,' Kevin said, but he was looking at Dad, whose eyes never left the hearth.

The three of us, Jamie, Tony and I, had sat on the back steps of my house for about half an hour trying to work out how we would approach the Lafferty house. We didn't know if we should go there, but at the same time we wanted to see Dan. We didn't know how he would be and what we should say.

We decided to wait until it was time for the rosary, then we would go in like everyone else and pray at the coffin – as long as we didn't have to look at Dan's dad. We were curious because none of us had seen a dead body before except in the films, but the thought of it was too scary.

People were arriving in droves at the house to pray over Tommy Lafferty's body, but it was still sunny outside. It didn't seem right. We slipped into the house and stood in the hallway hardly breathing as the house filled with people. We could hear the hushed tones coming from the living room and through the space in the half-open door I could just see Theresa Lafferty sitting on the chair, weeping with each person who came in and hugged her, passing on their respect and their tears. All you could hear were sniffs and sobs and sighs. I could see what looked like the edge of a coffin by the window. I strained my eyes to see more, dreading the moment I might catch a glimpse of the dead face, yet curious to see what it looked like.

The hallway was filling up and everyone was talking in whispers. A path seemed to clear when Father Flynn swept through the door, his prayer book in his hand. His big legs seemed to take the hall in three strides, and he nodded to people, his face sad but with a knowing look in his eye. I supposed that with him being a priest he would know where everybody went when they died. It was only the likes of us who had no idea and were crying when somebody left us. The priests always said they had gone to a better place. I often wondered where it was. It wouldn't have to be great or anything like that to be better than where we were. Just a better place would be fine. I was glad in some ways that Tommy was in a better place, because then he wouldn't have to work in the dark every day with the dust in his lungs and the sweat pouring out of him. But I bet that no matter where he was he missed Dan and Theresa and the rest of the family. I didn't understand all this stuff about a better place. But that was how it was.

The moment Father Flynn was about to go into the living room, Dan appeared at the door and they came face to face. Father Flynn immediately put his arm around Dan's shoulder and pulled him towards him, gently. For an awful moment, we thought he was going to kiss him, but much to our relief he didn't. The colour rose in Dan's cheeks. He obviously thought the same as us.

Dan managed a half-smile to us and we could only do as much back.

'In the name of the Father, the Son and the Holy Spirit . . .' Father Flynn's Irish voice boomed out the rosary and there was a general rustling in pockets and purses as everyone got out their beads.

Jamie, Tony and I counted the Hail Marys on our fingers. It seemed to go on for ever. Finally the end came. 'Hail, Holy Queen, Mother of Mercy, Hail Our Life, Our Sweetness and Our Hope ... To Thee do we send up our sighs, mourning and weeping in this vale of tears ...' We recited it parrot fashion, but our minds were far away in the hideouts where we made our own little dreams and fantasies. Nobody could touch us there, or so it had always seemed. But as we prayed and listened to the sobs from every corner of the room we each knew our lives were changing. Through the door I could see Dan sitting in the corner crying his eyes out. I could feel myself choking back tears until I could hold them no more. I kept my head down and the tears ran down my face and dripped off my chin.

When the rosary finished people started to filter away, but the living room was still full of women sitting around with handkerchiefs in one hand and beads in the other. There were long, sweaty silences, then some old person would utter some words of wisdom that seemed to be to nobody in particular.

'Oh Jeez, it was a quick call for Tommy all right. Too quick ... Too quick.'

'Oh aye, but it's not the now, it's the long winter nights she'll miss him!'

Theresa was sobbing softly and shaking her head at the thought. My mum sat next to her, holding her hand.

All the men were in the kitchen where my sister Ann Marie and some other teenage girls were clattering cups and gathering plates with mountains of sandwiches to hand round to everyone. Dan's uncle Brian was pouring whisky into glasses for the men, who were standing around with their black ties on and their faces serious. My dad's eyes were red as though he had been crying, but it might have been the drink. My brother Kevin stood at the opposite end of the kitchen with Jamie's cousin Arthur. They were both swigging from cans of beer and smoking furiously while they talked intently with each other. I thought I heard Kevin say something that sounded like, 'When Dessie and me get to Australia . . .' It was said during a pause in the conversation in the room and I think my dad heard it too, because he shot a glance at Kevin that could have turned him to stone. Kevin didn't flinch, though, and looked straight back at him.

Uncle Brian took Dan by the arm and ruffled his hair.

'Away and take some sandwiches and a bottle of lemonade outside wi' yer pals, son. Ye don't want to be standin' around in here wi' all the big people. On ye go now, son.' He motioned Dan to the table. Dan collected some sandwiches and wrapped them in a tea towel. We looked at him, hoping he would lift some fairy cakes as well, and were glad when he did. The four of us shuffled out of the back door.

It was getting dark but it was muggy and warm, and we sat down on the grass at the top of the garden. Everything around us seemed to be so quiet. Even the birds weren't singing and the sound of the odd dog barking seemed to make the gardens that backed on to each other lonely and empty places. We all ate our sandwiches in silence, nobody quite sure of what to say.

'Did you see him, Dan? Did you look?' I couldn't believe Jamie had just come out with it. Tony and I looked mortified, but we were also curious. We all looked at Dan. He looked at each of us.

'Aye.' He took a deep breath. 'I saw him. He was funny-looking . . . like he was sleeping. But he's not.' Dan looked at the grass.

'Did you touch him?' Jamie ventured.

'Oh for God's sake, Jamie,' I said, exasperated.

We all waited for Dan's response. It seemed to take ages.

'He was freezing, like ice. No, colder than ice. It wasn't like my da at all . . . it's not my da.' His voice began to quiver and he looked at me with tears in his eyes. 'Oh Kath, why did he have to die? He was just my da. He was great . . .' The tears ran down his face and his body heaved as he sobbed. I put my arm around his shoulder and Tony leaned over and touched his leg. Jamie sat with his knees tucked up to his chin, fighting back tears.

'It would have been better if it had been my da,' Jamie said, tears in his eyes. 'At least my ma would get peace.'

Nobody spoke. We all just sat waiting for Dan to stop crying. Eventually it was Tony who broke the silence.

'I wonder if Miss Grant has dried out yet?' We all looked at each other and burst out laughing, remembering how fantastic and scared and excited we had felt just a few hours ago.

'Do you think she'll ever find out?' Jamie asked, stuffing a whole fairy cake into his mouth.

'She grabbed my arm when I was coming off the bus and the ugly bitch looked me full in the eye. She thinks deep down it was me, but she'll never know. And that's the good part. As long as we stick together, she'll never know,' Tony said, looking at all of us, willing us to stick together.

'Don't worry,' I said. 'She'll never find out. It's our secret till the day we die.'

There was another long silence as we looked at the crescent moon that was just visible as the sky grew darker.

'Did you ever see your dad's dead body, Tony?' Jamie asked. I looked at him, then at Tony. You just never knew what Jamie was going to come out with next. Tony's face went very serious. He didn't say anything for what seemed ages. Then he took a deep breath.

'Look, guys, er, it's not the way I said it was . . . er, everything. I just didn't know how to tell you, because I was scared you would think I was just an asshole, but I . . . well, I kind of lied about my dad.' His voice was beginning to shake. We had never seen him like this. He never showed any kind of weakness. We were stunned.

'What do you mean, Tony?' I said. 'Is your dad not dead? Was he not a pilot? What . . . what do you mean?'

Tony sat up straight and stretched his legs out in front of him. Then he shifted around uncomfortably before settling down with his legs crossed. We all sat waiting desperately to hear his story.

'Well, it's kind of a long story . . .' he began. His mother had gone over to America to work as an au pair in the home of a US pilot and his wife. She worked there for months, but fell in love with the pilot, who made her pregnant. He loved her even more than his wife, who was not a good woman by all accounts, but he could not leave her because they also had kids. The pilot moved Tony's mum out of the house so their secret could be safe and put her into a little house in the country, and that was where Tony was born. Until he was eight years old, he always just thought his dad worked away from home. He visited most weekends, but left in the middle of the night, though sometimes he would stay over. He always brought Tony presents. But his mom always cried and cried for hours when he left. Then one day, about two years ago, a letter came and his mom was in bed for days not able to speak to anyone. He used to hear her at night weeping and sobbing. He wasn't sure what was wrong, but guessed it must be something to do with his dad. Finally she told him that he had been killed in a plane crash.

'It was a long day when she told me that,' Tony went on, 'because she also told me the whole stuff, about him being married and all to someone else, and that was why he was hardly ever there. I was mad at him at first for making her life like that, but then if it wasn't for him I wouldn't be alive. And he was really a good guy. He loved me, I think. He was always buying me stuff . . .' Tony's voice trailed off as he remembered.

'Jesus, Tony, that's terrible,' I said. 'It must be terrible now, living with the Polack who doesn't like anybody, when you had a really good dad.'

'I hate the Polack,' Tony said, his face reddening.

'At least you've got a dad,' Dan said.

'Yeah, but he beats the shit out of me . . .' Tony's voice began to tremble. 'You know what he does, he takes his belt off his trousers and beats my bare back and legs. He's a goddamn monster. And he hits my mom too. He hits me when he's mad at her because he knows it will upset her. He's like . . . he's like some kind of torturer. I hate him.' Tony was in tears now. We were all shocked. We had never seen him cry before. We sat in silence. Tony sniffed and sobbed into his hands. I wanted to put my arms around him, but I didn't know what to do.

From the house we could hear someone singing.

'Oh the pale moon was rising, above yonder mountain . . .' One of the men was belting out the old Irish song that everybody seemed to sing at parties. The wake had started and the men would sit up all night by the body of Tommy Lafferty, telling stories and singing and drinking. We all sat and listened to the song that told the story of a beautiful woman who was the rose of Tralee. It seemed a sad song somehow. All of the songs they sang seemed sad. They were all about loving somebody who was far away or who died, or about dreaming of going home to some place they could never get to because the sea was so wide. Every now and then the back door would open and someone would leave, the men and women all hugging each other and crying. Tommy Lafferty was in a better place. But who would hug him and cry with him? I wondered. And who would laugh and sing songs with him when all the men had had too much to drink? I looked up to the night sky and wondered if he was missing us already.

Chapter Five

In my dream there was a coffin and I was edging slowly towards it. The faces of everyone in the room seemed to be larger than life, with blotchy, rubbery cheeks and swollen eyes. They were slurping tea and looking at me with wild, mad eyes. I crept up beside the coffin and looked inside. Tommy Lafferty was lying there with his face as black as it would be when he came up from the pit. He had on a white satin shroud and entwined in his joined hands were rosary beads. I reached into the coffin and put my hand on his black face and felt the icy-cold forehead. Colder than ice it was. Suddenly his face broke into a big toothy smile and he sat up in the coffin laughing like a crazy man and grabbed my hand. Everybody in the room shrieked with laughter as I tried to pull my hand away.

I woke up at the bottom of the bed, struggling to get my hand free from the grasp of a dead man. I was sweating. But at least there was nobody holding my hand. I lay in the quiet of the dark, my breathing slowly coming back to normal. Then I heard the sound of raised voices. It was my dad and Kevin. I sat up on the bed, straining my ears.

'I don't need your permission, so that's where you're wrong.' Kevin's voice sounded angry and indignant.

'You're goin' nowhere. You're hardly out of school and you know nothin' of the world. Australia! Who do you think you are? Some kind of bastardin' adventurer?' Dad was emphatic. But Kevin's voice was becoming hysterical.

'You just don't get it, do you, Da? There's nothin' for me here apart from the family. This place is a shithole where my only future is the factories or labouring. Well, if I'm going to labour I'll do it in the sun, somewhere there's a chance my life can be different. Can you not see that? Can you not get it into your thick head? I don't want to be like you. I don't want to end up like you, bumming about the pub, pissin' my life up against the wall.' There was the almighty sound of something falling over and glass breaking. I leapt out of bed and raced downstairs.

I was horrified when I barged in the door of the living room. The coffee table was overturned and cups were smashed. Dad was on top of Kevin and had him pinned on to the couch. Mum was crying and trying to pull Dad back. But his face was crimson with rage and drink. Kevin's was too and he looked as though he was drunk. There were tears in his eyes.

'I should take you outside and batter you up and down the street, you ungrateful, big-headed bastard.' Dad had his shut fist up against Kevin's face.

'Martin! Don't! Martin! For God's sake, both of you!' Mum was sobbing and trying to keep me back.

'Dad! Stop! Kevin! Stop!' I was in tears.

Kevin turned his face towards me, then he looked Dad in the eye and grabbed his fist away from his cheek. His cheek looked red and angry.

'Don't you hit me, Da! 'Cos you'll regret it. I'll hit you back, by God I will! Don't make me do something I'll have to live with for the rest of my life! Now get your hands off me. You're a drunk, a useless excuse for a man, and I'll never be like you! Do you hear? Never!' Tears streamed down Kevin's face. Dad released his grip and got unsteadily to his feet. He walked out of the room, the tears spilling out of his eyes. I wanted to run to him. I wanted to run to Kevin. I wanted to stop my mum crying. But I didn't know what to do, so I just cried all the more.

Kevin was sobbing as Mum picked up the broken crockery that was strewn across the carpet.

'Mum, I'm sorry . . . I'm sorry.' He tried to help her. He pleaded, 'Mum, why can't you understand? I have my own life to live. There's nothing in this place for me. You want me to be happy, don't you, to make something of my life? I know I have a chance in Australia. Mum . . . please, it's my big chance . . .' Kevin wiped his face with his sleeve.

'I know . . . I know, son,' she said. 'But Australia . . . It's so far away. It's the other end of the world. You'll be lost to us . . .'

'I won't, I'll keep in touch. But I want my own life, for me.'

Mum sat down with the pieces of broken cups in her hand. She sighed.

'I know, I know. You have to do what you feel is right. But Kevin, you shouldn't have insulted your father like that. He'll be broken over it. Don't you think he has little self-respect as it is, without you hurting him like that?'

'But he talks at me as if I am a nobody, as if I was put on earth just to do what he tells me. Well I'm not.'

I watched his face as Mum tried to explain to him. She told him it wasn't Dad's fault he was the way he was. Nothing seemed to work for him. He had just given up and turned to the drink. But he was a good man in his day, bright too, and with dreams like Kevin and other young men. Somewhere along the line it all got lost and now he was bitter and angry. But he loved his family and he loved Kevin more than anything. He was just the kind of man who couldn't show his feelings to a big lad like him, so it came out in anger and frustration. Kevin would have to apologize. Swallow his pride and give his father some kind of way out of the situation.

Mum was right. I knew and so did Kevin. But he wasn't ready yet. He said he was going for a walk. He needed to be alone.

I helped Mum clear up and make some more tea. She poured a cup for me and we sat at the kitchen table drinking it in the quietness.

'Will we never see Kevin again?' I ventured, the thought too much to bear.

'Oh, we'll see him. But not like now, Kath. He's going all right, and we can't stop him. I've already lost him . . .' Tears were in her eyes as she stared into space.

We sat in silence. Then she got up and poured a cup of tea and took it upstairs to Dad. I listened at the bottom of the stairs and could hear snatches of his conversation through his sobs.

'I've ruined it for everyone, Maggie. Kevin's right. I'm no use . . . I'm a waster and always have been. Look at you . . . You're beautiful, Maggie, and you're old before your time because I gave you nothing. Now my boy has grown up and he wants to punch my face. He's gone now, Maggie, gone for ever. He's as dead to me as Tommy Lafferty lying in his coffin.'

I drank my tea and tried to imagine Australia. It always looked sunny and dry and hot on the television, and Skippy the bush kangaroo was always solving everybody's problems. So was Flipper. It didn't seem such a bad place. But it was far away, further than anywhere I could ever imagine, and that was where Kevin was going. My stomach had butterflies at the thought that I might never see him again. I couldn't bear to think of that. Surely he wouldn't leave me. Not Kevin. I climbed the stairs and went to bed thinking of Australia and Flipper and Skippy. My mind was so full up I would never sleep.

I could tell by the light that it was too early to get up for school. It seemed like all the birds in the world were singing outside my window, and from my half-opened eye I could see that it was daybreak. I glanced across at Ann Marie's empty bed and for a second wondered where she was, but then I realized that it must have been the noises that were coming from the bathroom that woke me. Someone was being sick, so I guessed it must be her. I listened and I could hear her retching and sighing. I got out of bed as she came back into the room. She looked the colour of pancake mix.

'You sick?' I asked, sleepily.

'No ... er ... yes,' she sniffed, climbing back under the covers. 'And keep your trap shut about it!'

I went into the toilet and opened the window. I couldn't understand why she was telling me to keep my trap shut. When I was sick everybody knew about it. My mum used to sit beside me and hold my hand. Why was Ann Marie wanting to keep it a secret? I went back to bed and slept.

When Mum came in to waken me I had been miles away in a scary dream. I was with Tony and we were swimming in the sea further and further away. We were laughing and smiling. Tony looked really happy, not like he had been when he was telling us about his dad. He had a beautiful smile on his face. We swam further away from the shore, our arms stretching out in front of us. Then I looked around and Tony wasn't there. I spun around and there was nobody, only me and the sea that went on for ever. I dived under the water, but there was no sign of him. I was terrified. Everyone was leaving me. Tommy Lafferty, Kevin and now Tony. I was looking around anxiously for him when my mum put her hand on my shoulder and shook me. I sat bolt upright in the bed, rubbing my eyes. Thank God it had only been a dream.

I couldn't get into the bathroom because Ann Marie was being sick again. Finally she opened the door and swept past me. She looked awful. She must have a bug, I thought.

It was the last day. No more school for the whole summer.

No more dragging yourself out of bed and up the hill to sit in front of Miss Grant, wondering when she would go off the rails and start hitting people. No more knife-edge if you put your hand up and got a mental arithmetic answer wrong. No more catechism. No more rattling your hands with the ruler if you as much as opened your mouth to talk to the person next to you. No more torture, at least for the next seven weeks. We would be out there in our own world. It was a magic feeling and there was a smile on my lips as I got dressed.

Then I remembered Dan and what he must feel like wakening up this morning in a house with his dad in a coffin in the living room. It was unreal. I tried to imagine the house, how quiet it would be, everybody talking in whispers because the corpse was in the room, not that he could hear them. Dan wouldn't be at school because the funeral wasn't until tomorrow, so we would go and see him after we escaped.

I was washing my face in the bathroom when I looked in the mirror and saw right into my eyes. They looked back at me, pale blue and soft. Then I remembered confession. There was always confession on the last day of school, so that Father Flynn could send us out for the summer with our souls all spotless clean. It was important, because if anybody got drowned or run over by a car during the holidays, as quite often somebody did, they would go straight to heaven. Always start the holidays with a clean slate, he would say as he strode up and down the class preparing us for confession, booming at us to examine our conscience and spit out every little white lie and every big coal-black sin we must have committed since our last confession a month ago. Get rid of all the filth from your soul, he would say.

I was dreading it. Because if I was really going to make a true confession I would have to tell him about Shaggy Island, and I couldn't even imagine how I would begin to do that. He was sure to come thundering out of his box and drag me out by the hair. And maybe I would have to tell him about Tony kissing me. I knew he would never understand that. Nobody would. Worst of all, I should really be telling him about what we did to Miss Grant's clothes, because that was definitely a sin. Maybe even more than one sin. But if he got to know the culprits behind that, we would all probably be flogged to death in front of the whole school. Too risky.

I spat the toothpaste into the sink and decided that the only way round it was to add extra lies on to my standard list of sins. But the thought of going into that tiny, dark confessional with Father Flynn on the other side whispering and questioning made me feel sick. He would hear the guilt in my voice. He would smell it. What if he started questioning me closely like Perry Mason, and led me into a trap where I spilled the beans on the whole gang? I looked in the mirror. My eyes were gazing back. They looked shifty.

Downstairs Mum was busying around the kitchen making tea and toast and shaking cornflakes into a bowl for me. It was her day off as she had worked on Saturday, but I could see she had already been up for hours, because the washing machine was at full speed slopping stuff around. Ann Marie sat at the table, her face pasty, sipping tea.

'What is the matter with you, Ann Marie?' Mum said, looking at the untouched cornflakes in front of her. 'Are you not feeling well? Are you sick?'

'I heard you vom—' I only got half the word out before Ann Marie shot me a glance that could have knocked me down. I suddenly remembered. I had to keep my trap shut.

'What?' Mum said.

I kept my head down and ate my cornflakes. Mum looked from me to Ann Marie, then back to Ann Marie, who sipped her tea. Her face seemed to flush.

'I'm not very hungry, Mum, but I'm fine. Oh God! Is that the time? I'd better get movin'.' She got up and put her bag over her shoulder in one movement, and before Mum could say any more she was out the door. Mum watched her as she went down the path and out of the gate. She had a worried look on her face. I couldn't understand why. But I was glad I kept my trap shut because Ann Marie would have sulked with me for the rest of the week if I had said she was vomiting.

'Last day today, Mum,' I said to get her out of her daydream.

'Aye, summer holidays. Oh, I wish we could go somewhere, y'know, for a week or something. Maybe a caravan . . . something like that.'

'Do you think we will? Oh, that would be brilliant. Can we go? Can we go, Mum?' The very thought was exciting.

'We'll see. Your dad has got a few weeks' work and maybe we can sort something with your auntie Margaret. They're all going to a caravan in Girvan or something. We'll see.'

I knew deep down we wouldn't be going anywhere. We did this every year. We talked about it, the possibilities, the half-baked plans, but most of the time we never went anywhere, except on day trips to the seaside or to Butlins. They were all right though, and if you went on two or three of them it was just like going on holiday. That was what we told ourselves anyway. You never really knew you weren't on holiday, and the only time it annoyed you was when some of your pals came back after a week or two somewhere with stories of what they saw and people they met, usually in Ireland or on a caravan site on the coast in Scotland. We went once or twice to Mum's sister Auntie Nora in Donegal and it was brilliant. She lived near a caravan site on the seaside and we used to meet loads of people and have great laughs watching all the grown-ups dancing and having a sing-song at night. Sometimes there would be jaunting carts you could get a ride on and it was fantastic.

But the ones who really made us jealous were the kids who

went to Blackpool. There was a place there called the Pleasure Beach and it was like one great big playground of terrifying rides and ghost trains and fruit machines that you could win a fortune in. But you needed money to go on a holiday like that, so most of us just imagined it and we were as good as there.

On the way to Tony's house I met big McCartney, the man everybody knew as the tick man who collected the weekly cash for a large furniture and clothing store chain. I never knew his first name, and really he looked like the kind of guy who didn't need a first name. Everybody knew him as McCartney, but my dad only ever called him Slippy Tits, though not to his face. Big McCartney swanned around the streets like some kind of public figure on missionary work. Almost the entire village was up to their eyes in debt with him. It was the only way to buy anything, from furniture to school shoes and clothes. It was always great when you came home with your new outfit for Easter Sunday, but before the week was out McCartney was at your door with the latest list of payments in the big red book he tucked under his arm. If you didn't pay, you had to double up the next week and so on until it became a nightmare. People used to get up to all sorts of tricks to try to avoid him when he came knocking at the door. They would hide upstairs or in a neighbour's house when they saw his blue van pull into the street. Sometimes people would be climbing the fence as he was at the front door and he would run round the back and catch them.

But eventually they would have to pay, and the ones who got into big debt with him had to hand over their family allowance books so he could collect the money and take it off their bill. My dad said it was taking the bread out of the mouths of children and he hated McCartney for that, even though he didn't have our family allowance book. Dad never really had much to do with him, but he still called him Slippy Tits just the same. I wondered if it was because of the way he looked. Dad said he had children all over the village. McCartney was very tall and dark, kind of like a movie star from the old films. He had a thin moustache like David Niven and wavy hair all slicked back. He would drive his blue van from street to street and sit it outside people's houses like a big advert that they owed him money. He smiled at everyone, even if they were telling him to bugger off, because he knew that in the end they would have to pay or their furniture would end up out in the garden. When he came to our house he was always being really smooth with my mum, commenting on her hair or telling her she was wearing a nice blouse. She would always ignore him and just hand him the money then show him the door.

As I passed him on the way to Tony's he gave me a nod.

'How's young Miss Slaven?' he said cheerily.

'No bad, McCartney.' I made sure I didn't smile. If my dad didn't like him then he was no friend of mine. He breezed on and into the gate of a house, whistling furiously as he rapped on the door.

Chapter Six

In the chapel we all sat in silence, waiting our turn for confession. Candles flickered at each side of the altar and occasionally an old woman wearing her mantilla would be kneeling in fervent prayer beside a statue. I was always fascinated to watch them praying, their lips moving as they made soft whispering noises, kind of whistling through their teeth.

If only I could get this morning over, I pleaded, as I looked up to the statue of the Sacred Heart, I promised I would never do anything bad again. The Sacred Heart stared straight ahead. He had heard it all before. He could see out of the back of my head, and he knew what I was going to say even before I said it. I asked him if Dan was being punished by losing his dad because of what we had done to Miss Grant's clothes. I thought if I concentrated enough, like St Bernadette, maybe I would see a sign on the Sacred Heart's face. But nothing. Tony nudged me.

'Kath, what'll you say if he asks about Miss Grant?' he whispered.

'Nothing,' I said. 'Just say I don't know anything. He can't see your face so he won't know anything. Just deny it,' I said, hoping Tony couldn't hear the edge in my voice.

'What about you, Jamie?' Tony nudged Jamie, who was on my other side.

'Nothin', say nothin'. He'll just be trying to get information, but he won't know anything for sure. Stuff him,' Jamie said.

We all sat waiting for our moment. There were only two more to go before us. We knelt down to prepare our conscience, but all of us knew we would just be adding on extra lies.

Finally it was Jamie's turn, and he rose confidently and swaggered into the confessional. He was gone ages. When he emerged, his face was crimson. Tony and me looked at him anxiously, and much to our relief he winked and gave us a concealed thumbs-up.

It was my turn.

'Bless me, Father, for I have sinned, it has been four weeks since my last confession.' I knelt down in the musty confessional and blessed myself as I spoke. I could hear Father Flynn through the grille taking a deep breath.

'Yes, my child. And what sins do you have to confess to the Lord God?' Father Flynn's voice sounded gentle, coaxing.

There was a standard list of sins that everybody said, and that were easy to explain. Lies, cheek, pride, envy, swearing, even stealing. The more difficult one was about impure thoughts. I reeled off my sins.

'I told lies nine times.' I always added an extra two just in case I was forced to lie in the confessional. 'I was cheeky to my sister three times. I forgot my night prayers twice, and I swore six times,' I said, my eyes shut tight, trying to will myself through it.

'Any impure thoughts? What about impure thoughts?' The question jolted me even though I had been expecting it, because I knew I was guilty. Thoughts of Shaggy Island flooded my mind. I felt my face burn.

'Well? Any impure thoughts? Have you done or thought dirty things?' Father Flynn pressed on.

'Y . . . yes, Father?' I ventured. I would have to say something.

'Who with? Who did you do it with?' His voice was edgy.

'What?' I was confused.

'Who did you do it with? The dirty things? Who with? Was it yourself? Did you touch yourself? Or did you touch a boy? Or did he touch you?' Father Flynn offered more options than I had ever imagined. He spoke fast, determined to get an answer.

I didn't know what he was talking about, what he meant. But I had started it by admitting I had had impure thoughts. I had to cover my tracks. Suddenly I had a brain wave.

'Er, Father ... Er ... I looked at the men's underwear in the catalogue.' I could hardly believe I'd said it. I was cringing. Imagine admitting that.

'What? Like the boys and men in their pants?'

Father Flynn's voice was loud and I flushed to the roots of my hair in case everyone could hear him outside.

'Y ... yes,' I whispered, mortified.

There was a silence that seemed to last an age.

'And did you enjoy the school trip, my child?' I was stunned but relieved that he had changed the subject, though I knew what was coming next.

'Yes, Father, it was brilliant.'

'And did you hear what happened to Miss Grant? She was made to parade through the town in her swimsuit in the pouring rain because someone stole her clothes.'

'Yes, Father, I heard ... I mean, I saw her coming on to the bus,' I knew I could do this.

'There is a belief that someone on the trip stole her clothes. Now, my child, if you know who that was, then this is the place to cleanse yourself of that most heinous of sins. You do know that, don't you? And that God will forgive you here and now and not another word would be said about it? You know that, don't you?' He sounded like a kind, decent father who would make sure you were protected at all times. But I was having none of it. I thought about him kissing Dan and making him terrified and upset. I was telling him nothing. I had to protect the gang at all costs. Something filled me with a new confidence. Maybe it was God. Maybe it was the Devil.

'I know, Father. But I don't know who would have done that. I can't think anyone would have done that, Father.' I was so convincing that I even convinced myself.

There was another silence while Father Flynn digested my words. Then he sighed, and told me to make an act of contrition.

'I absolve you in the name of the Father, the Son and the Holy Spirit.'

I was off the hook. Absolved and cleansed. I could die right now and I would have my wings on by the time they were carrying my coffin up the aisle. I came out of the confessional and smiled at Tony and Jamie, who were sitting waiting for me.

When I knelt down to say my penance I asked the Sacred Heart to try to understand why I had to tell the lies in the confessional. I didn't mean to be bad, but if he was really honest with himself, Miss Grant had had it coming to her. The Sacred Heart stared straight ahead.

After school had finished we stopped in to see Dan. We all sat in his back garden in the sunshine. It was the first day of the summer holidays and we should have been bursting with excitement at being free at last. But all four of us just sat there, deflated, wondering who was going to talk next. We had tried to cheer Dan up by telling him about the confessional and how Father Flynn was fishing to find out who stole Miss Grant's clothes. The only time he laughed was when I told him that I had confessed to looking at the pants in the catalogue.

'I bet he looks at the men's pants as well,' Dan said.

'More like the boys' pants,' Jamie said.

It was Dan's dad's funeral tomorrow and it was beginning

to dawn on the whole family now that they would have to close the coffin and would never see his face again. Dan said his mum had been crying all day and all night. He was getting to hold a cord at the graveside as they lowered his father into the hole in the ground. It seemed to make him feel important. But his face was sad.

I was surprised to see McCartney's van in the street again when I was on my way back to the house, because he had been doing his calls when I saw him in the morning. His van was about four doors away from my house and I wondered where he was. I went round to the back door of my house, which was open a little, and I could hear conversation from inside. It was my mum's voice, protesting, and there was the voice of a man, persuasive, insisting. It wasn't my dad.

I strained my ears.

'Listen, Maggie . . . A lovely woman like you . . . you wouldn't have to be paying every week. I can work the books . . . my fiddle. You know what I mean? Oh Maggie! Oh Maggie! Oh, I'm so excited, Maggie. Oh Jesus, Maggie! You're lovely . . .' The voice was pleading.

'No! Look . . . please don't! Get your hands off there! Don't!'

I sneaked around to the kitchen window and peeped in. I was horrified. It was McCartney. Big Slippy Tits. He had my mother pinned against the door and seemed to be pushing himself against her. His hand was on her thigh at the front and he looked like he was pushing her legs open. She was struggling even more and her face was red.

I was filled with rage and panic. The bastard. I had to save her. But I couldn't let her know I had seen this or she would die. I had to think fast.

Suddenly I was bursting in the back door screaming and crying that I had hurt my leg and the pain was murdering me. McCartney jumped back from my mother and she almost leapt across the kitchen towards me. I screamed all the louder and my legs buckled as though I was about to collapse. As I was going down on to the floor I half opened my eye to see the shocked McCartney standing looking at me. He was as white as a sheet. He held his big red book over the front of his trousers and seemed to limp past me. He must have hurt his leg as well, I thought.

As soon as he was out of the door I began to calm down.

'Where's the pain? Where is it sore?' My mother knelt beside me anxiously feeling my leg.

'Oh! Oh! There! Oh! That's it!' I was trying desperately to feign agony.

'Can you move it? What happened?'

'I was jumping off the wall and I went over on my ankle. Oh, I think it's easing up a bit now.' I moved it slowly, careful to screw my face up at every movement.

My mother went to the sink to give me a glass of water. She looked straight into my eyes and right through me. She knew I was faking. Her face fell. How could she ever explain it? I wanted to tell her she shouldn't be ashamed. I felt terrible, because I knew that she'd done nothing, and that McCartney was trying to touch her and she was pushing him away, but I couldn't tell her because she would be mortified that I had witnessed it. I wasn't entirely sure what was going on, but I knew that McCartney was trying to get her to pay him behind the door, as my dad used to put it. If he ever found out what Slippy Tits had done, he would pull his lungs out. Mum looked as though she was going to cry. I tried to stand up, faking a limp, but she could see it was all an act.

'I'll make the tea,' she said, turning away from me.

I limped into the garden and sat on the grass watching her at the sink wiping tears away from her face.

The coffin rested at the front of the chapel and I slipped past it to light a candle below the statue of Our Lady. It was hard to imagine that Tommy Lafferty was inside there all cold and stiff in his white satin shroud. I glanced at the brass plate screwed on to the light oak wood. Thomas Daniel Lafferty RIP, aged 40. I wondered where he was, if he could see us, if he could see Dan and his mum and his brother and sister making their way down the aisle to sit at the front of the chapel. All Dan's family were there, his uncle Brian and his wife and all their children. Dan's mum kept looking at the coffin and sobbing. Dan bit his lip and tried not to cry, but it was no use. I knelt in front of the statue and prayed for Tommy Lafferty, for God to let him into heaven as soon as he could and for Dan and his mum not to feel sad for ever. I prayed for Tony that he would love me for ever, and that the Polack would stop hitting him. I prayed for my mum and dad and Kevin and Ann Marie. I prayed that none of us would get caught for stealing Miss Grant's clothes.

It was a long, dismal mass, with Father Flynn speaking for ages about Tommy Lafferty and how he was one of the most decent men in the village, but that like a good Catholic he was always prepared for God and to go to a better place. He said God had chosen to take Tommy back and that he had only loaned him to us. He said that death comes like a thief in the night, and we must always be ready.

I thought of lying in bed at night when the streets are quiet and you can't sleep, and all you can hear is someone's high-heeled shoes clattering along the road from time to time. You never know the minute that God is going round the houses looking in people's beds and wondering who to take. Like a thief in the night. The thought made me shiver.

Ann Marie's face was chalk white and she squeezed out of her seat, past Mum, Dad and me. She looked as though she was going to be sick again. Dad looked at Mum, but said nothing. She looked worried. It crossed my mind that Ann Marie might be dying.

At communion there were sniffs and sobs from all around the packed chapel as everyone sang the sad, slow funeral hymn. Even my dad poked his thumbs into his eyes to stop the tears coming out.

Everyone sang: 'They are waiting for our petition, silent and calm; their lips no prayer can utter, no suppliant psalm.'

I pictured all the souls in the dark never-ending corridor of purgatory trying to find a way to get out, but always ending up back at the same place. You were years in purgatory and you only ever got out if people kept praying for you, then eventually someone would give you a hand up and you were in heaven. You were made then. But purgatory seemed like a depressing place, and it must be frustrating waiting your turn among millions of other souls. But at least it wasn't hell. You had no chance if you were down there.

When the mass ended, Dan's Uncle Brian and Theresa's brothers all carried the coffin on their shoulders. They were big, strong men but the tears rolled down their faces, and everybody wept as the procession passed each seat along the aisle. Dan held his mother's hand and his face was flushed and wet with tears when he passed my seat. He looked straight at me and he sobbed his heart out. I felt helpless. There was a lump in my throat and my chest felt tight. I thought I was going to burst. My dad put his arm around my shoulder. God had come like a thief in the night. It wasn't fair. I wondered who would be next.

After the cemetery I walked away on my own. I wanted to be alone because I didn't want everyone to see my tears. I sat by the railway line and cried my eyes out. I was even crying out loud because I knew that nobody could hear me as the whole village was at Tommy Lafferty's funeral and most of them would be in the pub by now. So I jumped when I heard a voice.

'Kath? I've been looking all over for you. What're you doing, sitting here all by yourself?' It was Kevin. I immediately tried to compose myself and wiped away my tears. But he could see. He sat down beside me and handed me his handkerchief without saying anything. We sat for a while saying nothing, watching the heat rise like waves in the distance. He took off his jacket and tie, and rolled up his shirt sleeves. His strong arms were golden brown from working outside. He lit a cigarette and took a long, slow puff.

'You know about Australia then, Kath?' Kevin leaned back on one elbow so he was facing me.

'Aye.' I stared straight ahead.

'Are you upset with me, Kath?' He reached out and gently turned my face towards him.

'You're going away, Kevin. You're going away to leave me. I'll never see you again. And you're my only brother ... it'll be as if you're dead or something. Why are you going away, Kevin? Why? Do you not like us?' I blurted it all out.

Kevin knelt in front of me and took both my hands.

'Oh Kath! Wee Kath! So much to learn. Listen, darlin'. It's just that this place, you know, it has nothing for young guys like me with no qualifications. I'm not clever like you. I'm never going to get a good job or go to university or all the things you'll get because of your brains. I'll never get a decent job because I'm a Catholic with no qualifications, so I'll be digging ditches or working for a brickie in the pissin' rain until I'm old and riddled with rheumatics.'

'What's wrong with that? At least you'll be here with your family ... with me.'

'But I want a chance of a better life, Kath, a better life. And when I make enough money I'll come back here and open my own business . . . a shop, or a pub, or something like that. You'll see.

'Dessie and me are going on this cheap offer for people to emigrate to Australia. They're desperate for workers, young blood like us, and it will be a great chance.'

I pictured him in Australia, working stripped to the waist in the blistering heat, or swimming in the sea, or shearing sheep like the way you saw in the movies. It was all tough guys and sweat, but everybody seemed happy and joking all the time and drinking big frothy pints of beer. It was nothing like here and I knew deep down that a boy like Kevin would have a great time there. I would miss him so much. He was the best friend I ever had. He would read to me when I was in bed sick, and the way he read made the story come alive from the page. One time he read *Heidi* to me and when I slept that night I was Heidi climbing the hills in Switzerland, running to meet the snowy-haired old grandfather. Kevin was the best brother anybody could hope for.

'But what if you don't come back? I'll be left with Ann Marie and she hates me. She never talks to me or takes me anywhere,' I said.

'I will come back. And if I don't . . . well, you'll just have to come and see me. I'll be rich enough to send your fare, and you can come and bring Mum, and Ann Marie too, and we'll have a great time.'

He made it all sound marvellous. He told me stories of the Great Barrier Reef where there were fish that were all kinds of colours, and of the outback where kangaroos and koala bears were running wild. It was going to be the most fantastic place and he would write me letters every week like a diary and I had to do the same. When I looked around me at the dreariness of the houses all cluttered together and the sameness of street after street, I was beginning to warm to it, but I couldn't bear the thought of saying goodbye to him.

'When will you go?' I asked.

'Can you keep a secret?' he said. I nodded.

'It'll be about two months yet. Dessie and me are doing some extra work out on McBride's farm to get enough money, then we'll be ready. But Mum and Dad don't know yet. After the other night, I'm going to have to work on Dad and try to get him on my side. I don't want to fight him, Kath, and I shouldn't have said the things I said to him. I'd had too much to drink. But he has wasted his life and I will never do that. I can be somebody, I know I can. Now don't tell anyone until I say, OK?'

I nodded that I wouldn't. He stood up and pulled me to my feet.

'C'mon home and we'll help Mum make the tea. Dad will be in the pub with all the men from the funeral, so it will be a long day on the drink. Let's just hope he doesn't want to box me when he comes home.'

Chapter Seven

The days were long and hot, and sometimes when we sweltered under our T-shirts, we peeled off. The boys were always bare-chested and I would have preferred to be that way too, but Mum said that now that I was nearly eleven, I had to keep my vest on. I knew what she meant and knew that some time in the future I would have the big fleshy breasts that Ann Marie had. The thought filled me with dread because everyone was always kidding her on about them and making her blush. But she seemed to enjoy having them. It seemed to get her noticed. Maybe I would get to like them.

It had been two weeks since Tommy Lafferty's funeral and Dan had hardly been out with the rest of us. He was always helping his mum around the house and going to the shops. He was the oldest of the family and was trying to get a job to bring in some money, so he was always busy. Jamie and Tony were around but everything seemed flat and boring. It wasn't much fun playing at the Man From Uncle when there was only three of you, and with two of you on the one side chasing just one Russian spy.

Tony and I were spending more time together, wandering off into the fields and woods exploring and climbing trees and building a camp. We used to call it our house and we would bring a picnic and sit inside and eat as if we had lived there for years.

Sometimes we would swim in the burn and Tony would

77

be wearing just his shorts and I, as usual, had to wear my vest. It was when he pulled off his T-shirt one day that I noticed the huge black bruise on his back. It looked as though he had been hit by a stick, but there were also red welts on his back as though he had been hit by a belt or a whip. We were splashing around in the water, and Tony must have forgotten the marks were there when he took his shirt off, then remembered when he saw the shocked look in my eyes as I noticed the bruising.

'Tony,' I said, stretching my hand out to gently touch the bruise. 'Jesus! Your back, Tony . . . What happened?'

He winced as I touched his back and pushed my hand away. He didn't say anything for a moment as we both stood in the water up to our waists. The sun was splitting the trees and throwing shadows across the stream. There wasn't a breath of air. Tony's face looked sad and angry at the same time. He turned away from me and waded back to the embankment, where he sat down brushing the water from his legs and reaching under his T-shirt on the ground for a packet of cigarettes. I followed him out and sat beside him, turning to lean on one elbow so I was facing him. He drew on the cigarette deeply and the smoke came billowing out of his nostrils. I was fascinated. He seemed to be in another world. Eventually he spoke.

'It was the Polack. I told you, Kath, he beats me up, the crazy bastard. I hate the shit.' Tony was sitting with his arms clasped around his knees. I could see the bruise on his back more clearly in the light. It was all the way up his rib cage. There were other little bruises on his arm as well, like finger marks.

'What happened, Tony? Why did he hit you? What was it for?' I asked.

'There doesn't need to be any reason, Kath. He just takes lunges at me. OK, sometimes I give him a bit of cheek, but mostly he just comes at me for something he says I haven't done around the house. He sometimes comes into my room and shuts the door. Then I know I'm in for it.' Tony's voice was racing.

'Usually it's after he's had a fight with Mom or something. Then he just comes in and grabs me. I punch him back or try to grab his hands but it makes him worse. He says he's going to put me in a boys' home or something. I heard him talking about it one night to Mom, and she wasn't even trying to stop him . . .' His voice began to trail off as tears came to his eyes.

'Oh Kath! What am I going to do? I think he's going to kill me, or kill my mom . . . or maybe I'll kill him, the bastard.' Tony was wiping tears away from his face.

I didn't know what to say. I wanted to take him home and ask my mum and dad if he could live with us for ever. I wanted to get the police or somebody to protect him. But I had no idea what to do.

'What do you mean, send you to a boys' home? He can't do that. Your mum would never let him.' The very thought of Tony being sent away filled me with dread.

'They can if they want, Kath. I heard him talking. He was saying to her that they both got on a lot better when they were on their own and that they would have a better chance if I got sent away to a school somewhere or a home,' Tony said.

I couldn't believe what I was hearing. Through his tears Tony said that the Polack had beaten up his mum a couple of times and that she was scared of him. He said that she had started drinking and that sometimes when he came home from school she smelled of drink. She wasn't the same with him since she married the Pole and now he was trying to split them up. He wished he could kill him or get rid of him in some way.

'He sits there every night in the bed-room counting his money. I sneaked up one night and watched through the crick in the door. He's got loads of money stashed away in a tin box he keeps below the floorboards. There's loads of notes. One of these days, Kath, I'm going to creep in there and steal every bastard penny he's got. That'll teach him.' Tony had the same angry look on his face that he had the day we took Miss Grant's clothes. It made me scared.

We both lay back on the grass, watching in silence as the wispy clouds drifted across the sky. I wished we could be this way for ever. Just Tony and me, living someplace where everybody was happy all the time. No angry people fighting or plotting against you. No teachers hating you. But most of all nobody ever dying. I could feel the sun burning my face. Tony spoke. He turned his face towards mine. His eyes were a little red, but the blue looked pure and piercing in the strong sunlight.

'I love you, Kath. I'll always love you. Even when we're big and grown up and no matter what happens to us, I never want to marry anyone but you.' Tony never took his eyes off my face. I didn't know what to say. I felt a lump in my throat.

'I know,' I said. 'I know, Tony ... I love you too.' I felt a little awkward saying it but I took his hand. 'Don't worry, Tony, it'll be all right. You'll see.' I squeezed his hand. We lay still, feeling the sun dry the water on our bodies. We didn't need anybody else.

I was sure she was dying. Nearly every morning I lay in bed listening to Ann Marie being sick in the bathroom before she went to work. Every time I asked her about it she told me to shut up, that it was none of my business. I guessed that everybody else knew about it but they had decided not to tell me she was dying because I was too young. But I knew all the same.

I was even more convinced when I came home one afternoon to find both my mum and dad crying and Kevin standing in front of the fireplace looking very grim-faced. As soon as I walked into the room they rushed me back out. I felt like saying to them that it was all right, I already knew Ann Marie was dying, but I didn't have the heart. I went upstairs to my room. I knelt down at my bedside and said a decade of the rosary that Ann Marie wouldn't suffer too much before she died. I asked God why he had to take her to a better place when she was so young and seemed to like the place she was in. I thought it might be punishment for what she was doing in Shaggy Island. I could feel my stomach in knots. I didn't really know Ann Marie even though we had slept in the same room since I was born. She was different from me and Kevin. Her head was in the clouds and she was always slagging me off for reading books all the time. She had dreams of going to work in Spain or in London as a chambermaid in some big hotel where she would meet a rich man who would marry her and buy her everything. Now she was dying and none of that would ever happen. She hadn't been anywhere except the chocolate factory she worked in, and the furthest she had been was the dancing on a Friday night at the next town about two miles away. It was all pie in the sky. Maybe that was why she was crying at night. Maybe she knew she was dying and was just so disappointed that she hadn't got any of the things she had dreamt about. My heart went out to her. I promised myself that I would do everything to help her in the short time she would be here. I started straight away by making her bed and folding her nightdress. I puffed up her pillows and stood back looking at the neat bed. I pictured Ann Marie lying there in her white shroud with her arms clasped across her chest like the way they did in the movies. The thought scared me. I decided to go and meet her at the corner when she came home from work so I could walk with her. I would make an extra effort to be nice to her every day. But I had to make sure she didn't know that I knew she didn't have long to go.

I stood at the corner and watched Ann Marie in the distance with two of her pals walking up the road from the chocolate factory just outside the village. She was still wearing her white cotton overall and had her bag slung over her shoulder. They were all having a good laugh, smoking cigarettes and giggling. Ann Marie was laughing too, but when she got closer to me I could see that she looked as if she was in another world. She caught my eye, and I waved to her. She looked a bit confused to see me, but waved back and smiled a little. She was so brave, I thought. I was seeing Ann Marie in a different light now.

'Hi,' I said when she reached me. 'Want me to carry your bag?'

She looked suspiciously at me.

'I've no money, or chocolate . . . not till Thursday.'

'Oh, it's OK, I don't want anything. I just came to meet you, Ann Marie,' I said, as if it was a normal, everyday thing for me to do.

Ann Marie looked bemused but handed me her bag and we walked along the road.

'Where's your wee boyfriend then?' Ann Marie nudged me as we went past Tony's house.

'Who?' I said, pretending not to know what she was talking about.

'The wee Yankee, Tony. Don't give us your patter. The two of you are joined at the hip,' Ann Marie joked. She looked happy, not dismissive, the way she normally was with me. I decided to share some of my thoughts with her.

'He's my very best friend, Ann Marie. Tony's great. He's going to be my friend for the rest of my life.' I didn't want to say too much.

Ann Marie stopped in her tracks. She looked at me and her eyes seemed softer than I had ever seen before.

'Wow. That's more than a friend, Kath. Maybe Tony's the man you'll marry, eh?'

'I think so,' I said, trying to sound as if I had considered the notion for some time.

Ann Marie smiled, but she looked far away in her thoughts. I wondered if she had a boyfriend she loved. She never seemed to have any boyfriends for any length of time. They were always hanging around her, then you would never see them again. I felt sad for her because now she was going to die and wouldn't even get the chance to get married. But I had to pretend I didn't know anything about that.

'Do you want to get married, Ann Marie? Do you ever want to get married?' I said.

Ann Marie stopped and looked up at our house. Her face looked disappointed and as though she was going to burst into tears. Then she tried to smile.

'Ach, who'd have me?' She forced a laugh. I immediately jumped in to defend her.

'Loads of guys, Ann Marie. I've heard Andy Murphy and Joe Burns both saying they fancied you. Everybody fancies you . . . Honest.'

Ann Marie sighed and took her bag off my shoulder.

'C'mon, smarty pants. The dinner will be ready.'

We went into the house and I followed Ann Marie up to our bedroom. She looked around, bewildered at how tidy it was.

'I made your bed. And I tidied up everything,' I said eagerly,

She looked at the room and then at me. She had a funny puzzled expression on her face.

'What are you playing at, Kath? Is there something you're looking for?' she asked.

'No, nothing. Nothing at all. I, er . . . I'm just trying to help.'

We went downstairs to eat. The atmosphere round the table was terrible. Mum and Dad's faces were like fizz and Kevin poured the tea silently, glancing from time to time at Ann

Marie and then at me. It must have been like this at the Last Supper, I thought.

Finally the silence was broken by Dad. He looked at me.

'I didn't know there was a stooshie at the school trip, Kath,' he said.

'Stooshie?' I said with the most innocent look I could muster.

'Aye. I hear that frustrated old bint Miss Grant got her clothes stolen at the beach and had to walk through the town in her swimsuit in the pouring rain. Jesus, that must have been a laugh. I'd love to have been a fly on the wall of that bus.' He was laughing between mouthfuls of food.

I decided I had better say I had heard about it too.

'Aye, it was a laugh. Er ... I heard somebody stole her clothes and the next thing she came on to the bus soaking wet. She was raging,' I said, stuffing food into my mouth so that I could get the dinner over quickly and make a sharp exit.

'Who would do a thing like that?' Mum said, shaking her head.

'Somebody with a big future,' Kevin chipped in. 'Anybody with the guts to do that is going places. Good on them. Grant is a dried-up old hoor by all accounts.'

'Tut. Mind your tongue, Kevin,' Mum said.

I kept eating and slurping my tea. Dad persisted.

'I heard it was a few of the kids who did it, Kath. In fact, I heard it was that wee Yankee fella, Tony, your pal,' he said, looking me in the eye.

I felt a flush rising in my face. Everybody looked at me. Kevin had a glint in his eye. He could see that I knew a lot more than I was letting on.

'Tony?' I said, sounding surprised. 'Oh no. He was with me and Jamie and Dan all day. No, it wasn't him.' I tried to sound convincing, and made a swift mental note to add another lie when I went to confession.

They all looked at me. I was sure they knew I was lying, but I didn't flinch. I remembered watching a war film where the British woman spy was being tortured and questioned by the Gestapo. She never moved a muscle. And neither did I. But I felt hot.

'I don't know so much about that Tony fella,' Dad said, pursing his lips. 'I hear he's a bit of a smart arse. He seems to be the leader of the pack at the school, according to what I hear. Maybe he's not the right kind of company for you, Kath.'

There was a red mist coming down over my eyes. What did he know about Tony? What did he know about the bruises and red marks on his back from that Polack bastard who beat him nearly every day? What did he know about Tony's mum drinking? Nothing, that was what. I was raging, but I wouldn't dare say anything or turn my tongue on my dad. My eyes were filling with tears.

'T . . . Tony's all right. OK! He's not bad. He's good. He's my best pal and I . . . I'm his. And . . . you don't know nothing about him. So he's my pal. So just . . . just . . .' I was stuttering on the verge of tears. Kevin saw I was about to lose the place and interrupted.

'He's only a wee laddie. There's no badness in him. Leave the boy alone, Da. If Kath wants to play with him then that's up to her. Jesus, what do we know about kids' pals? It's their own wee world.'

Dad could see how deeply upset I was and backed down a little.

'I know that, I know that. But all I'm saying is that if he is trouble, then it can lead to trouble for everyone that goes around with him. You know . . . if you fly with the crows you get shot with the crows.' He softened as he looked at me.

I downed the last of my tea and pushed my chair back.

'Tony isn't trouble,' I said, standing up. 'I'm going out to play.' I walked as straight and upright as I could towards the

ANNA SMITH

back door. No matter who they thought they were, they could never tell me anything bad about Tony. I'd loved him from the moment I saw him and nobody could ever ruin that for me. Tony was mine for ever. I could feel their eyes on me as I opened the back door, walked out of it and closed it softly behind me.

Chapter Eight

Barney Hagen was a hero. He had been in the war, and he had never been the same since the Japs took him prisoner. They said that when he came home he only weighed five stones and that his cheekbones were almost sticking through his face. They sent him to the Swiss mountains to fatten him up and so that he could breathe pure fresh air. But when he came back home to the village he was never the same man. When they talked about him as a young soldier going to war I could see in my mind this brave boy in an army uniform, with his face all clean and smiling, but with a strong expression because he knew how grave things could be when you went to war. But it was hard to picture him like that when I saw what he was now.

He was only about forty-seven, but he just looked to me like an old man. His face was grey and sad. His hair was almost gone and he wore a flat cap most of the time, even in the house. Barney didn't go out much these days. After the war everything seemed to fall apart. My dad said that he was only a boy when the war ended, but he remembered that at first Barney had been treated like the hero he was when he came home. They carried him shoulder high through the village and held a feast in the church hall in his honour. But as the years went on Barney just didn't seem to be able to cope. His wife left him because he spent most of his time in the pub drinking so he could forget the torture and the horrors of the

Jap prisoner-of-war camp. After she went away, Barney spent even more time in the pub, where he used to sit in a corner by himself, drinking and staring into space. Sometimes his face would twitch and he would tremble. Dad said nobody would go near him then because he was reliving the nightmare of the war and he would never really escape from it.

Eventually Barney stopped going to the pub and mostly just stayed at home, drinking or just looking out of the window. He walked with a limp because his leg had got withered after an infection set in from an insect bite while he was living in the stinking camp. The leg got worse the older he got and he had to depend on people coming into the house to help him or to go to the shops for him.

I was always a little scared of Barney, because when I walked past his house he always seemed to be sitting peeping out from behind the curtain. Sometimes he would wave and his face would almost smile. I always waved back, but it was a kind of half-hearted wave because even though I was only glancing at him, I could see his eyes and they looked as if they were staring right through me. I knew that some kids were friendly with him and called into his house to run messages for him, but the fact that he was crippled and sad made me afraid of him.

It was a blistering hot day and I was on my way to the shops for Mum, when I passed Barney's house. I automatically looked in and there he was at the window. When he saw me he strained his neck and pulled back the curtain. He rapped the window and I stopped in my tracks. He beckoned me to come in, but I stood for a moment wondering what to do. What if he was a murderer? I could go in there and never be heard tell of again. Nobody would have a clue as to where I was until Barney died of gangrene or something and then they would find me starved to death in his attic or the coal cellar.

Barney could see me hesitating and he smiled and waved me in again with a reassuring look in his face. His eyes looked softer and I felt sorry for him. He was a war hero, but now nobody really cared about him.

I walked up the path and took a deep breath before gently knocking on his door. He took a while to come and I guessed it was because of his bad leg. Finally he opened the door and there he was standing before me. I was awestruck at how frail and old he looked. I could hardly believe it was the same man that my dad had told fascinating stories of, how he had been captured and lived in a pit of water for weeks while the Japs tortured and killed his friends one by one. He said they even pulled their fingernails off.

My eyes swiftly looked to his nails to see if they were there and I was surprised to find that they were.

Barney could see my fear and shock. He stood back as if to invite me into the house.

'Would you go a wee message to the shops for me, pet? It's just that with my leg an' stuff I can't get about, and I'm out of bread and things.' Barney raised his hand in a kind of pleading way. He looked sad. I studied his face for a moment then decided that he wasn't a murderer.

'Aye. Yeah, I'll go for you, no problem . . . er . . . Barney.' I was a bit surprised at how informal I was with someone I hadn't met before, but he was so well known in the village that I felt I knew him. I stepped into the hall and watched him make his way to the living room with one hand on the wall and the other on a walking stick. He dragged his bad leg behind him. It looked as if there were no muscles in it and it kind of flopped as he shuffled along.

His living room was dark and it smelled of greasy food and stale tobacco. It looked gloomy compared to the scorching sunlight I had just left. I glanced around the room, my eyes swiftly catching picture stories of Barney's life. There was a black and white picture of a young boy in an army uniform, standing to attention, his hair all shiny and slicked back. He was carrying his army cap tucked under his arm. He had dimples in his face and strong white teeth. In an alcove there was a dark green baize frame with a bunch of medals and ribbons attached to it. They looked like gold and silver and they were the only things that gleamed in the house. They made the place look sad.

My eyes rested on the medals and I thought what a hero Barney must have been to win all these. He must have seen my interest and he limped over to the alcove and lifted the medals to bring them across to me. I watched him slowly cross the floor, then come towards me smiling proudly.

'Have a look at them, darlin' . . . It's Kath, isn't it? Martin Slaven's lassie. I see you all the time passing with your wee pals. You're always out and about at something, are you not?' Barney was smiling and his eyes didn't look sad any more.

I looked at his medals and ran my fingers across the cold metal and the silk ribbons.

Each medal had an engraving for some battle and they had the name L. Cpl Barney Hagen written across the bottom.

'They're brilliant, Barney,' I gushed, sincerely. 'You must have done loads of things in the war. It must have been amazing. Did you kill loads of Japs and Germans? Was it amazing?'

Barney's face suddenly stopped smiling and I stopped talking in mid sentence. I looked quickly at his withered leg and I could have kicked myself for blurting everything out when Barney was obviously still remembering and suffering. How could I have done that after everything my dad had said about him? I was ashamed at my thoughtlessness.

'Sorry, Barney. I didn't mean to . . .'

'Aw, it's OK, darlin'. No problem. I'm just a bit tired of it all sometimes. But maybe another day I'll tell you some stories. How does that sound?' His face was happier and I felt relieved.

'Great. I'd like that.'

'Right, now if you go to the shops and buy me some milk, bread and sausages I would be very grateful, Kath.' He went into his pocket and handed me a pound note. 'Oh, and get yourself a wee sweetie, Kath, OK?'

I took the money and told him I wouldn't be long. I let myself out and walked quickly out of the gate and down to the shops. My head was full of wars and bombs and fearsome insects eating the legs of young soldiers who had dreams of going home to the girls they loved.

I watched the birds soar across the sky, dipping and diving like kamikaze bombers crashing towards the ground, then with scarcely a flap of their wings they were up and away again. The starlings made a black pattern across the blue, rising and falling, rising and falling. I was hypnotized by their fluid movement. I was alone, lying on the grass near the old railway line with the sun on my face and my thoughts a million miles away. I was lost without Tony, who had gone with his mother to visit an aunt for a couple of days. He had looked different lately. Since the start of the summer holidays he had begun to look pale with dark shadows under his eyes. He said he didn't sleep at night and he showed me more bruises from the Polack. Tony wasn't the same fun any more. He looked sad. His eyes had lost their sparkle and now they looked haunted. He was worried about his mum, who was drinking more and more. She had been found asleep on a park bench in the village square and everyone was talking about her. Afterwards she couldn't come out of the house for a week because the Polack gave her a black eye.

I closed my eyes so that I could relive the moment when Tony and me were in the sea that afternoon when he kissed me. It was a great picture and I hoped I would keep it for ever.

I didn't see the shadow approach and I flinched when I felt the blade of grass tickling my face. It was Kevin.

'So this is where you've been hiding.' Kevin plonked himself down beside me.

'Hi, Kev, what is it? Is it teatime already?' I couldn't understand why he had come looking for me.

'No, no. Er ... Kath ... I just wanted to talk to you about something.' His voice sounded hesitant. I raised myself up on one elbow and looked quizzically at him.

'What ... what is it, Kev?' My mind started to race. Something was wrong.

Kevin pushed his hair back two or three times, which he always did when he was nervous or worried or trying to explain himself. He looked at his hands, picking his fingernails, then finally looked at me as I sat wide-eyed with anticipation.

'Well, Kath, it's ... it's ... er ... It's about Ann Marie. Er ... she has to go away.' He seemed to take a deep breath then went on. 'Er ... Ma and Da said I should talk to you about it.'

This was it. I knew it. They couldn't bear to tell me themselves about Ann Marie dying so they sent Kevin. Oh God! My insides turned over. Kevin looked flushed and upset. I decided to save him the agony. I blurted out:

'It's OK, Kev ... I know.'

He looked startled. 'You know?'

'Aye. I know. I heard her vomiting. Every morning. I've known for weeks.'

Kevin's face was shocked. He struggled with his words.

'Jesus, Kath. I didn't know you knew about stuff like that. I ... I ... er ... mean, you're only ten. Jesus, I can't believe you knew.'

I tried to be brave.

'Aye, I knew weeks ago, Kev. I knew for sure when I walked in that day and you and Mum and Dad were all there with faces down to the floor. I've been trying to help Ann Marie. I feel so sorry for her. It's not fair! How can God do that, Kev? How can he take her away to a better place when she's only sixteen? Sometimes I think God doesn't care about us!' I was angry and sad.

Kevin looked bemused.

'Kath, it's not really anything to do with God. Well, not really.'

'Aye it is! He's the one that comes like a thief in the night, picking people out of their beds! Why doesn't he take some old fart rather than a young lassie like Ann Marie? It's not fair!'

Kevin's eyes were screwed up as he tried to figure out what I was saying.

'Kath, what are you talking about? A thief in the night?'

'You know . . . like Dan's dad. That's what Father Flynn said at the funeral. God comes like a thief in the night and takes you away and that's you dead. Now it's Ann Marie he's going to take away . . .' My voice trailed off.

Kevin's face looked as if it was going to burst, then his eyes began to smile.

'Kath, you don't think Ann Marie's going to die, do you?'

'Of course I do. She is, isn't she? Isn't she, Kev?' I knew the moment I said it that she wasn't going to die and my heart leapt in my chest. Kevin burst out laughing and put his head in his hands.

'Aw, Jesus! Kath . . . Aw, Jesus! Ya poor wee coull' He laughed and grabbed me to his chest. 'I can't believe you thought she was dying. My God! You must have been off your head with worry!' He released me and looked into my face.

I was thoroughly confused now. I was thrilled that Ann Marie wasn't dying, but if Ann Marie wasn't dying then what was the big deal? Why was everyone going around with their faces ready for a funeral and why was Ann Marie weeping into her pillow at night and vomiting every morning?

'What's going on, Kev? Tell me,' I insisted as he lit a cigarette.

He sat up and composed himself, then he began.

'Er, Kath ... Ann Marie ... Ann Marie's ... well, she's, er, going to have a baby.'

My eyes almost popped out of my head. How could she have a baby? She wasn't even married. She had only just left school a year. A baby? How? Then thoughts of Shaggy Island flooded my mind and I felt my face redden. Oh God. Was that it? A baby?

'A baby? God, Kev. What's Mum and Dad saying? Are they raging? Jesus, is Dad going mad?'

'Aye, it's been a bit like that over the last few weeks. That's why we've all been going around with long faces. But listen, Kath, you have to understand this, and that's why I'm here to see you and talk to you. Now you mustn't tell anyone in the world, not even Tony, about Ann Marie. You see, it's a big shame on the family that's she's in trouble like this and not married. I mean, she doesn't even have a steady boyfriend ...'

I tried to keep my face straight and hoped that Shaggy Island wasn't written all over my forehead.

Kevin continued: 'You see, Kath, Ann Marie has to go away, now that she's pregnant. She's going over to Auntie Nora's in Donegal to have the baby, and then it'll be adopted, and when she comes back everything will be fine. Everybody will just think she's been working over in Donegal for a few months.'

This seemed very strange to me. You're having a baby, you go to Donegal and then give it away. Like an orphan baby. Except it's not an orphan because its mother is alive and its father too, whoever he is.

'But what about the baby, Kev? It's Ann Marie's baby. Does she not want it? I'd love to have a wee baby in the house. It would be magic.' The thought of a little baby being bathed and put to bed and then coming in beside you in the morning was brilliant.

Kevin looked very serious.

'You see, Kath, it's not as easy as that. It's not like you can just have a baby and not be married. It's such an embarrassment for the family. I mean, Mum and Dad will be shamed and Ann Marie . . . well, she'll never get a husband if she's got a baby. Who's going to take on another man's child?'

I couldn't understand this kind of logic.

'But what about the baby? I won't be ashamed of it! It's just a baby!'

Kevin shifted restlessly. He didn't look like he believed any of what he was saying.

'It's not just the practicalities of it. You see, Kath, Father Flynn was down at the house and speaking to Mum and Dad and he talked of the shame and stuff and he more or less told them this is how it's done. There was no choice really. I mean, there's lots of Catholic couples in Ireland who can't have babies and they'd love to adopt one. It happens all the time.'

None of this made any sense to me. I felt a rage rising inside me. Father Flynn. Who was he to come and tell anybody what to do? After what he'd done to Dan I could never look at him straight in the face without seeing him kissing Dan in the sacristy.

Before I could stop, I heard myself saying it.

'Father Flynn? Father Flynn? He's a poof!'

Kevin burst out laughing. 'What? Oh, Kath, ssssh. If anybody hears you, Jesus, you'll roast in hell.'

I was on my feet. There was no stopping me now.

'He is! He is! He's a big poof! Ask Dan! No, don't, 'cos he won't talk about it. But he told us. Father Flynn kisses him after he comes off the altar. After mass even! He pulls him on to his knee and kisses him on the face! Even on the lips! Aye, and another thing, he does it to other altar boys as well!

95

He's a big poof, and he's telling our Ann Marie she can't have a baby? That's not fair!'

Kevin was shocked. He didn't know what to say. His mouth was half open as he sat looking up at me, watching me bluster and rage. He pulled me back down and pointed his finger right in my face.

'Now listen, Kath. Have you any idea what you're saying? Jesus, Kath, you're saying the parish priest is a pervert! Do you know what that means? Are you making this up?'

But Kevin knew I wasn't making it up. He knew me too well. We both sat in silence. The birds kept soaring in the sky. Everything looked the same, but it wasn't. It never would be.

I could almost feel Kevin's anger about Father Flynn. Kevin had never really swallowed the full Catholic stuff and it was one of the sources of conflict between Dad and him. He had never been an altar boy and when he was a child it was a different priest at the chapel. But now this revelation opened up a whole new image of the priests who he had little respect for anyway. I knew he wanted to go up to the chapel and pull Father Flynn out of the confessional. But he couldn't. He could do nothing. And he knew that. Who would believe it anyway? Who would anybody believe? A wee boy like Dan or the parish priest who knew everything and could help you any day of the week, even if your daughter was pregnant. His word was as good as God's because he was so much closer to God than any of us could hope to be. He more or less got through right to the man himself as soon as he made the sign of the cross.

Finally Kevin said, 'OK, Kath, OK. Jesus! Poor wee Dan! Listen, Kath, I'll fix this for Dan, I promise you that. Before I go to Australia ... But anyway, about Ann Marie ... I'm afraid the decision has been made. Ann Marie has agreed to go to Donegal and when she comes back she can start again. Hopefully she'll think twice the next time. Or better still, maybe she'll find herself a husband.' Kevin stood up and flicked his fag end away. 'Maybe it's for the best, Kath,' he said, but I knew he didn't believe it. 'C'mon, pal, let's go home.' He walked away.

I sat for a moment and watched him as he went. His shoulders seemed to sag a little and I thought I saw him shake his head. His hand went up to his eye and I wondered if he was crying. But no. Not Kevin. I got to my feet and ran to catch up with him. I walked alongside him all the way home. But we said nothing.

Chapter Nine

We had been catching minnows in jam jars and now we sat at the edge of the stream and watched the tiny fish dart about their murky prison. They buzzed round and round the jars, bumping into the side, confused but too stupid to know that they couldn't get out.

'Maybe it's cruel to do that.' Dan was lying on his stomach watching the minnows.

'What? Fish don't have a brain. They don't know they're trapped. That's why they keep hitting the sides,' Jamie said, chipping stones into the pool that had been created by the makeshift dam at the foot of the waterfall.

'Well, brain or no brain, they look a bit upset. I'm putting mine back.' Dan lifted his jar and headed towards the water.

He waded in and poured his jar over some pebbles that were barely submerged in water. The minnows struggled briefly, their bodies thrashing furiously, then they were carried away by the current. We watched as they disappeared like quicksilver into the stream.

'There,' said Dan, triumphantly, 'they're free now. They look happy.'

We all watched, and in the silence we could hear the water bubbling through the pebbles then rushing faster and more furiously as it flowed downstream.

Without another word, Jamie, Tony and me picked up our jars and poured them into the stream. It had taken us ages to catch them, and now here we were dumping them back in the water. We watched as they struggled, then swam swiftly to freedom.

'Looks great, doesn't it?' Tony said, staring intently at the fish. 'One day I'm gonna be like that. Like the fish. Just free to do what I want . . . run fast or walk slow . . . just keep goin' and see what happens to me. I'm gonna be free.' Tony's eyes looked dark and sad.

'What do you mean, free, Tony? It's not like you're in prison like the Bird Man of Alcatraz, for God's sake,' Jamie said, sitting down and opening the sandwiches he had brought for the picnic. We all followed him and took our sandwiches out.

Tony was eating, but he seemed far away. Then he spoke. 'I'm gonna run away.' It was as simple as that. He didn't make a great elaborate statement, and he spoke softly. But we knew he meant it. We all looked at each other, afraid of what was going to happen next.

'What, like . . . er, run away from home?' Dan asked.

'Yeah, away from home. From the Polack. From . . . from . . . er . . . Mom. I can't take it any more. I've had enough and I'm gonna run away. I got plans. And . . . er . . . I got plans to get money too.' Tony tossed away the crusts of his sandwich and they floated downstream. He guzzled a drink of diluted orange squash he had made up in a sauce bottle.

'What about your mum, Tony?' I asked, feeling panic rising in me that he was going to leave us. 'I mean, your mum would die if you ran away. She'd be worried sick, Tony.'

Tony looked at me and then the others. He knew that we knew what had been happening in recent weeks, with the drink and his mum being found outside.

'You know Mom. She's . . . well, she's . . . I just don't want this any more. It's bad. And I'm not stayin' around. I hate it.'

'Tony, you're only eleven. I mean, where would you go? The

cops would catch you before the day was out and bring you home.' I was trying to think of ways to stop him, but I knew there would be no way.

'That's where you're wrong, Kath. You see, I've got a plan. I'm goin' to steal the money from the stash the Polack keeps below the floorboards, then I'm gonna hide out for a day or so ... in the woods or somethin', then I'll get a train to somewhere. I dunno, maybe the coast or somethin'. Hell, maybe I'll even go back to the States.'

Dan and Jamie were looking at each other, then at me, then at Tony. They knew he meant business and the only one who could stop him was me. But I knew that it wouldn't work.

'Why don't you all come with me? We could all be together. I'll get enough money ... It'll be all right. We can look after each other.' Tony looked pleadingly at us. But he had a determination in his eyes. I had seen it before. Even if we wouldn't go, he would go.

All of us sat pondering the possibilities of an amazing adventure. It was tempting. It would be like the movies. To run away and be free of everything. I could see that Jamie was turning the idea over in his head. He wouldn't have to watch the brutality in his house any more, with his crazy dad getting drunk and hitting his mum. He was a big lad for his age and the thought of fending for himself, like some of the heroes we read about or watched on TV, appealed to him. Dan looked sad. He knew that no matter what, he could never leave his mum. Not while she still sobbed every night in her bed for his dad. Dan was the man of the house now, all the grown-ups kept saying, and he knew he would never be free. I thought of everything that was happening in my house. Of Ann Marie packing her bags to go to Donegal and give her baby away. Of Kevin with his secret that he was going to Australia. Of Mum and Dad and the same no-hope days. I would love to be free. Free to run and roam and sleep outside at night or in a barn or something. Free to go to the seaside and spend all your money in the café on fish and chips, then go to the pictures and stuff your face with sweets. And all the time, I would be with Tony. We would be together and we would look after each other. But then I thought of Mum and Dad and how everyone would be hunting high and low for me. They would cry their eyes out. No, I couldn't run away. But my heart sank, because I knew that Tony could, and he would. And soon.

The way Barney told the stories, I was right there in the middle of the war. Right in the prison camp with the stifling heat and the stench of men dying in their own vomit and shit. I could smell the fear. I could see the cockroaches and the rats that ran over their feet at night. And sometimes a man would scream out in the blackness when he awoke to find a rat gnawing at his hands. During his vivid stories, I was rigid with fear as Barney sat on his chair, sucking his cigarette so deeply there were shadowy pockets in his cheeks, as he took me with him to the Jap prison camp. I watched his eyes narrow as he remembered with bitterness the beatings and the torture. Then they would go all misty when he spoke of the day it was all over and they became free men. But they would never be free, he said. On the day the troops threw open the gates, Barney said it was the sweetest moment. They all sang and cried and hugged each other's emaciated bodies when the American and British soldiers rolled up to the camp in their jeeps and trucks. But Barney said by the time he was on his way to the US hospital, the horror of what he had been through felt even worse. And he never was a free man again.

'I'm sorry, hen.' Barney sniffed and brushed away a tear. 'I didn't mean to go all soft. It's just that sometimes it all seems so painful.' He put his hand on his chest. 'I feel it right in here. Like a physical pain. I know you're maybe too young to understand this, darlin', but although the camp was like being in hell, it's actually been harder being here all these years. You see, in the camp, you were all the same, struggling and fighting every day in the hopeless, stinking hole that it was. There was nothing to look forward to. But back home, here, I had to try to be like everybody else. Everybody thinks I should have been able to put it behind me, but I can't ... I can't. It haunts my every waking hour.' He stopped and put his head in his hands.

I sat quietly, scarcely breathing, not knowing what to say or do. His stories had been more and more dramatic every day I had visited him, but I had never seen such pain. I got out of my chair and went across to him and very hesitantly, gently, put my hand on his shoulder and squeezed it. Without lifting his head, he put one arm around my waist and pulled me close to him. He was holding me so tight with one arm I thought he was going to squeeze the life out of me. But I couldn't say anything because I was afraid to hurt him even more. Then he looked up at me with his bloodshot eyes and his face all wet with tears. He stroked my hair and touched my face. His hands felt rough, but I felt so sorry for him. He held me like that for a moment, then I eased myself gently from his grasp.

'I'll get you a cup of tea, Barney,' I said, walking away from him into the kitchen. 'Maybe you can show me some more of the medals and maybe even the gun you kept,' I shouted from the kitchen.

As I poured the tea I thought about Barney holding on to me, and I thought about Father Flynn grabbing Dan. And then I remembered there were always stories at school of someone whose uncle or family friend had been interfering with the children and he had to move away from the village. But it didn't feel like that with Barney. He just seemed sad and lonely and I think I was the favourite of all the kids who sometimes called in to him.

When I brought the tea and biscuits in he had pulled himself together and was limping across the room with the medals and some kind of object inside a yellow cloth. He spread the medals on the table. He explained to me what they were for. One for saving an injured soldier who he carried on his back for two miles behind enemy lines. One for leading his platoon to safety after crossing a raging river in the dead of night. Another, he said, was just for turning up for the war. Then he very deftly unwrapped the yellow duster. There it was. A real gun. A pistol, just like the ones on *The Colditz Story*. My eyes opened wide.

'Can I touch it, Barney?'

'Aye. It's OK, there's no bullets in it.'

I lifted the gun and examined it. It felt cold and heavy, much heavier than I would have believed. I put my hand on the trigger.

'It's amazing, Barney. Did you kill people with it?'

'I did . . . I did, Kath. And they were just boys like me.' He stroked the gun as though he was recalling each time he had fired it.

'Where are the bullets, Barney?'

'Oh, they're kept separate. Never store the gun and the bullets together, for you never know when someone could come in and shoot you dead in your bed. I know where the bullets are, but nobody else does.'

He let me play with the gun as he puffed his fags and disappeared behind a cloud of smoke. I stood facing the mirror over the fireplace and held the gun in my hand, pleased with my reflection. I pointed it at the mirror. I looked just like one of the French Resistance or the British woman spy in the film *Carve Her Name With Pride*. I would have been great in the war.

Barney looked miles away. He was pouring himself another whisky, and I decided it was time for me to go.

I put the gun back on the table and he lit a cigarette, puffing it in hard and sniffing. He swallowed hard and I thought he was going to cry again.

'OK, I'm away, Barney,' I said, as I backed out of the room. I don't know if he even saw me go, because he had seemed to slip into another world, the one he could never really escape from.

It had been raining for two solid days and I thought it would never stop. We were bored rigid, stuck in the house with nothing to do. I had gone to Tony's house and Jamie and Dan joined us, sitting on the floor in the hall playing cards for matches.

We were playing poker and the stakes were high. Tony sat back and drummed his fingers on his chest, just like Maverick.

'I'll raise you five grand and I'll call you.' He stroked his chin.

'I'm out,' Dan said, surrendering his hand.

'Me too,' I said, spreading my pair of kings and an assortment of cards that didn't match.

Jamie covered the bet, his face showing nothing. He turned over his cards. Three aces and two queens. He looked triumphant.

'Not bad, boy ... not bad,' Tony said in his toughest American accent. Then he turned over eight, nine, ten, jack, queen, all hearts. 'Tough shit,' he said, pulling a pen he had been using as a cigar from the side of his mouth. 'You got a lot to learn, boy. Better luck next time.' We could never beat Tony at poker.

His mum came out of the kitchen with her raincoat on. Her face looked tired and drawn. She looked nothing like the woman I had seen knocking at the window the very first time I saw Tony in his garden. Now she looked sad and her eyes were a little bloodshot. She seemed jerky, and nervy, but as ever made us all welcome.

Tony looked a little embarrassed in case she was going to say anything or appeared to have been drinking.

'Tony,' she said, 'I've put out some sandwiches and biscuits for you all, and there's juice made up. I have to go to the shops and get some things in, so you boys all behave until I get back. OK?'

We all nodded sincerely, ready to get stuck into the food as soon as she was out of the door. She caught Tony's gaze as she brushed past him and he looked pleadingly at her. He knew she was going to the shops to buy drink and that she would bring it back concealed in her bag before taking it to the bedroom.

'OK, Mom. Er . . . how long will you be?' Tony asked.

She told him about an hour and he looked satisfied.

As soon as she was outside, we were in the kitchen and at the food. As we tucked into the corned beef sandwiches, Tony told us he had a plan.

'Do you guys want to see something interesting?'

I more or less knew what was coming. I knew he was going to take us upstairs and show us the Polack's money that was stashed below the floorboards. I sensed we were in for another rollercoaster ride.

'Yeah. Sure, Tony. What?' Jamie said, stuffing his sandwiches into his mouth.

'I'm gonna show you the Polack's money box. I've never actually been right through it, but there's lots of dough there. Fancy a look?'

We all glanced at each other. It was too good to miss.

'What if he comes in and catches us?' Dan was always cautious.

'He won't be home for three hours yet. Jeez, we could be in and out six times by then,' Tony said, downing his juice and wiping his mouth with his sleeve. 'C'mon, guys, let's go.'

We followed behind him in single file along the hall and stood at the foot of the stairs. It looked dark up there. Jamie,

Dan and I all looked at each other as Tony took the stairs two at a time. We hesitated.

'What if he comes back early?' I said, picturing the Polack walking in and finding us all with our hands in his money box.

Tony turned around and gave us that challenging look we had all seen before.

'He won't. He won't come back. And anyhow, doesn't that make it all the more exciting? C'mon, guys, what are you, scared?'

Jamie pushed past me and started up the steps.

'Scared my ass,' he said with a perfect American accent.

Dan and me followed, but not quite as fast.

In the bedroom the Polack's big trousers were draped over a basket chair and the way they were hanging you could almost see the shape of him. The big black leather belt with a fat metal buckle was threaded through the loops and Tony caught me looking at it and knew what I was thinking. I guessed this was the belt he used to beat Tony.

He pulled back the rug from the side of the bed and carefully eased out the floorboard. Then he stuck his arm in all the way up to his shoulder and brought out the tin box. We all looked at each other in anticipation. He wiped the sweat from his top lip. He was nervous, even though he tried to act tough. He must have been terrified in case the Polack landed in on us, for Tony knew he would be history.

He reached under the drawer of the bedside cabinet and produced a tiny key. He held it up to us and raised his eyebrows and smiled broadly.

'Watch this, guys,' Tony said. He opened up the box and our eyes almost popped out of our heads as we saw the wads of money. There were fivers, tenners and twenty-pound notes. I had only ever seen about two twenty-pound notes in my life and I was thrilled.

'Jesus, he's a piggin' millionaire,' Jamie said, crouching down beside Tony, who was inside the box rummaging around.

'How much is in there, Tony? Thousands?' Dan said.

Tony lifted bundles out and began to count them. There were at least twenty bundles of what looked like hundred-pound wads, and there was more lying loose.

'I'd say there's about eight or ten thousand pounds here. Look,' Tony said, raising the box up to us. 'Smell it. Real dosh. More than that asshole would ever need.'

'God,' I said. 'He must be like a miser or something. I mean, he's got all that money, but you said he hardly gives your mum anything. What does he do with it?'

'He just keeps it. That's what he's like. Maybe he's planning to leave some day and he needs cash. Well, let's hope so. I'd be glad to see his Polack ass out the door and Ma and me would have some peace again.'

Tony kept rummaging and suddenly underneath the cash we saw what looked like a passport. But it was in a foreign language and it looked ancient. He pulled it out to examine it. He opened it up. We all gathered round. There was a faded black and white picture of a young man with a mass of curly dark hair and a stern expression on his face. There was no mistaking, though, it was the Polack. It was the first time I had ever seen his name. Tony had never even told us what his name was, he only referred to him as the Polak and so did we. Anton Zadrovic, it said below the photograph. We couldn't make out what else was written, but we could read quite clearly the country. It didn't say Poland. It said Lithuania. We all looked at each other.

'I thought he was Polish,' Jamie said.

'So did I. We've always thought that,' Tony said. 'But this says he's Lithuanian.'

We didn't understand any of it and wondered why he had always said he was Polish.

Tony sifted through some more papers. Then he suddenly stopped. We all saw it at the same time. The swastika. It was familiar to us who had played the war games a million times. We had been to Colditz and back and we knew a Nazi when we saw one.

We could hardly believe our eyes. Tony pulled out what looked like an old newspaper.

On the front page was Hitler in an open jeep being driven through a street with masses of people lining the road. He was making the Nazi salute, as were the crowds. There was a swastika at each side of the top of the page. The paper was flimsy and yellowing. Tony opened it very carefully. There it was. The picture. Staring back at us. The Polack. The same face as the passport photo, but this time in the uniform of a Nazi SS soldier. He had a rifle over his shoulder as if he was guarding some Jewish prisoners. We couldn't understand what the words said, but we could see they were telling a story about him. There was a picture on the same page of Jewish prisoners being transported to camps. We recognized the word Auschwitz.

'Holy shit!' Tony said. 'Holeee shit! He's a goddamn Nazi! Jeeesus, man. The Polack's a goddamn Nazi! The bastard! The murdering Nazi bastard! God! I can't believe this! Wow!'

We were almost speechless. We could scarcely take it in.

'Jesus, Tony,' I said breathlessly. 'I can't believe that. The Polack . . . he's really a Nazi! Jesus! This is like a movie! Can you believe this? Look! He's got a rifle over his shoulder, just like the one he uses now when he's out shooting rabbits!'

Jamie and Dan were shaking their heads, their eyes wide open.

'What a lying, cheating scumbag!' Jamie said. 'Do you think your mum knows, Tony?'

'No way . . . no way. He told her his family were Jewish and got gassed in the camps and he was left an orphan. He said he became a Catholic when a Polish family took him in after months of living on the streets. What a lying shite!'

Tony looked further into the box. There were Nazi medals and ribbons, all with the Third Reich inscriptions. And more newspaper clippings showing the Polack, again with his SS uniform on. One was in what looked like a camp and the headline was Kovnow, Lithuania.

'He must have been some kind of Nazi hero,' Dan said. 'Look at all the stuff.'

Tony sat back on his heels. He was trying to decipher any words that sounded familiar so he could understand what the clippings said, but it was no good.

'A Nazi! My God! It all makes sense now,' Tony said. 'I mean, he's such a bullying, evil bastard. He obviously got plenty of practice.'

We were mesmerized and trying to take in what we were witnessing when suddenly we all jumped together as we heard the front door slam.

'Shit!' Tony said, stuffing the papers back in the box. 'Shit! Shit!'

'Hullo! Hullo! Anybody home?' It was unmistakably the Polack's gruff voice.

'Oh shit, Tony! We're done for! He'll kill us! Jesus!' Dan was on his feet.

'Sssh! Sssh! Stay quiet as a mouse. The first thing he does when he comes home is go to the fridge and drink a pint of milk. We've got time. We'll slip into my room. Now slowly. No noise.' Tony deftly put the box back and like a cat burglar slid open the drawer and replaced the key.

We crept in a thin, terrified line into Tony's room. In a second he had a game of Ludo open on the floor and we were rolling the dice as if we had been there all day. We heard the footsteps coming up the stairs and our stomachs turned over. At the same moment as the Polack pushed open the door, Tony roared: 'Oh yeah! And it's the nation's favourite Tony Keenan who wins hands down again!' We looked at him, marvelling at his improvisation.

The big Pole looked around the room. We were scared to look up from the board.

'Tony,' he rasped. 'What'ya doin' in here? Does your mother know you have all these people in here?'

'Sure. She said it's all right. She even made us some sandwiches,' Tony said innocently.

'What'ya doin' up the stairs? I hope y'not pokin' around anywhere y'shouldn't be or y'know what y'll get, boy.' The Pole stood scratching his belly.

We glanced up at him, then back to the board, praying he couldn't see our guilt.

'No, no. We're just playin'.' Tony got up. 'In fact, now that I've won again, I think we'll go out and play some football. C'mon, let's go, guys.'

We were up like a shot. I thought I would burst if I didn't get out of that room. We clattered downstairs and into the kitchen, pushing each other to get out of the door.

To our amazement Tony stopped dead at the back door. He turned to face the closed kitchen door and gave a Nazi salute with his finger across his top lip. 'Heil Hitler! You Nazi bastard!' he whispered, and we all piled out of the door.

Chapter Ten

I could hear my mum crying in the night and I put my hands over my ears to make it stop. There had been movement and talking coming from their bedroom all night and I could hear Dad's voice, soft and gentle, as if he was trying to comfort her.

I knew it was about Ann Marie. She had been packing her bags for days, getting ready for her trip to Donegal. Almost every night I was wakened in the middle of the night by the sounds of her sobbing into her pillow. I lay scarcely breathing, wishing I could say something. But I wasn't sure if she knew that I knew she was having a baby. She wasn't all that fat, just a kind of bump at the front, but I noticed she didn't undress when I was in the room. She was also wearing a lot of baggy shirts belonging to Dad, or one of Mum's bigger blouses, so she didn't look pregnant. I suppose that was so that nobody outside would find out.

I hadn't spoken much to her about going to Donegal, except to talk about the times we used to go there on holiday to live with Auntie Nora and her family. It was only a small village, with a few bed and breakfast places and some pubs, but it was by the sea and everything always smelled great and fresh. Sometimes the winds would nearly whip you off your feet and you could be walking along the beach bent over against the gale, trying to get back to the house. Then the rain would come on so hard that it wasn't even landing on the sand but was going straight back up because the wind was so fierce. It fascinated me, and even though I was frozen stiff by the time I got into the house, I felt great. You could nearly fall asleep in front of the peat fire, and I used to get drowsy listening to Aunt Nora's husband Uncle Eamon telling stories at night. He was Irish and she married him after meeting him on a weekend bus trip to Bundoran. Dad was thrilled that she was going back to her roots, and I only vaguely understood what that meant. Mum and Dad were both born in Scotland and so were their parents, but their grandparents had come over on the boat. Dad used to say the only time he felt right in his heart and soul was when he put his foot back in Ireland. He said he couldn't really understand why he felt so strong when he wasn't born there, but he said it must just be in his blood, or maybe his soul had a memory. Sitting listening to them talking about stories carried down the years made me feel the same. If I ever wanted to go anywhere to live it would have been there. Sometimes there would be men who Uncle Eamon said were from the North and they would be staying for a couple of days. I never knew who they were and we never spoke to them, but when they came, he used to take them into the kitchen and they would talk for a while. Sometimes they just stayed one night, and we were told to say nothing about it.

Now here was Ann Marie talking about going and saying there was a job she had in the village and it was going to be great, but I think it was all just to convince herself everything would be fine.

Then there were the visits from Father Flynn. I was growing to despise him. He would come into the house and I would be motioned by my parents to leave the room. Father Flynn would always playfully ruffle my hair or pinch my cheek on the way out, but I could always feel myself glowering at him. I knew things about him that the rest of them didn't. They would faint if they knew what I knew.

One evening when he came in, it was just Mum, Dad, Ann Marie and me who sat in the living room. They must have been expecting him because Mum had bought a packet of gyspy creams and I was told not to touch them. I opened the door to him when he arrived.

'Hallo, Father,' I said, stepping aside to let him across the threshold.

'Kathleen! Howyedoin'?' His big Irish voice boomed as he strode past me.

He didn't wait for my answer. He was full of business.

I came into the living room and deliberately sat on the couch until Mum and Dad's faces were contorted trying to signal to me to leave the room. Eventually I got up and slipped out, unfortunately close enough to Father Flynn so he could grab my hair.

But I didn't go upstairs. I made some noises on the stairs by climbing two or three, so that they would think I had gone to my room, then I sat in the hallway listening at the door. There was a silence, then finally Father Flynn spoke as softly as his voice would let him.

'Now!' he said, and I could picture him leaning forward the way he always did, with his hands clasped, when he was making a point. 'Now! And how're tings, Ann Marie?' She didn't answer. Maybe she just nodded.

'And you, Martin and Maggie? Are ye all right?'

'As well as could be expected, Father . . . under the circumstances.' Dad sounded like he was trying to pick his words.

There was another silence. The air must have been thick in that room. I could feel the tension.

'Right now! Right!' Father Flynn began. His voice grew soft and I could barely hear.

'Now, Ann Marie, it'll not be long till it's all over and you can get yourself back to normal and, God willing, put this little, shall we say, fall from grace behind you.' I could imagine them in the room, sitting looking at him, anticipating his every word.

'About the parents,' he continued. 'They're getting pretty excited across the water now that the wee one is only about . . . what'sit . . . three months away. Oh yeah! Sure, they've a little nursery all painted and everythin'. They're goin' to be great parents, Ann Marie, and you'll never have to worry that the . . . er . . . the little one will want for anything.'

There was a silence in the room and I wondered if anyone was going to ask questions or even suggest that this should not happen. But no. I heard some papers being rustled.

'Now what you've to do, Ann Marie, is just sign here, which in effect is you giving up the child to its new parents . . . God bless them for relieving you and your loving parents from the burden . . . and then that's it. You can come back home when the time is right. And well, you know, your penance will go on for a long time, but you'll have saved your poor mother and father the shame of bringing an illegitimate child into the world.'

Silence. Then Ann Marie spoke.

'And . . . er . . . Father . . . er . . . will I ever see it again . . . the baby? Will I ever know how it's getting on? I mean, will I hold it or anything when it's born?' I knew by the sound of her voice that she was close to tears. She was stuttering and struggling with her words. I could picture Mum and Dad glaring at her. They knew she was hurting, but they knew that the priest was right. She couldn't have a baby out of wedlock.

Father Flynn cleared his throat.

'Ah now, Ann Marie! Ann Marie, Ann Marie! You know the situation. I've dealt with this in the privacy of the confessional, and you know the enormity of the stain on your soul for that . . . well, that yielding to the temptation. Now this is, if you like, how you must face your punishment . . . if you know what I mean. Nobody is going to look upon you any different.

You'll just have to buckle down now, girl, and get on with it.
You're paying the consequences. Now that's the way it is, girl.
There'll be another opportunity for you. You're a young girl
and you'll get a husband in the future. Even though you're
no longer a virgin, somebody'll want you for their own and
love you and give you many more children. Now let's look at
it that way, Ann Marie. Come on now, none of your crying.
You should have thought about that six months ago.'

There was another silence in the room and I heard the
papers being rustled again.

Father Flynn spoke. 'Right! That's it. Now that's a good
girl. That's the stuff. Yes, blow your nose, girl. Well, that's
that done! Now, Martin how're things with you? And Maggie!
How're things at that chicken factory? You must be worked
awful hard down there. They tell me people are doing twelve
and fourteen-hour shifts. Is that right?'

'Yes, Father. It's not easy, but you just bash on.' Mum's
voice was weak as though she was finding it hard to speak.
I heard the clatter of cups and I knew they would be coming
through the hall to go to the kitchen. I dived on to the stairs
and swiftly raced to the top and into my bedroom.

Ann Marie's suitcase was all packed and lying open at the
bottom of her bed. I peeked inside it. Her blouses and bras
were packed as well as her skirts and a pair of jeans that she
couldn't get into at the moment and her favourite yellow wool
cardigan. There was a big baggy cheesecloth smock dress. Then
underneath, tucked away, was a little white crocheted woollen
baby jacket with silk ribbons woven through the collar. It was
beautiful. I eased it out of the case and brushed it against my
cheek. It felt soft and fluffy. I pictured a little baby with its
pink face and tiny fingers and toes. Ann Marie's baby. But
she had to give it away. It would have a new mum and dad
who had a nursery all painted and ready. It wasn't fair.

*   *   *

Tony had a devilish glint in his eye when I opened the back door to him, and I knew straight away he had been up to something.

'Hi, Kath. What's doin'?' he said as I closed the door behind me and stepped outside.

'Nothing. It's boring. Saturdays aren't the same when you're on school holidays.'

'Not today, Kath. We're goin' out for the day, you, me, Jamie and Dan. We're takin' in a movie, then it's down to Luigi's for chips, ice cream, the lot.' Tony stood hands in pockets, a wide smile on his face.

'Aye. Dream on, Tony. What did you do, rob a bank?' As soon as I said it, I was thinking that he probably had.

'Not quite,' Tony said, as he dug into his pocket and pulled out a ten-pound note.

'Jesus!' was all I could say.

'I took it from Hitler's box. Fat old bastard won't even miss it.' He grinned. 'C'mon, let's go and get Jamie and Dan. We're going to have a feast of a day.'

I didn't even look back at the house in case anyone was watching me and asked me where I was going. We were off together down the road, just two kids like any other you would have seen on a Saturday morning walking in the street. Except we had secrets they could never even dream of. And better than all of that, we had a tenner between us. I couldn't wait to tell Jamie and Dan of Tony's latest exploits. I broke into a run with Tony chasing after me, both of us giggling at the sheer cheek and madness of it all.

When we got to Jamie's house we automatically slowed down because you never knew what you would find there. The back door was open and Jamie was in the kitchen with his young brother and sister who were getting out of their pyjamas. He was washing their faces and trying to get them dressed. His brother was screaming that there was soap in his eyes.

'Shut it. You've got to get washed,' Jamie said, rubbing their faces till they were pink.

He looked embarrassed at us catching him like this.

'Mammy's not well. She's in bed. But she'll be up in an hour,' he said quickly. The kitchen was like a bomb site and he hurriedly tried to tidy when he saw us glancing around.

'We're goin' to the movies, then the café,' Tony said.

'Me come too! Me come too! Me want to go to the café! Chips!' The wee brother's eyes opened wide.

Jamie quickly came out the back door.

'I'm skint. I can't go anywhere.'

Tony produced the tenner once again and held it up triumphantly.

'Don't worry, the Nazi's payin',' he said.

'Jesus! Jeesus, Tony, you'll get us all locked up,' Jamie said.

'Well? Are you in? Or are you going to sit about here all day like Julie Andrews?' Tony said, shrugging his shoulders and grinning as he spread his hands in front of him.

'Give me two minutes.' Jamie opened the back door and pushed past the children as he barged through the kitchen.

Seconds later his mum appeared in her dressing gown, looking awful. Her face was pasty and her eyes were shadowy. Her hair was sticking up and she was holding her ribs as she walked. Tony and I glanced briefly at each other, the same thought flashing through our minds. Jake had been at it again.

'Hi, boys,' Mary McCabe said, trying her best to sound cheery. She turned on the cold tap and banged the kettle under it. She winced as the simple effort of lifting the kettle seemed to hurt her ribs.

'I'm all sore today. Must have pulled a muscle,' she said, but by the look on her face she knew we didn't believe her.

The bathroom door at the end of the hall opened and Jake McCabe emerged clutching a newspaper under his arm.

'Shut that fuckin' door!' he growled, then broke into a racking cough which sounded as though he was about to spit up balls of tar.

Mary slammed the hall door on him. We watched, nervous of what might happen next.

The door was kicked open. Jake, his face crimson from coughing, came in with his eyes blazing. He walked up to Mary, who looked as though she was about to collapse.

'Don't push your fuckin' luck!' He spat the words out. Tony and me shrank back.

Jake shot us a glance.

'Fuck are you lookin' at? Piss off!' He slammed the door in our faces. We stood silently, scared.

Minutes later Jamie came out with his hair all slicked back and a clean T-shirt on. His face was shining. He looked lovely, but his eyes were sheepish.

'Christ, it's the Brylcreem boy!' Tony joked, making a grab for Jamie's hair, but he dodged out of the way.

'Let's have a walking race to Dan's house,' Jamie said and was walking on already with his arms swinging and hips swaying in that exaggerated way of the men in the walking races at the Olympic Games.

We all raced after him, walking as fast as we could, and for the moment we tried not to think what was going on back inside that kitchen.

Dan was hanging bed sheets on the washing line of his back garden and didn't see us as we approached. We stopped yards from him, crouching behind the wall, sniggering as we watched him carefully drape the sheets over the rope. He had a clothes peg in his mouth and his little sister stood by his side handing him pegs from a bag she had strapped to her waist.

'Seen any old knickers wi' a hole in them? I know somebody who lost a pair,' Tony said as we jumped out on Dan, startling him when he turned and saw us. He looked worried and tense at first but laughed when he saw the joke. He quickly put the stretcher on to the rope and pushed the washing up high. We watched as the candy-striped sheets billowed in the wind.

'Our Dan pees the bed!' It seemed to come from nowhere and the words hung frozen in the air, leaving us all stunned. Suddenly it dawned on us why Dan was hanging out his sheets, and why he had looked slightly startled when we surprised him. His face dropped and he turned on his sister.

'Get into the house, you! Quick! Git, before I kick your arse.' He lunged at the girl, his face beetroot red, and she dodged him, racing off towards the back door.

'See her!' Dan said. 'Wee shite!' He didn't look at any of us and kicked the ground.

Jamie broke the atmosphere.

'Listen, Dan, we're goin' to the pictures, then the café for a slap-up meal. Tony's got money he took from the Nazi. Hurry. He's got a tenner.'

Dan's eyes opened wide when Tony produced the tenner and waved it in the air. He laughed.

'You're a nutcase. What if he counts it and finds it's missing?' he said.

'Stuff him. You saw the box. He's got a fortune in there. He'll never notice. C'mon, let's get movin'.'

'What're we goin' to see?' Dan said.

'*Planet of the Apes.* You might recognize yourself,' Tony said, adopting an ape's posture, crouching down and holding his hands high above his head as he circled Dan. We all laughed. He walked exactly like an ape. We all joined in, but none of us could get down as low as Tony.

'Wait while I tell my mum. You know what it's like,' Dan said as he ran off to the house. He emerged minutes later in his denim jacket and jeans, munching on a banana sandwich.

'Just getting into the swing of things, Dan?' Jamie said, making a monkey face.

Dan aimed a kick at him but missed.

The sun was bursting its way through fat white clouds. We walked down the road, the four of us taking the full breadth of the pavement like the gunslingers from *The Magnificent Seven* strutting into town. There was a big afternoon ahead and nobody could touch us. We were on our own and had a tenner of the Nazi's money. It was great. Dan even broke into a skip, the shame of the bedwetting revelation vanishing for the moment to the back of his mind as we stood waiting for the bus to take us into town.

You could always hear Billy Cowan before you saw him. He had the biggest mouth in the village and here he was again shooting his trap off and goading the other kids in the queue for the cinema. He hated Tony, mostly because everybody else liked him, but also because he spoke like an American. That made Billy jealous because no matter how much he tried to be like the guys in the movies, he couldn't even sound like them. But he hated the rest of us anyway, because we were Catholics. He said he hated all Catholics, just like his dad who led off the Orange Walk every year. He said that Catholics should be in Ireland where they belonged in their stinking bogs and not over here, stealing all the jobs. I couldn't understand it. I had only been to Ireland on holiday. This was my home. We all felt edgy as we walked up to the queue. Tony and Jamie squared their shoulders while Dan and me fell in behind them.

'Look at Cowan,' Tony said. 'He's eyeing us up. I bet he starts on me again. I feel like wasting his face.'

'Let's just get in the queue and ignore him,' Dan said. 'We

122

might not get in if there's a fight. C'mon, never mind. He's a diddy anyway.'

All four of us took our place in the queue quietly. We looked up at the poster on the wall with all the hype about *Planet of the Apes*. We were getting quite excited.

'I heard it was real apes,' Dan said, wide-eyed. 'And that they trained them up.'

We all burst out laughing. 'What! Real apes? Wi' coats and hats on, and sitting around talking and stuff?' Jamie said, sniggering.

'No,' Dan insisted, 'I don't mean the talking. But I heard it was real apes they used and dressed them up. I mean, they do it in the tea advert on the telly, so it can be done.' He was convincing himself.

'No way,' I said. 'Look closely at their faces, Dan. They look too much like people. No way are they real apes.'

'We'll see, we'll see.' Dan was refusing to concede the point.

When the cinema doors opened everyone rushed forward and the commissionaire was out trying to get us into an orderly queue. We were almost at the ticket kiosk and Tony was fishing in his jeans pocket for the money.

'Right, lads! Hurry up before the Micks get all the good seats!' Billy Cowan nodded in our direction and urged his mates to push forward. They did. We ignored them.

After they got through it was our turn and Tony produced the ten-pound note. Billy and his pals were still hanging around, watching us.

'Hey, Yankee! Where did you get all that money, eh? Whose pockets did you dip?' His mates all shuffled around laughing. They were scared of him. Billy was thirteen but was already a head and shoulder taller than all of us and looked older. He was a known bully in the village and had a reputation in the Protestant secondary school he attended for being the best fighter in the first year. Some people said he even went to Shaggy Island at night and did the business.

'Hey . . . I'm talkin' to you, Mick. Are you deaf as well as stupid?' Billy persisted as Tony put the tickets and the change back in his pocket. He looked angry.

We all stood facing Billy and his pals in the foyer. Tony looked Billy in the eye.

'Why don't you piss off? We're goin' to watch the movie, OK?' Tony said matter-of-factly.

We walked past Billy, but only got a few steps when he piped up.

'How's your ma, Yankee? Still pished?' The words had barely left Billy's lips before Tony was on top of him, head-butting him to the ground. It happened so fast we didn't even see it. Immediately, the commissionaire was in, pulling the two apart.

'Right! Right! That's it! Are ye wantin' barred out? Is that it? Now, on your feet the two of you.' He pulled both of them to their feet. Tony's eyes were blazing. Billy looked a bit shocked and was clutching his stomach, trying to catch his breath.

'He kneed me in the balls!' Billy shouted, his face red with indignation.

'What balls?' Tony said, struggling to get at him again.

'Right! Right, now, I'll put the two of you out in the street.' The commissionaire tightened his grip, his face reddening.

Both Tony and Billy were silent, looking away from each other.

'C'mon, Tony, let's watch the picture. C'mon, it's nearly started,' Jamie said, pulling Tony by the arm.

'This is no finished yet,' Billy snapped at Tony as he turned to walk away.

We ignored him and walked through the swing doors into the exciting darkness of the cinema. The usherette shone her torch and led us to seats halfway down and we filed in silently.

Tony was still breathing fast by the time we took our seats. I could see in the darkness that there were tears in his eyes. I squeezed his arm gently, but he never took his eyes off the screen.

The picture started and from the opening words we were engrossed in the screen. Nobody spoke until halfway through the film, when Dan leaned forward and said:

'I'm sure they apes are real.' We all sniggered.

'Away and get the ice lollies,' Tony said, pushing a pound note into his hand.

We could smell the aroma coming from Luigi's Café as soon as we emerged, blinking, from the cinema into the late afternoon sunshine. The smell of chips frying mingled with the kind of earthy odour of herbs from Luigi's special sausages filled the air and made our mouths water in expectation. We made our way into the street, squeezing past the queue for the next showing of *Planet of the Apes*. I was glad to see that there was no sign of Billy Cowan and his cronies, though I got the feeling that this wasn't over yet. As we crossed the road, Jamie looked over his shoulder, scanning the crowd for Cowan.

'Hey, guys! Look!' We all stopped in our tracks, assuming it was Billy he'd spotted. But it wasn't. It was Miss Grant, standing at the entrance to the cinema by herself. She must be on a date. It was unimaginable to think that someone would actually want to go out with her.

'Can you believe it?' Tony said, smiling. 'Can you actually believe that anyone would want to go to the pictures with her? Or even that she would go to the movies and actually enjoy herself? Jeez. Poor guy.'

'I wonder what kind of pants she's got on,' Jamie said and we all laughed.

I watched Miss Grant shift around from one foot to the other in her high heels. She looked almost acceptable, dressed in a red knee-length skirt and white blouse with a black jacket over her arm. Her hair was all sorted and she was wearing lipstick. I tried to imagine her having a normal conversation and laughing with her boyfriend, but I couldn't get the picture in my head. She was looking at her watch, then peering up the road. I felt a sudden, surprising pang of pity for her. What if she was getting stood up? I knew from listening to Kevin and Ann Marie that it was the greatest shame in all the world to get a dissy. You became the laughing stock if it happened. Just about everybody knew, because nine times out of ten you would be meeting the date outside the pictures and everyone would notice if you ended up being on your own. Miss Grant kept looking at her watch.

'I think she's getting a dissy,' I said, as we walked backwards still watching her.

'I hope so,' Tony said. 'I hope she stands there till she faints face down in the dark.'

We followed our noses to Luigi's. We had more important matters on our minds than Miss Grant's love life. But I couldn't help looking over my shoulder to see if she was still waiting as the crowd started to file into the cinema. Soon she would be on her own. Serves her right, I thought.

Inside Luigi's we piled into a booth and the four of us tried to grab the plastic menu at once.

'How much have you got left, Tony?' I said, wondering if I could get a Luigi's special supper and a milk shake.

He emptied his pocket on to the table. Rolled-up pound notes and a ten-shilling note plus lots of silver. It looked like nearly six pounds. It was loads.

'We've got plenty. We can get a full meal each and a drink and still have some left,' Tony said, eyeing the menu.

'Brilliant! I'll have sausage, egg and chips, and a strawberry milk shake,' Jamie said.

'A Luigi's special for me,' I said. 'And a chocolate milk shake.'

Tony and Dan ordered the same when Luigi's wife Carla came shuffling over to the table, her big fat chest hanging down to her waist, which seemed to be held up by the bright red and blue grease-stained apron she had tied around her wobbling stomach.

'Okay-cokay, my boys ... and geerls,' she said, nodding and smiling in my direction as if we were old friends. I smiled back at her. I loved to watch Carla in the café, bouncing from table to table, waving and laughing in big exaggerated gestures. She seemed to love everybody. The only time you heard her shouting was in the back kitchen when she and Luigi were having a fight over something. It sounded brilliant. They used to scream at each other in Italian and you could hear pots and pans crashing. Then Carla would emerge with plates full of food in each hand, laughing and shaking her head, mumbling something in Italian as she weaved through the café. It was nearly as good as going to the pictures.

Nearly all the Italians I came across seemed to be louder and more expressive than anyone I knew. Dad said it was their hot blood due to being raised in a warm climate. They were really hard workers and seemed to own all the cafés and chip shops. Most of them who were here came over just before the Second World War and made good money, but I had heard stories that when the war broke out and the Tallies were on the side of the Nazis local people used to go and break their windows. That must have been terrible for them. Some of the Italians were also here because they had been held in various places as prisoners of war, and they just stayed on. I heard others broke the hearts of some girls while they were here, then went back home to Italy after the war.

When the food came, nobody spoke. We eyed up the plates full of steaming chips and Luigi's home-made sausage with the flavour bursting out as soon as you stuck your knife into it. We wolfed down the food, roasting our tongues and throwing back ice-cold milk shakes to cool us down. What a feast.

We leaned back in our seats, stuffed full, and slurped the remainder of our drinks from straws hoovering the bottom of the glasses.

Dan fidgeted in his seat and toyed with his straw. He looked worried. We all looked at each other. Eventually he spoke.

'Guys ... Er ... You won't say anything about the sheets, eh?' he mumbled.

There was an awkward silence.

'What sheets?' Jamie said. We all looked from Dan to each other. He looked relieved. We were glad that was out of the way. But Dan kept going.

'It's ... er ... not that I've always done it ... It's only in the last three weeks. Jeesus! I don't know! I just don't know!' His head was down.

'Forget about it, Dan,' Tony said. 'Jeesus, man! Who cares? It's no big deal.'

Our attention was diverted by Miss Grant walking through the door of the café. She shot a brief look in our direction, then sat in a corner. She was on her own. She had been dissied. We all looked at each other and nodded knowingly. I watched as she sat down. Her body seemed to slump, deflated, on to the chair. She looked at the menu, then put it back down. Her face was stern. Then she reached into her handbag and pulled out a handkerchief. She swallowed hard, then sniffed. She dabbed her eyes. Jesus. She was crying. She had been stood up and here she was all alone in the café on a Saturday afternoon, all dressed up with nowhere to go. Well, I thought, she probably deserved it. But despite my better judgement, I couldn't stop feeling sorry for her.

The boys all watched her, seemingly unfazed.

'Huh! Who cares if she's a poor bastard?' Tony said. 'It's probably her own fault.'

'I can't believe she's greetin'. I wish I had a camera,' Jamie said, unmoved by the scene.

Dan just watched, biting his nails. He seemed to be miles away.

Finally we got up and went to the counter to pay Carla.

'Okay-cokay. You like my Luigi's food? Good? Enjoy?'

'Brilliant, Carla!' we all chorused.

'Here . . .' She fished into a box and brought out a handful of sweets. Smiling, she dropped them into our hands. 'For my most best customers!'

'Cheers, Carla! Thanks!' we all said, stuffing the sweets into our pockets as we walked out the door.

Miss Grant was watching us intently. My eyes met hers briefly and I looked away.

Outside, we'd only walked about five yards when we saw them.

There he was, his hands on his hips, Billy Cowan, surrounded by four or five of his pals.

'Shit,' said Tony. 'There's Cowan come looking for trouble.'

'C'mon, let's go the other way. Let's leg it and we'll get the bus at the next stop,' Dan said nervously.

'That'll be right,' Tony said. 'And run away from him for the rest of our lives! No way. We'll just walk right on and ignore him. But if he starts, Christ, man, I'll kick the shit out of him.' Tony was raging. He could go so quickly from laughing and joking in the café to someone who was wound up, angry and ready for action. I was scared. But I banked on Cowan and his mates not hitting a girl.

Billy and his pals seemed to part and spread out, blocking the way as we walked towards them. Billy was standing in the middle of the pavement. When we moved on to the road, they moved on to the road. There was no way out. We were trapped.

Jamie and Tony squared up, ready to fight. Dan looked at me. I didn't know how to fight.

'Where do you think you're goin', Yankee?' Billy said, taking a step forward.

'We're going home, Cowan. That's where,' Tony said as we came to a halt face to face with them.

'Home?' he sneered, looking at all of us. 'Hey, McCabe!' He singled out Jamie. 'I heard your ma's goin' to the laughin' academy! She's mental!' he said, goading Jamie about his mum, who everybody knew was close to breaking point.

'Fuck off, Cowan, ya Orange bastard!' Jamie spat. His fists were clenched by his sides. My legs felt weak. Dan was breathing hard. I thought he was going to sprint away.

'Who are you callin' an Orange bastard, ya Fenian shite!' Billy's face was contorted with rage.

'You,' Tony said, walking towards him. 'You, that's who. Now piss off, before you get your ass kicked.' We were almost walking through them as Billy's pals seemed to stand aside. Suddenly it happened.

'Your ma's gettin' shagged by big McCartney! She'll let anybody shag her for a free drink!' For the rest of his life, Billy Cowan would wish he had never said that. I had never seen anyone turn the way Tony did. The colour seemed to drain from his face into his T-shirt, and he swivelled around and was on top of Billy before he knew what hit him. Two of Billy's pals jumped on Tony's back, but he kicked upwards like a horse and knocked one flat on their back. He pulled the other one over his shoulder. Jamie jumped in and punched one of them to the ground as he tried to get up. Another jumped on Jamie. Dan leapt in and started punching everyone and anyone, shouting, 'C'mon, ya bastards. Are ye want it?' I couldn't believe my eyes. I was standing jumping from foot to foot. Tony was killing Billy. He was straddling him on the ground and swinging punches at his face. The blood was pouring from Billy's nose and mouth. I saw a tooth pop out on to the road. Tony's face was crimson and he couldn't stop punching. His eyes were full of raging tears. I screamed at him to stop, but he didn't hear me. He was lost in a frenzy of rage. I tried to jump in and pull him back. But it was all chaos. I was rooted to the spot.

Suddenly there were the big hairy arms of two men dragging Tony off Billy and pulling Jamie and Dan back.

'Are you all right, Kath?' It was Kevin and his pal, big Dessie O'Hanlon. Relief flooded through me. They were laughing at the antics of the boys and trying to hold Tony back.

'Wait a minute, tiger! Jesus! You're a strong one!' Dessie was saying as Tony was still throwing punches and kicking even when he held him in mid air.

Billy staggered to his feet and tried to kick out at Tony, but his foot was grabbed by Kevin and he fell to the ground again.

'Do you not know when you're beat, son?' Kevin said. 'Now away to your mammy and get your nose wiped.'

'Fuck off you. I'll get my da down and he'll sort you out,' Billy was saying as he backed off. His lip was burst and his nose looked broken.

'Aye! Well ye'd better tell him to bring the rest of the Lodge, 'cos your da couldn't beat Casey's drums. Now piss off home before I lose my temper.' Kevin lunged at Billy, who ran backwards giving him a two-fingered gesture of defiance.

Tony, Jamie and Dan looked like warriors. There was blood on their clothes and Tony's knuckles were bruised. Big Dessie finally put him down and he turned away, tears in his eyes. He walked off quickly past the bus stop and in the direction of the village. We all went with him, Kevin and Dessie walking behind us. Then Kevin and Dessie stopped, said something to each other and Dessie waved and went in the other direction, towards the pub they must have been in.

Kevin walked after us as we ran after Tony. When we caught up with him, he was sitting on a wall at the side of the road with his head in his hands, crying. We all sat down quietly.

'You all right, son?' Kevin said, trying to ruffle Tony's hair, but he flicked his hand away and sniffed.

'Leave me! Leave me alone!' Tony fumbled with stones in his hand, then chipped one into the distance.

We all stood around in silence, awkward. Jamie broke the ice.

'Hey, Tony! Cowan was killin' you if I hadn't jumped in!' Jamie had his cheekiest smile on as he provoked Tony. It worked.

'That'll be right! My ass! He would have been history if *he* hadn't pulled me off him.' Tony gestured at Kevin, who sat with his arms folded, mildly amused.

'Aye, that's right! I'll tell you this much, Keenan. You've got a big future with those fists of yours. Only thing is, if you were a boxer, something tells me you wouldn't hear the bell!' Kevin said.

'And what about Dan? Jesus, Dan, I didn't know you could fight. You were jumpin' about there like Rocky Marciano!' Jamie danced around, shadow-boxing with Dan, who was ducking and diving.

The atmosphere picked up. Tony stood up and wiped some blood off his lip, spat and pulled a cigarette from a packet in his top pocket. He sucked in the smoke and blew it out hard. He looked at me through the cloud of smoke and I smiled at him. He smiled back.

'C'mon, let's walk to the next bus stop and get home,' I said, wanting to be back on my own ground.

But Kevin stayed sitting on the wall.

'Listen, guys,' he said, motioning us to stay where we were. 'Listen. Er . . . I want to talk to you about Father Flynn.' Kevin looked at Dan. I was shocked. Dan looked at me as though I had committed an act of treachery.

'Kath! Kath! God's sake! What did you tell him for?' Dan gasped, his voice high and stunned.

I opened my mouth to speak, to tell him that it just slipped out, that I didn't mean to tell. To tell him that I didn't mean any harm and that it would be all right because Kevin wouldn't do anything. But inside, I couldn't believe Kevin had brought this up. Before I got the chance to say anything, Kevin spoke. His voice was in command, gentle but firm. Everybody listened. Everybody loved Kev and they knew he would never do anything to hurt them.

'Just hold on a minute. Don't get all excited. I want to talk to you, to all of you, about this bastard Flynn. Now, Dan, don't worry. Nobody will ever know what went on. But for you and for the rest of the wee boys that this is happening to, I'm going to get rid of Flynn. Somebody has to. And I can do it, I know I can. It's right. But you have to trust me. You have to believe that I can fix it. And most of all, you have to tell the truth.'

'I'm not going to no police!' Dan said, nervously. 'They'll just take me away and put me in a home or something. No way!'

Kevin put his hand out and touched Dan's shoulder.

'Dan, listen to me. There will be no police. No way. I won't put you in that situation. But I'm telling you one thing. If Flynn is kissing you just now . . . well, in six months he'll be doing much more.' Everything went silent as we took in Kevin's words. We tried to picture what that meant. Much more. We knew stories of people who had slipped into bed beside their nieces and nephews, men and guys you just thought were all right, until you heard that. We tried to picture what Father Flynn would be doing. But we couldn't. It was still unthinkable that he was actually kissing the altar boys. Dan looked white and his eyes filled with tears.

'He already is,' he said, his head going down.

'Bastard!' said Jamie. 'C'mon, we'll go and pan all his windows in!'

'No! We won't do that,' Kevin said.

'What can we do?' I said. 'Who's going to believe Dan? Everybody thinks Father Flynn is a saint.'

'Yeah, Kevin. What can you do? Nothin', that's what,' Tony said, throwing his fag end into the air and kicking it.

'That's where you're wrong!' Kevin looked at Dan. He put his arm around his shoulder. Dan sniffed and kept his head down. Suddenly it all came home to me. The bed-wetting, the nail-biting and the look he always had lately. I thought it was because his dad had died. But it was more than that. Much more.

Kevin spoke, softly. 'We're going to the Bishop! Today! Right up to his big fancy house, and we're going to sit him down and tell him what is going on. What do you think, Dan?'

'He'll tell my mammy and I'll get killed. What if I get put in a boys' home?'

'Listen, son,' Kevin said. 'Trust me. I know these people. I know how they like things kept quiet. They won't want a scandal. But they'll get rid of Flynn and that's the most important thing. But you need to be brave, and you need to tell that Bishop everything that is happening and who else it is happening to. Do you understand?'

There was a silence. Everybody looked at Dan. His face was terrified at first, but then he looked angry. He glanced up at Kevin.

'Will you be there, Kev?' Dan said.

'We'll all be there, son. Every one of us,' Kevin said, looking around us all.

We all looked at each other. We didn't know what to say. But we were going with Kevin to the Bishop's house, that much we did know.

Chapter Eleven

We had to walk for ten minutes across town until we got to the big private road that led to the Bishop's house. This was the first time I had been as far away as this without my mum. I had only ever been allowed to go on the bus to the town nearest the village if I was going to the pictures or the café, but now it felt as though we were nearly in Glasgow. I saw a sign for Hamilton, but I had no real idea where I was. The journey on the bus had seemed like an age, and we hardly spoke a word. I sat beside Tony, who smoked two cigarettes but said nothing. Kevin sat with Dan, who stared out of the window most of the time. We went through small villages then countryside until the faster road that led to the town where the Bishop lived. Every now and again on the journey, I noticed that Kevin would pat Dan's arm reassuringly, and Dan would look at him and try to smile. But there was no smile there. Not like the way it used to be, before his dad died and before any of this stuff came out about Father Flynn. I wondered how long it had been happening for. I felt angry. Jamie said nothing. He just sat with knees up on the seat in front, staring out of the window. The skin was broken on his knuckles and he picked at it. I knew that he was thinking about his mum and what Cowan had said about her going to the 'laughing academy'. That was what they called the mental hospital and it was where they took you if you went crazy. A lot of people had gone crazy in the past few years. I heard people say it was the Valium or something. But Mary McCabe never seemed the type to be crazy. She was always working and having a laugh with the neighbours. Everyone asked her to parties because she was a great singer, but they were always afraid because if Jake was with her he would always pick a fight at the end of the night and she would end up getting a black eye. But lately she had been doing funny things. People had seen her crying and walking the streets late at night on her own. I sat next to her at mass once and the tears rolled down her cheeks and she had to get up and go outside.

Jamie was always worried about her and tried to help in the house by running to the shops and sometimes even cooking chips for his sister and brother's dinner, because his dad was drunk and his mum was upstairs crying. I wished Kevin could fix it for Jamie too, but I knew he couldn't.

We all stopped in our tracks when we saw the Bishop's house. I had never seen a house as big as this in real life. It was like a castle, with turrets and little windows and what looked like a tower at the very top of the building.

'That must be where he keeps the people who don't put enough money into the plate,' Kevin said, half joking, half bitter.

The street on the way up to the private road he lived in was lined with big old trees with fat leaves on them and the houses were huge stone efforts with wide windows and lawns that looked like tennis courts. There were no people though. I assumed they would be sitting inside on velvet chairs with their china cups drinking tea and reading great big newspapers. I wondered where the children were. I never knew any rich children and it would have been good to see what they looked like and what they wore.

We walked up the driveway, the gravel scrunching under our feet. I felt my hands go sweaty. Dan took Kevin's hand.

Tony, Jamie and me all looked at each other, then at the house. Nobody was sure what was going to happen. I was thinking that maybe we had made a mistake. Maybe we should have written the Bishop a letter. I hadn't seen him since my confirmation and he seemed like a good man, making us all laugh with his big cheery face, before he gave us the gentle slap on the cheek that was meant to be for all the sins we had committed. But I wasn't sure I wanted to meet him like this. If my mum and dad ever found out I was here, they would kill me stone dead.

It was too late though. Kevin was already banging the huge brass knocker against the vast dark brown door. We waited. We were hardly breathing. I felt my mouth go dry.

To my relief, a woman opened the door. She was older than my mum, but quite nice-looking, with greying hair and lovely soft blue eyes.

'Hallo!' Kevin said, straightening up. 'Bishop O'Toole there? Er . . . we'd like to speak to Bishop O'Toole,' he said as if he was somebody.

'Oh! Er . . . I don't think so. Have you an appointment?' The woman looked confused and worried because she couldn't remember making an appointment for the Bishop to see a big guy and four kids.

'Well, no, we don't have an appointment actually. But it is very important, and urgent, and we have to see the Bishop right now. So could you go and get him please!' Kevin sounded like a much older man. The woman looked a bit intimidated.

'But Bishop O'Toole has people coming for dinner and he's busy right now. If you haven't an appointment then you'll have to come back on Monday and I'll make some time for you then.' She stepped back into the house, but Kevin put his foot in the door.

'Listen, missus, I don't care if the Pope of Rome is coming to dinner! Could you just go in there and tell the Bishop I want to see him as a matter of urgency. And tell him it's about Flynn ... er, Father Flynn.' I could see the anger and the colour rising in Kevin's face as his voice got louder.

Just at that point, as the woman was shrinking back, a voice came from inside the house.

'What is it, Mrs Mulhearn? Who's there? What the blue blazes is all the shouting?' Suddenly Bishop O'Toole appeared, like a vision from the shadows of the hallway. He looked irritated. He was in his shirtsleeves, but still with his dog collar. I was quite surprised because I assumed priests always wore jackets all the time. I hardly recognized him without his big hat and all the robes he had on that day of the confirmation. But I knew his voice straight away. It was soft and Irish and he sounded as though he was singing when he spoke. He appeared at Mrs Mulhearn's shoulder. We all swallowed hard as his eyes flicked around the group standing determinedly on his doorstep. His eyes finally rested on Kevin, who was holding Dan's hand. I could see Dan's knees shaking.

The Bishop's expression changed and became softer, but he looked suspicious. He pulled open the door and Mrs Mulhearn stepped away.

'My name is Kevin Slaven and this is Dan Lafferty ... er ... your ... er ... Bishop O'Toole.' Kevin couldn't bring himself to say 'your Grace' to the Bishop.

'Yes, boys. What can I do for you?'

'We want to talk to you about Father Flynn ... er ... Bishop,' Kevin said, standing his ground.

The Bishop looked at everyone then at Dan. Dan's face went white. He took a step back. Kevin held on to his hand tightly. The Bishop stepped back from the door and opened it wide.

'Well, now, you'd better come in, hadn't you?' He motioned us all inside. 'Follow me, lads ... and lasses,' he said, striding down the hall. 'Mrs Mulhearn? Bring some orange squash for our visitors, please, to my study.'

*   *   *

The Bishop sat down behind the big desk, pushing his chair back to make room for his stomach. His cheeks were pinkish and jowly and he had full red lips which he licked and seemed to nibble with his teeth as his eyes surveyed the five visitors who had invaded his privacy. He took a deep breath and pushed his wavy black hair back from his forehead. He stroked the crown of his head as if he was trying to make sure it was still there. The grandfather clock in the corner ticked like a time bomb in what seemed like a never-ending silence. The four of us stood in a row facing the desk, with Kevin a step in front of us facing the Bishop. Tony, Jamie, Dan and me all exchanged glances. Dan looked at the floor. His knees were still shaking.

'Now then!' The Bishop spoke. He motioned us to chairs a few feet away from his desk. 'Sit down, boys and girls.' His eyes softened when he looked at me. I tried to smile back. 'Now! Tell me your names again.' He smiled inquisitively.

Kevin turned to us as we sat on the high-backed dark brown wooden chairs, our legs dangling inches from the floor. He pointed all of us out and told the Bishop who we were.

Bishop O'Toole sat with his hands clasped over his stomach. I looked around the room. It was dark and shadowy with chairs and tables you could see your face in. I could smell the leather and the furniture polish. The sun streaming through the stained-glass window made brilliant blue and gold colours on the papers that lay on the Bishop's desk.

A huge picture of the Sacred Heart with its flaming heart exposed looked kindly down at us. Dan was staring at it as if it was going to talk to him. There were other oil paintings in the room of saints and one massive painting that looked like the story of the resurrection of Christ with the stone pushed away from the tomb and all sorts of people walking around with surprised and peaceful looks on their faces, and with Jesus like a ghostly figure amongst them, his halo glowing in the sunlight. It was a beautiful room, but it felt cold and a shiver ran through me.

'Well now, Kevin.' The Bishop leaned forward. 'You want to talk to me about Father Flynn? What's the problem? He's a fine priest and a good man. I'm sure you know that. But what have you come to tell me, Kevin?' Bishop O'Toole's voice was gentle and fatherly.

Kevin took a deep breath and straightened himself up. He pushed his hair back.

'Well, Bishop, you see, it's very delicate ... er ... and I have to tell you that I don't come here lightly, with some daft complaint. It is a very serious matter. Er ... well, there's no easy way to say it, so I'll just say it ... Father Flynn is interfering with the altar boys, sexually, and I've come here to tell you so that you can do something about it.'

The Bishop's face flushed, then he went pale around the mouth. He breathed deeply through his nose like a bull ready to charge. I swallowed hard. The clock seemed to tick louder. Dan stared at the Sacred Heart. Tony stared at the Bishop and Jamie looked at his feet swinging beneath him.

The Bishop sounded completely calm. 'And what evidence do you have of this very serious allegation, Kevin?' He sat back and looked across at the stained-glass window.

Dan shifted in his seat. Kevin spoke. 'I have the evidence, Bishop, of a young boy, Dan Lafferty, who is sitting here and absolutely terrified because of the whole business.' Kevin turned and looked at Dan, who looked from him to the Bishop.

'And exactly where and how is this happening?' the Bishop said. 'And exactly what has been done about it? I mean, has the young boy Dan spoken to his parents, or to police? Or has he just told his pals?' There was an edge of sarcasm in the Bishop's voice. It riled Kevin.

'No, Bishop O'Toole. Dan hasn't spoken to the police. He's

ten years old, for God's sake. He wouldn't know where to start. But by God he's telling the truth. He's a good lad from a fine Catholic family, and his father was just killed at the pit. Now I expect he'll get a hearing from yourself, because he's not the only boy it is happening to.'

The Bishop's eyes narrowed.

'You mean there are others apparently being defiled at the hands of your parish priest? Well now, Kevin, this is indeed a serious affair, a most serious affair.' The Bishop was trying to keep calm, but his voice was beginning to crack.

'Yes, there are other altar boys. It's not just Dan. Apparently he pulls them on to his knee in the sacristy after mass and kisses them. But according to Dan, he actually does more than that,' Kevin said.

The Bishop pushed his chair back and eased himself to his feet. He looked massive. He walked from behind his desk, his shoes clicking on the highly polished wooden floor. He stood facing all of us, with Kevin standing at his side.

'And you, Dan,' he said, looking at Dan. 'Do you want to tell me all about this, my child? Do you want to tell me all about the terrible things that Father Flynn is supposed to be doing to you?'

There was a look in Dan's eyes that I hadn't seen since the day of the school trip when he told us about Father Flynn. I could see that he sensed the Bishop didn't believe him and there was anger building up in him. We all watched him, waiting for him to answer, willing him to be brave.

He looked at the picture of the Sacred Heart, then to the Bishop. Dan took a deep breath and spoke.

'Yes, your Grace.' His voice quivered a little. 'Yes, I'll tell you. Er ... Father Flynn has been kissing me on the face in the sacristy. He just does it all the time now. I know there are other boys because they talk about it and they call him a big poof.'

Tony looked at me, his eyes wide. The Bishop blushed to the roots of his hair.

'That's a disgraceful way to talk, boy! You should have your mouth washed out with soap!' He spat the words out and turned away from us, walking towards the window.

But Dan wasn't finished.

'I don't care! I don't care what you say, your Grace! It's true! I'm just saying what the other boys call him. But he does kiss us, honest, and ... er ... that's not all.' Dan's voice began to shake. I could see tears welling up in his eyes.

The Bishop turned his head slowly towards us and he started to walk across the floor.

'Well? Come on, lad, let's hear it.' He faced Dan.

Dan burst into tears, his whole body shaking. I thought I was going to explode with rage and fear.

'Leave him!' I said, putting my arm around Dan's shoulder as the Bishop stood over us.

But Dan spoke through his tears. He pulled himself away from me.

'He ... er ... h ... he puts his hand inside my shirt and under my vest and rubs my chest!' He sobbed, his voice angry and desperate. 'I hate it! I hate him! He kissed me right on the lips when he did that! I hate him. I wet the bed and everything now! Oh God! Oh God! Make him stop!' Dan's body crumpled as Kevin pulled him towards him and he buried his head under Kevin's arms wrapped around him.

Tears came to my eyes. I wiped them away quickly before they spilled over. Tony looked at me and bit his lip. Jamie's eyes darted around the room as though he was about to smash the place up.

The Bishop stood his ground. But his indignation and sarcasm had gone. He knew. He lowered his eyes. He looked as though he had heard it all before. He took a deep breath.

'Come on now, my boy.' He pulled a cotton handkerchief

from his pocket and handed it to Dan. 'C'mon now, there's a good lad. Don't be upsetting yourself. You'll be fine now.'

Dan sobbed and sniffed and blew his nose. His face was flushed and his eyelashes wet with tears.

'So what happens now?' Kevin said, folding his arms defiantly. 'I take it you do believe the boy? You must have heard stories before about priests abusing their position like this, because I've heard them, though I never really believed them until this happened. So what are you going to do about it?'

The Bishop moved back behind his desk, and sat forward, playing with the gold ring on his wedding finger.

'What happened to that orange squash now?' As he said it, Mrs Mulhearn came in through the door like a ghost, with a tray of drinks. She passed them around and looked concerned as she saw that Dan had been crying. She smiled at him, and left the room.

We all gulped the orange squash, our eyes flitting from Dan to the Bishop.

'Well?' Kevin insisted. 'What are you going to do about it? You're not going to pretend it didn't happen, are you? Because this is not going to go away.'

The Bishop looked angry, his eyes blazing at Kevin.

'I find you rather an impertinent young man,' he snapped. 'Did St John Bosco's not teach you to respect the clergy and the office of a bishop, an office for which you don't even have sufficient respect to address with the correct title? Or did it teach you to barge into someone's home making accusations and demands?'

Kevin's face flushed. 'Aye, it taught me respect, Bishop. I've got plenty of respect. For decent Catholics who work like navvies and fork out their last every week for the parish plate to pay for the upkeep of a bloody mansion like this and to keep the likes of you going in good red wine and steak!'

I thought I was going to faint. I couldn't believe that Kevin had just spoken to a bishop like that. A man like the Bishop was closer to God than anyone, and here was Kevin more or less calling him a drunken sponger. Jesus, if my mum and dad could have heard him, they would have killed him. Tony, Jamie and Dan were all standing with their mouths half open. They couldn't believe their ears.

The Bishop got to his feet, his face ashen.

'Get out of my house! You dare to speak like that in the presence of the Sacred Heart of Jesus looking down at you!' He jabbed his finger at the picture. 'You have no right to criticize the way I live. You have no idea what the life of a priest or a bishop is like . . . the loneliness, the pressure. You criticize, with your teenage insolence and your high and mighty indignation, but you do not know. No, you do not know . . .' His voice trailed off, quivering . . .

Kevin was not intimidated.

'No, Bishop, I don't know . . . I don't know about the loneliness or the difficulties. But that is not my business. I'm just a daft boy. But I'll tell you this. No priest, no man, should abuse the innocence of a child for their own perverted satisfaction. You know that and I know that. And you can spit and rage all you like, but you had better get rid of that bastard!' We all gasped out loud when he swore. 'Because if you don't get rid of him, so help me God, I'll have it all over the papers and you'll be out of a job so fast your arse won't touch the ground.'

Kevin turned and strode across the room, leaving us four standing gawping at the Bishop, who looked as though he was about to collapse. We looked at each other and scurried after Kevin. As we swiftly left the room I was the only one to look back and see that the Bishop was standing as though he was rooted to the spot. I wondered if he had heard this before, not just about Father Flynn, but about other priests. No, I told myself, that could never happen. Priests weren't like that.

I felt kind of sorry for the Bishop because he seemed like a good man, but I was mad too. He should have told Dan he believed him and that he would do something. He should have told him that he would protect him and the rest of the kids. But he just let us go.

Chapter Twelve

The sound of Mum's voice whispering to Ann Marie roused me from sleep.

'C'mon now, Ann Marie. It's nine o'clock. The bus is in two hours and you've got one or two last-minute things to do,' she said as she gently shook Ann Marie's shoulder.

I felt a heaviness in my chest as I opened my eyes. This was the day Ann Marie was going to Donegal. Pictures flooded into my mind. Ann Marie was on the boat all by herself, then she was met by Aunt Nora, then was giving the baby away. I shut my eyes to make the scenes go away, but they kept coming back. I tried to imagine what Ann Marie was thinking as she sat up and swung her feet over the side of the bed. As she got up, she pulled her nightdress over her head and stood naked, gazing out of the window. I peeked with one eye and saw her running her hand across her stomach, which was now quite swollen with the baby inside. Her breasts were heavy, with big pink nipples that looked like they were going to burst. There were tears in her eyes. I pretended to be asleep as she shuffled around the room getting herself dressed and sniffing. She pulled on a big wide dark blue shirt that belonged to Dad and a pair of crimplene trousers of Mum's with elastic round the waist. It made her look much older because before she got pregnant I had got so used to her wearing tiny mini skirts or tight bellbottom jeans. Now she looked like somebody's wife who couldn't afford decent clothes. When she was dressed I faked a yawn and opened my eyes, throwing the bedclothes back. I sat at the side of the bed and watched her snap her case shut. She looked at me and her lips moved like a smile, but it wasn't a smile.

'I wanted to get you something for the trip, Ann Marie,' I said, getting to my feet. 'But I didn't have any money.' Then I swallowed hard and said, 'I'll miss you.'

Suddenly she threw her arms around me. Tears sprang to my eyes. I wanted to tell her that I loved her, that I knew she was being sent to Donegal to have her baby and give it away, and that I thought it was so unfair. I wanted to tell her to keep on going and stay in Ireland and just keep her baby, and when I grew up I would come and help her look after it. I wanted to say sorry for all the rotten things I had done and for getting her into trouble sometimes if she annoyed me and I told on her. But none of it came out. I just squeezed and squeezed her and she held me so tight I thought I would be right through to the baby any minute. When we let each other go, our faces were wet with tears. Ann Marie rubbed my eyes with the palm of her hand and I sniffed and sobbed.

'Jesus,' she said, dabbing her eyes, 'you'd think I was going away for ever. It's only for a few months' work.' She kept up the pretence. But I knew deep down that she knew. I kept up the ghost as well.

'I know . . . I know. But it won't be the same.'

'Aye. But look at all the space you'll have in this room all on your own. You can throw things everywhere.' Ann Marie tried to make light so that we could go downstairs and face Mum and Dad. She walked out of the room ahead of me and I stood looking around. A thought flashed through my mind of how big this room would be for me and how I could move the beds around any way I wanted now that I was on my own. But the room felt empty already, and it had never felt empty before.

* * *

Downstairs, I was forcing my feet into my shoes without undoing the laces when I heard Mum and Dad's conversation in the kitchen.

'Aye, Barney's in a bit of bother by the looks of things. Mind you, if it's true, he deserves all he gets.' I don't know why, but I just knew he was talking about Barney Hagen.

'But if it's just gossip, and the badness of some kids, then it's a terrible label to put on a man.' Mum seemed to be defending him.

'That's typical of this hole of a place. They wouldn't let you live,' Dad said. 'Barney Hagen is a poor wreck of a man because he nearly gave up his life defending the very kind of ungrateful bastards in this village who couldn't spell courage and who would tell tales that would get you hung. I don't believe there's any truth in the rumours, but I heard they were getting the police involved.'

Everyone looked up at me and I looked from Mum to Dad to Ann Marie.

'What?' I said.

'Nothing,' Dad said.

I sat at the table and Mum put a bowl of cornflakes in front of me. I suddenly didn't feel very hungry, with the thought of what they were saying about Barney Hagen. I didn't really know what they meant, but I got the impression he had been doing something bad with kids. I remembered my last visit and how sad he had been, and how he put his arms around me. But there was nothing funny about it, not like the kind of stuff I'd heard about Father Flynn. I pushed the bowl away from me.

'I'm not too hungry this morning,' I said.

'What? You? Not hungry in the morning? Well, that's a turn-up. Are you sick?' Mum said, feeling my forehead.

'No, no, I'm fine. I'll just have some toast,' I said, buttering a slice and lifting a mug of steaming tea.

There was a silence. Then Dad said: 'Kath! Did you not tell

me you were in Barney Hagen's house a couple of weeks ago and you went his messages?'

'It was last week,' I said, trying not to blush.

Everyone looked at me. I felt my face go red. I slurped a mouthful of tea. I don't know why, but I felt guilty. I felt as if I was going to be found out for doing something. But I hadn't done anything and neither had Barney. He was just a sad old crippled war hero. I wished they would all shut up.

'Yeah,' I said. 'I went his messages a few times. And I was in his house. He showed me his medals. They're brilliant. All shiny like new. And he told me amazing stories about the war. Did you know, Dad, that Barney got his bad leg after being kept in a pit of water for five weeks? It was a big insect that bit him, right through to the bone it bit him.' I rushed my story about Barney, hoping I could convince them he was sound. I knew he wasn't a bad man.

Mum sat down. They all looked at me again.

'Kath,' Mum ventured, 'have you ever noticed anything strange about Barney? I mean, like the way he behaves towards you?'

I knew what she meant. I didn't know how to answer. If I told them about Barney hugging me and stroking my hair, they would hit the roof and have the police at his house. I could just imagine it. Barney getting dragged out and everybody in the village knowing it was me who did it. Anyhow, he hadn't done anything to me. And even though lately I had dropped my head to avoid seeing him waving me in as I passed his house because I was always with Tony and the boys, I wanted to defend him.

'No,' I said, as convincingly as I could. 'Barney's all right. I think he's just lonely. He's got nobody. He just tells me stories and stuff. I feel sorry for him. Other kids go his messages too and they go into his house and sit with him but he wouldn't hurt a fly. He's a good man.'

I was careful not to mention about the gun. I knew that would cause trouble.

There was another silence.

'Right!' Dad said. 'Listen, Kath, I know you think he's all right and that, but we're hearing a bit of a different story, and we don't think you should go back there again. OK? No more visits to Barney's and no more messages. I think he'll be getting a visit soon from the police, by the way people are talking.'

I could feel anger rising in me.

'Why doesn't everyone just leave Barney alone? God's sake, Dad! He's just a sad old man! These people who are saying bad things about him are rotten 'cos they're just rotten people who make up things. I know they're all liars!' I thought about Barney crying that day and felt tears in my eyes.

'People in this village have too much to say about everybody,' Ann Marie said, her voice bitter. 'If they would just mind their own business and live and let live we would all get on better!' Everyone went quiet. We all knew what she meant and how she felt. She didn't have to fight and shout that she wanted to keep her baby and defy all the gossips and holy willies who seemed to run everyone's lives. Mum and Dad knew how she felt and they kept silent. Mum bit her lip and stirred her tea. Dad got up from the table silently and walked away. He looked ashamed.

Brendan O'Hanlon's red van pulled up outside the gate and we all knew it was time to go. We had been standing around in the living room for what seemed like ages. The whole place felt like it was weighed down by the silence that hung in the room. Ann Marie's case was in the hall, sitting there staring us all in the face, like a monument to her fall from grace. The battered old case sat there looking as if it was punishment for what she had done. As much of her life as she could cram into it was in the case and when you looked at it, it seemed to amount to nothing. Mum fussed around getting jackets and packing sandwiches in a bag for Ann Marie's journey. Dad's eyes met Ann Marie's fleetingly as he lifted her case and opened the front door.

'C'mon then. Let's go if we're going. The bus won't wait, neither will the ferry.'

He walked down the path.

I stood in the room with Ann Marie and Mum. They looked at each other. Mum went over to Ann Marie and smoothed down her jacket the way she used to do when she was a girl going to school in the morning. Ann Marie's lip quivered. I walked out to the van.

The two of them followed in silence, both afraid to speak, their throats and chests tight with emotion.

We piled into Brendan's van for the journey to the bus stop where Ann Marie would take the bus that would get her to the ferry terminal more than two hours away. It was important that she didn't walk to the bus with her case because someone might see her and start gossip about her. She had to slip away unnoticed. That was how it was done. We tried to make a joke about how we were all stuffed in like sardines, and Brendan recalled how both our families used to crush into his van when we went to the coast for the day. They were great days and I pictured the hazy sunshine as I looked out of the window at the overcast sky and the dismal grey houses and streets whizzing past. They were great days. If only they could have stayed that way.

I was glad the bus stop wasn't too far because the awkward silences were only broken by Brendan telling more stories of the old days and laughing like a drain. Everybody smiled as he recalled things but it was more out of politeness. I guessed that he knew about Ann Marie, and as he was Dad's closest friend and his son Dessie was Kevin's best pal, their family could be trusted with the story.

I suddenly thought of Kevin and imagined that he must have said his goodbyes before he went to work.

'Where's Kevin?' I asked, just to make sure.

'He's at his work. He said cheerio to Ann Marie this morning,' Mum said.

'He gave me ten pounds,' Ann Marie said. 'I was really shocked. That was great of him. Not such a bad guy after all.' She nudged me and we smiled.

The van stopped at the bus shelter and we all got out and Dad lifted out Ann Marie's case. Brendan stayed in the van. Dad looked at his watch and fidgeted awkwardly as though he would like to get on with it and get away. Mum pulled her jacket around her and shivered even though it wasn't cold. Her eyes were red and she kept biting the inside of her jaw as if she was trying to fight back tears. Ann Marie strained her neck trying to watch for the bus. I was almost overwhelmed by the urge to tell them to stop all of this right now and go back to the house. But I couldn't. I was only ten and what did I know? I heard the drone of the rickety old bus in the distance and then saw its nose as it pulled over the brow of the hill. We all looked at each other, and I thought for a moment everyone looked surprised, as though we had all come this far but somehow believed it would never really happen. But it was happening. The bus was empty apart from an old man in a flat cap, and as it pulled in with a hiss of brakes, the driver jumped out of his seat and came down the steps.

'Howyedoin'?' he said, smiling broadly. Then he saw that nobody was really smiling back at him. He looked at Ann Marie and there was a flash of recognition in his face. She wouldn't be the first lonely, frightened, tear-stained girl he had taken on this journey in similar circumstances.

'Right, folks,' he said, lifting the case and opening the luggage compartment. 'I'll get this little lot put away and then I'll make sure you get right to the ferry. No problem.' He was like the family doctor who moves in to smooth everything over when there is confusion and fear. He went back on to the bus and sat in his seat. The old man in the flat cap sat up and stared out of the window, suddenly interested in the little drama that was unfolding in front of him. We all shifted around. I thought I was going to die. Dad was first to make the move.

'OK.' He seemed to take a deep breath, then moved towards Ann Marie and took her in his arms. He squeezed her and she buried her face in his shoulder. They held together for what seemed like ages. 'You're still my girl,' he whispered, wiping her tears away. 'No matter what, you're my lass. Everything will be fine, Ann Marie. You'll see.'

She looked at him through tears. Mum threw her arms around Ann Marie and sobbed. Tears rolled down my face. Dad came and put his arm around me. 'C'mon now,' he whispered. 'It's not the end of the world.' I wiped my tears.

Mum and Ann Marie held on to each other for ages and the driver looked away as if he felt he was intruding. The old man stared sadly as if he had seen it all before. Finally they let each other go. Ann Marie came forward and hugged me as tight as she had done in the bedroom. I sobbed into her chest. She spoke through her sobs but her voice was cracking. 'Now you take care of our bedroom and make sure it's not like a bombsite by the time I get back. Understand? Or you know what you'll get.' She was trying her best to act tough but her lip was trembling.

'W . . . will you write to me?' I managed to croak.

'Course,' she said. 'An' you keep me up to date with all the news . . . Promise?'

I nodded. 'Hurry back,' I said, as she turned away from me. 'I'll watch for you.' She turned and smiled at me. Dad was holding Mum in his arms, trying to stop her from sobbing. Then Ann Marie was on the bus and at the window waving to us. The driver revved the engine and gave us the thumbs-up. The old man just stared. Ann Marie waved, but now her face was all crumpled as she broke her heart. And mine.

Chapter Thirteen

W e were cooking bacon and sausages on the fire at our camp in the woods and we inhaled the aroma, our mouths watering in anticipation. We were starving from swimming the length and breadth of the dam we had built that had become our Olympic pool as well as the crocodile-infested jungle pond into which Tarzan would swing from surrounding trees. It just depended on whoever we were at any given time. It was great to be out here, just the four of us laughing and carrying on as if there was nothing else in the world but this. I hardly thought about Ann Marie when I was at the camp, even though Shaggy Island wasn't that far away as a constant reminder. She had written me a couple of letters saying how she had settled in and was working in a guest house down the road from Auntie Nora's. She said she was enjoying great walks on the beach and the gusts of wind were giving her an appetite for all the food Auntie Nora was stuffing her with. I thought about her every night before I went to sleep, willing my thoughts to cross the water and make her feel as if I was right there with her. But out here, I was a million miles away from all of that.

Tony had been stealing money on a regular basis from the Nazi's box and he had worked out a clever plan of stuffing strips of newspaper in the middle of each wad so that the bundles all looked the same and the Nazi could see at a glance how much money he had. We all prayed that he wouldn't take

157

the elastic bands off one day and decide to count the money properly. If he did, Tony was a goner. We laughed our socks off at the picture of him, his big dark eyes bulging when he saw how he had been robbed. Jamie was the best at doing impersonations of him shouting and rushing around the room. We told ourselves it wasn't stealing because he was a Nazi and we knew what the likes of him had done in the war. Barney Hagen told me and I saw it on *Colditz*. Stealing from them was too good for them, we had decided. We sat back and enjoyed the fruits of Tony's exploits – sausages and bacon and lumps of bread, washed down with bottles of lemonade and chocolate bars for afters. This was the life.

'If only we didn't have to go home,' Tony said, watching the flames flicker on the fire.

'Yeah, I know,' Jamie said. 'I wish we could just live our lives like this, out in the wild. Like the way they did in the wild west, digging for gold and stuff. It would be great.' Jamie tossed twigs into the fire, one by one, watching the flames devour them.

His house was getting worse. Jake McCabe had had them all out in the street again just a few days earlier, and this time Mary was in such a state the doctor had to be called to put stitches in a cut on her head and give her something to calm her down. She was running up and down the garden with the blood pouring from her head, screaming and bawling, with Jamie running after her, trying to get her inside. We could hear Jake smashing the house up. It had been hours before everything was quiet and finally the lights went out. Everybody in the street must have heard it because the walls were so thin, sometimes you could hear your next-door neighbour going up the stairs. But nobody helped Mary.

The doctor was going to get the police, but she told him it wasn't Jake who hit her but that she fell and cut her head on the table. Nobody believed her though.

'As soon as I'm big enough, I'm going to waste his face,'

Jamie said, his eyes narrowing as he pictured the scene of him giving his dad the hiding of his life.

'Would you like to run away, Kath?' Dan said, hoping I would say no. He couldn't bear the thought of leaving his mum and his brother and sister, especially after his dad had died. But we had all noticed the change in him since the visit to the Bishop's house. He had stood up for himself that day in front of everyone, even the Bishop, who was trying to scare him off. Dan was a lot tougher now, and though he was still an altar boy, he said that Father Flynn had suddenly stopped trying anything with him. But Dan knew he could never run away from home.

'I wouldn't like to run away,' I said. 'Not like the way Tony and Jamie are talking. I mean, my mum and dad would die, and Kevin would probably find us anyway and he would go crazy. But I would like to go to Ireland and see Ann Marie.' They all looked at me. I wasn't sure if they knew the truth behind her going to Donegal. But I could never tell them.

We watched in silence as the fire began to sink and the daylight faded from the sky. Somewhere deep in the woods, the spooky call of an owl signalled the approach of darkness and we all looked at each other, knowing it was time to go. Suddenly, as the shadows crept in around us, the thought of sleeping in the woods didn't seem so attractive, and we hurried our steps out of the trees and into the open fields where we could see the houses of the villages at a comforting distance.

By the time we got to Tony's gate there was just the two of us, as usual. Dan had jumped the fence to his house, eager to get home to his mum. Jamie hung around as long as he could with us because he didn't want to go back in, but eventually he went, his hands thrust deep into his jeans pockets and his head down.

We both stopped a few yards away when we saw the blue van at Tony's gate. I couldn't understand what big Slippy Tits

McCartney's van was doing there at this time of night. Surely he couldn't be collecting money. Tony looked embarrassed. I was confused. Then I saw and understood. In the darkness I could just make out the shadows of the two figures kissing in the front seat before the woman sidled out of the van and closed the door. McCartney drove off, swiftly, not even giving us a second look. Tony's mum turned, startled when she saw Tony, then gave him a big wide smile.

'Tony? Is this you just getting home?' She looked furtive. She ran her fingers across her lips, as though wiping them would mean that she hadn't just spent the last hour with McCartney, doing whatever they did in the back of his van or at his house. The rumours were true. No wonder Tony went crazy when Billy Cowan slagged him off at the pictures. Tony didn't answer her. He just looked at her sadly. She tried to pretend she didn't notice. 'Good thing I met McCartney. He gave me a lift back from your auntie Jenny's. I couldn't have faced the walk.' She only made it worse by building up a story that we all knew wasn't true. Tony didn't even answer her, but watched as she went up the path, a little unsteady on her feet. We said nothing for a while. Then Tony spoke.

'She's with him all the time, Kath. I just don't know what's going to happen if the Nazi finds out.' There was a kind of panic in Tony's voice.

'Maybe they're in love,' I said, then could have kicked myself at the absurdity of it. What difference did it make if they were in love? The Nazi would still go berserk. But I had seen a film like that once where the woman got the man she loved and everything worked out well in the end.

Tony looked at me as if I was daft and said, 'Jesus, Kath. Even if they are in love, she's married to that bastard in there and he's a crazy Nazi. He'll kill her. Anyway, McCartney's just as big an asshole.'

'I know,' I said, remembering the scene I had witnessed when I walked in on him with my mum.

'See you tomorrow,' Tony said, turning and walking away.

'See you,' I said, watching as he turned the handle on his front door.

Chapter Fourteen

We were all helping move tables around the village hall in preparation for the big send-off party for Kevin and Dessie O'Hanlon before they went to Australia. There had been an air of excitement and trepidation around the village for the last few days. Kevin and Dessie were two of the most popular guys in the place. The girls all loved them and hung around them in the pubs, and even after mass there was always some girl making an excuse to talk to Kevin as he walked home with us. He used to laugh and wink to me whenever a girl would come up and join us on the walk home from church with some spurious reason to be with him. I would laugh and take his hand, just to make sure she knew that I was the only girl he really cared about.

Whenever I thought about those days it made me really sad. I couldn't bear to think of life without Kevin, and I had been trying to put it out of my mind for the last few weeks, but now the time was coming close when I would have to say goodbye.

Kevin seemed to be on a great high all the time. He was joking with Mum when she was getting all his clothes washed and ironed ready for the trip. She loved it when he kidded her on and crept up behind her and threw his arms around her neck. She would laugh and give him a slap, but afterwards, when she was ironing, I would see her wiping her tears away. Dad seemed to be worse than ever. He was drunk more often and hardly even spoke to Kevin, no matter how much Kevin would try to draw him out. Kevin used to ask him to go for a drink with him, but almost every night Dad would say a flat no and Kevin would lift his jacket and go by himself. The atmosphere between the two of them dragged the whole house down. I had heard Dad say to Mum one night when he was drunk that he could never forgive Kevin for turning his back on his family. Mum tried to reason with him, but there was no telling him. I was only hoping that by the time we had the party everything would be different.

It was going to be a great night. Most of the village was going, well most of the Catholics. There were a few Protestants who Kevin used to work with, but mostly they didn't really mix with the rest of us. The band was going to be made up of two young pals of Kevin's who played guitar and another who played the organ. Kevin said they knew all the hits and there was going to be some great dancing. Two old men were going to be brought in to play the accordion so that the mums and dads could get in some dancing as well, and there would be a sing-song.

Everyone had made food for the buffet and there was a ten-shilling cover charge and all the money raised between that and the raffle would go towards sending Kevin and Dessie to Australia. It was costing them next to nothing to get there because the Australian government was so desperate to get people over to settle in their country that they were more or less paying families to emigrate. Loads of people from all over the country were going with promises of great jobs and new houses.

Father Flynn was going to be at the party as well and would make a speech wishing the boys well. Kevin had told Mum that he didn't want him there, but she brushed him off and told him there was no question of having a celebration without the parish priest to start it off.

When the day finally came around, Jamie, Tony, Dan and me were exhausted carrying plates of sandwiches and food from the houses to the hall throughout the day. It was blazing hot and on the way home from our final trip we bought ice creams and sat in a field, glad of the rest.

'Guess who's coming to the party?' Tony said, staring into the distance.

'Not Bishop O'Toole?' Jamie said, smiling.

'No, worse than that,' Tony said. 'That Nazi bastard. Can you believe it? He never takes his arse out of the door, and he's coming to the party with Mom. He'll just waste it for everybody.'

'No he won't,' Jamie said. ''Cos my da's coming with my ma and if anybody's going to waste things it will be him. Christ, I wish he would die!'

'Jesus!' Dan said. 'How can you say that?'

'I don't mean to annoy you, Dan, but your da was great. Mine's just a waster. My ma's not even going to enjoy herself, and she hasn't been out for ages.'

I could see the night ahead of us and had a feeling it was going to be eventful.

'It'll be all right,' I said, trying to cheer them up. 'Kevin and his mates will make sure everything's fine. You'll see.' I didn't really believe it, though.

We sat in silence for a while, each with their thoughts inside their own homes.

'Did you hear about Barney Hagen?' Dan said.

'What?' I said, suddenly concerned there had been more stories.

'The cops were at his house this morning. I heard my mum say to her pal that he had been interfering with weans and that they might even charge him,' Dan said, pleased that he knew something we didn't.

'Old bastard. He's probably just like Flynn,' Jamie said.

165

'Hey, Kath, is he not your pal? Do you not go his messages?'

My face went red and I spluttered. 'Yeah! He's not like Flynn! Nothing like him. He's just an old man. He's not doing anything to anybody. I don't believe that story. Jesus, Barney was a hero in the war,' I said.

'What if it's true?' Dan said. 'You'd better watch yourself, Kath.'

I stood up and everyone followed. 'C'mon, let's go. It will soon be time to get ready for the party.' We all walked home and nobody mentioned Barney Hagen again.

I didn't tell them that I had been to Barney's house the day before, despite being told not to go back there. I had knocked at the door but Barney didn't answer. I sat on the step for a minute, then shouted through the letterbox, but still he didn't answer. I knew he was inside because he didn't ever go anywhere, and I could smell the tobacco. I knew he knew I was out there but wouldn't come to the door. I felt guilty for not visiting him sooner, because now he would be thinking that I was one of the kids who was starting the bad rumours, and he would feel I had betrayed him. I would go back and see him tomorrow, and this time I would make sure he let me in.

Dad had stayed out of the pub all day after much coaxing by Mum and promised to be on his best behaviour. Whatever agreement they had come to must have been a good one, because he was even half talking to Kevin, who had just stepped out of the bath and was buzzing around the house with a towel wrapped around his waist. Kevin looked beautiful. His body was bronzed and hard with muscles from working on the building site. He was a full head bigger than Dad and his eyes and face shone as he looked in the mirror, combing his hair and admiring himself.

'You really want a mirror that kisses back, don't you?'

Dad grunted from behind his newspaper. It was his way of communicating and Kevin enjoyed it.

'You have to admit it, though, Da,' he joked. 'The women in this village are really going to take it bad when I go.' He smiled and posed in the mirror, enjoying the banter.

'Oh aye.' Dad kept it up. 'God's gift itself. The poor women will have to put up with the likes of Slippy Tits McCartney if they want a real man now.'

'He's not a real man. He's a spiv. It's a real man the women love,' Kevin said.

'Oh I don't know,' Dad said. 'He seems to be doing quite nicely. I hear he's dipping his wick down the road at the Polack's house,' he muttered, grinning.

Kevin looked over his shoulder as I left the room and he must have thought I hadn't heard.

'No wonder, Da. I mean, that woman's no' a bad bit of stuff,' he confided. 'But she's tied to that fat-arsed man. Christ! No wonder she drinks!' The two were talking like old friends, and Mum was delighted as she put down mugs of tea on the mantelpiece.

'You shouldn't talk about her like that,' she said. 'She's had a real hard time.'

'Aye! I'll bet she's having a hard time. So is McCartney,' Dad chuckled.

'You have the mind of a sewer,' Mum scolded.

'I'm only saying what the whole village has been saying for months,' Dad said. 'It should be good fun at the party tonight, because Slippy Tits is coming, and him without a woman on his arm. It could be the kind of a night you have to lock up your wives.'

'That'll be right,' Kevin joked. 'No woman is going to look in his direction as long as I'm there.' He pouted in front of the mirror, eyeing his profile one way then another.

'I'll tell you something,' Mum said, lifting cups from the

table. 'I know for sure that the Pole is coming, for Sara spoke to Mary McCabe today and said she was looking forward to it, but that she was a bit worried that the Pole had decided to go, especially when he never goes anywhere.'

'Could be good fun,' Kevin said, strutting out of the room.

Tony, Jamie, Dan and me all made our way down to the church hall at the bottom end of the priest's garden. It had been built years ago, before Father Flynn had been there, and looked more like a big long wooden garage than an actual hall, but it was where all the dances were held as well as all the meetings of the Legion of Mary and the St Vincent de Paul groups.

We watched fascinated as the band tuned up on the stage of the empty hall.

'One two, one two.' The singer with the Beatle-cut hairdo looked casual but confident as he tested the mike.

The drummer rattled his sticks across the drums in a fast, dramatic beat as if to fill the place with the excitement of what was to follow. Every now and then there would be an ear-splitting screech from the speakers and the sound of one of the band rasping, 'Aw, for fuck's sake!'

It must have been great to be up there and be somebody in front of the whole village, I was thinking. Just singing your songs and everybody staring at you, hanging on your every word.

The hall was beginning to fill up with people arriving in dribs and drabs, bagging their tables nearest the makeshift bar built with two long tables joined together. The old caretaker walked across the floor shaking slippery powder and immediately we were racing up and down the wooden floor sliding and falling. He shouted at us to get up and we did, brushing off the dust from our party clothes.

Jamie, in his black jeans, was already sneakily helping himself to sandwiches from underneath the covers in the buffet. He was always starving and took every opportunity outside of his house to stuff himself. My mum used to say there was no bottom to his stomach.

I was dressed in my lime-green silky sleeveless top that buttoned down the back and I thought I looked great. It had been sent to me by a cousin in America, and even though it wasn't new, it looked fantastic against my auburn hair, or so my dad had said when he saw me all dressed. I had my cream jeans on and I had been warned to be careful not to dirty them, so I was constantly checking them to make sure. Tony was wearing a black shirt and it made him look older. His face was thinner now and with his tan and blond hair he looked just like a film star. Dan was wearing a T-shirt that was too big for him and blue jeans with huge turn-ups at the bottom. His hair was all kept down by Brylcreem because every time he washed it it sprung up like a hedgerow.

As more and more people came in, the band struck up for a trial song.

The singer caressed the microphone as he pouted and sang Lazing on a Sunny Afternoon. He was just like the guy in the Kinks and the people at the tables nodded to each other approvingly.

We went outside into the early evening sunshine and watched as dozens of young people arrived, some with carrier bags of drink. They were all laughing and carrying on, and some of the older people frowned as they looked at their gaudy clothes and hairdos.

Mum and Dad arrived with Dessie O'Hanlon's parents and Dan's mum, and they sat close to the bar. Dad looked happy and relaxed and I was immediately relieved. Mum had on a white cotton dress with bold red roses on it. It hugged her figure and she looked the youngest I had seen her for ages. Since Ann Marie left she had been getting up every morning with her eyes all red. But tonight she looked fantastic. Dan's mum was smiling and seemed happy. She hadn't been seen out anywhere for ages, but now she had her make-up on and her hair done. Dan's face lit up when he saw her and I guessed he was pleased that she looked so well.

Jamie looked edgy when his mum arrived on her own. She looked around her, nervously, her face thin and her eyes darting around the hall. Mum noticed her and immediately shouted her over, patting a chair, signalling for her to come and sit with them. Mary McCabe was relieved and moved across to join them.

I heard her speak softly to Mum.

'Oh Jesus, Maggie, I hope to Christ he doesn't come. I had an unholy row with him this afternoon and I threw a cup of tea in his face. He went off his head. But I just got off my mark and by the time I came back he was sound asleep. That's where I left him. God forbid, but I hope he never wakes up.' She said the last bit so quietly I barely heard her, but I was shocked. Mum just squeezed her hand.

'Never mind, Mary. We'll have a good night. Maybe he'll sleep right through the night.'

'Fat chance,' Mary said, then turned to me and ruffled my hair. 'Aren't you the little madam now,' she said. 'God, you're looking great, Kath. Not be long now till you're grown up. You and our Jamie and your wee gang. God, you'll all be gone soon enough,' she said, and her eyes looked sad.

Kevin and Dessie O'Hanlon came strolling in with two other mates and three girls. They all looked as though they were straight from the movies. Kevin was laughing and punching Dessie, who had his arm around one of the girls. I thought they must have been drinking because they were all carrying on and were really happy. Kevin was wearing his dark blue Levis and a tight white T-shirt to show off his muscles. His denim jacket was slung over one shoulder. They took their seats close to the band and immediately

Dessie was at the bar ordering pints, and Babychams for the girls.

The hall was getting packed now and Jamie, Tony, Dan and me were standing at the doorway watching as the band were getting ready to start.

Suddenly Tony nudged me and I looked over my shoulder. It was the Nazi and Tony's mum. She had that faraway look in her eye that she always seemed to have of late, and the Nazi was ushering her by the elbow. I thought he might be supporting her because she was a bit tipsy, but I decided it was probably because he wanted to push her into whatever seat he chose, in case she would sit with any friends. The Nazi grabbed hold of Tony's hand as they walked past us, and Tony resisted.

'C'mon, sit with us, Tony. You're not standing around here like a stray dog. C'mon.' The Nazi yanked Tony's arm. Tony resisted.

'No. I want to stay with my pals. Leave me.' He pulled his arm free.

The Nazi stopped in his tracks and still held on to Tony's mum's arm. He looked as if he was squeezing her arm and she winced slightly, looking pleadingly at Tony. Tony's eyes were raging, but I knew he was worried that the Nazi might take it out on his mum and embarrass her in public.

'OK, OK, I'm comin'. But just for a little while.' Tony went under protest, looking over his shoulder at us.

I turned around just in time to see Father Flynn coming striding up the path, his big frame filling the doorway.

'Hallo, Kath,' he said, slapping my bare arm, which stung. I rubbed it and looked up at him. I hated him so much.

'Hallo, Father,' I said, looking away.

'How's yerself, Dan? And Jamie? Howya? Mother of God, this looks like a bit of a do, eh? A bit of a do all right!' His eyes roved the hall, taking everything in. He looked half mesmerized and half disgusted that all these people should be out having a good time. He looked at the bar disapprovingly and clocked everyone who was standing there, nodding at them with that look of disdain he always had. He walked right across the floor and down to the stage, climbing up the side stairs and chatting briefly to the boys in the band before taking hold of the microphone.

'Right now, right now, your attention, please, ladies and gentlemen,' he boomed. The din in the hall diminished to a few mutterings. I looked at Kevin, who was sitting back on his seat, smoking a cigarette and eyeing the priest with disgust.

'Now, I just want to say, everyone have a good time. It's all for Kevin and Dessie here, fine boys. Now God be with us all. And let's hope nobody lets themselves down,' he said and walked off the stage full of his own importance and pleased at the hold he had over everyone. The noise level rose again and the priest roamed from table to table, sitting down or standing chatting to people. He was always slapping somebody's back or joking with somebody. Everybody had great respect for him, but we knew what he was and we all looked at him with disgust.

'I feel like getting up on the stage and telling everyone about him,' Jamie said.

'Me too,' I agreed.

The party was in full swing and everyone was dancing to the beat of the band, who were belting out great songs from the charts. Kevin was hardly off the dance floor, gyrating and swinging his hips with the girls who were fawning over him. Dessie always seemed to be kissing some girl and I thought at one point that he was going to suffocate because he was kissing one for so long. If Father Flynn had seen him he would have hauled him off as if he was a dog after a bitch in heat.

Tony had managed to slip away from his mum's table and we were all together hanging around the bar area and nipping back and forwards to the buffet to help ourselves to sandwiches and cakes. Every time somebody's back was turned, Jamie was drinking out of their pint and giggling as he urged us to join in. Tony took a couple of swigs of beer but Dan and me didn't touch it. We just kept out of the way of anyone who looked as though they might pull us on to the floor to dance and embarrass us. I hadn't noticed Slippy Tits McCartney coming in, but when I turned around he was standing at the bar, knocking back whisky and half-pints of lager. He nodded to me and I looked right through him, feeling quite pleased that he looked a bit embarrassed. I could tell from the look on his face that he wondered if I had seen what he was trying to do to my mum that day when I walked in on him. Tony wouldn't even look in his direction, but he watched closely as his mum slipped away from the Nazi and came past McCartney to go to the toilets. The two exchanged furtive smiles. I glared at McCartney, who knocked back another whisky.

Mum and Dad were shaking themselves about the dance floor and I was mortified at their attempts to dance like the young ones. But they didn't care. Dad had had a few drinks and he felt as though he was twenty again, and by the look on Mum's face she felt sure they had wound the clock back and were young and in love again. He kept throwing his arms around her and she was giggling.

Dan's mum was reluctantly being glided around the floor by James Hennessy, a bachelor whose fiancée had died in a car crash ten years ago and who had never really found another woman. He had a bit of money because he owned the local bookie shop and most of the men and a few women spent a lot of time there at the weekends hoping to bag the big winner. Everyone knew Hennessy, and even though he was the bookie who usually always won, he seemed to be a good guy. Dan looked at them a bit suspiciously but was happy when he saw his mum smiling.

Mary McCabe looked miles away, smoking nervously and

fidgeting. She kept glancing at the door, hoping the vision of Jake would not appear. But the look on her face said it all. When I saw her expression I turned and saw Jake McCabe standing in the doorway. His face looked mean and his mouth was tight as though he was about to spit. He didn't move from the door for a few minutes, but just stood watching everyone. Jamie moved further away from the door and pulled me with him.

'Shit!' he said. 'Look what the cat's dragged in.'

'Maybe he'll be all right,' I said, trying to console him. 'Maybe he'll just stand at the bar and drink. He'll probably not bother anyone,' I said, knowing there wasn't a hope.

We moved closer to my mum's table and sat at the edge of it. I felt a bit embarrassed as Dad put his arm around me and kissed me on the cheek, his lips wet from beer and smelling of tobacco. Dan, Tony and Jamie sniggered. I pulled away from Dad a little.

'I hope he stays where he is,' Mary said to Mum, jerking her head in the direction of Jake.

'Don't you worry yourself, Mary,' Dad said, putting a protective arm around Mary. 'Jake McCabe will do you no harm tonight, darlin'.' I felt really proud of my dad. Sometimes he could be a real hero.

Kevin came bursting up and dragged Mum on to the dance floor and was throwing her around like a rag doll. She was laughing as he took her in his arms and spun her around.

'Jesus, Martin,' Mary said, looking at Mum and Kevin. 'For a minute there I thought it was twenty years ago and it was you throwing Mary about like that. Kevin's so like you.'

Dad laughed, but stared into the distance as if he was remembering those nights when he promised Mum that he would love her until the day he died and she believed their lives would be like one long happy dream.

'Aye, dreams, Mary . . . dreams,' he said, swigging his pint.

* * *

Halfway through the night everyone was getting stuck into the buffet and coming back to their tables with plates piled high with sandwiches, sausage rolls and cakes. Tony, Jamie, Dan and me were making our fourth visit of the night and I was beginning to feel bagged up. Jamie looked as if he was a bit drunk and was laughing and larking about all the time. I wasn't sure I liked him like this. He looked as though he could get out of control, and somewhere in his eyes there was a look of his dad. It didn't bear thinking about.

McCartney stood at the bar by himself, but was joined from time to time by some of the young boys and the occasional woman who stood flushed and fluttering her eyes at him. I couldn't understand why anyone could like him. At one time, when there was a crowd at the bar, a young woman, who was only about thirty and who I knew was married, squeezed in beside him and was talking to him, smiling up to his face. He was chatting to her, but his eyes were everywhere. Suddenly through the sea of bodies at the bar I saw her slip her hand in between his legs and he flinched slightly, then smiled at her with a lecherous look on his face. I was horrified as she kept her hand there, moving it up and down. McCartney's face seemed to change its expression and he leant forward and whispered something to her. He put his drink down and went outside. A second or two later she followed him. I looked around the hall to see if her husband was there, but I couldn't see him.

'I know what they're up to,' Tony said, nudging me. 'Did you see them?' he asked, knowing that I had.

'Jesus,' I said. 'If her man finds them he'll kill her.'

Before we knew where we were, the four of us had sneaked outside the hall and stood in the silence. We knew it was wrong, but curiosity overcame us. I remembered Shaggy Island and that night with Ann Marie and the shock I got, but still something in me wanted to see what McCartney was doing. We heard whispered tones coming from the side of the hall and we tiptoed round. In the darkness, I could just make out McCartney's figure as he huffed and puffed over the young woman, who was lying on the grass with her pants at her ankles. She had her hands on his backside and we all looked at each other in disbelief as we heard her say quite clearly, 'Oh McCartney! Oh! Oh! Now! Faster! Faster!' We were horrified. What did she mean, faster? Her moans were getting louder and more like one long wail. McCartney was telling her to sssh.

'Christ,' Jamie said. 'You'd think he was riding a horse.' We all burst out laughing and ran away.

Chapter Fifteen

Inside the hall, the young band had taken a break and the two old guys with accordions were playing tunes that made the mums and dads dance and shimmy round the floor. We were stunned when we saw the Nazi pulling Tony's mum around in some kind of waltz. He danced like he knew what he was doing.

'That proves he's a Nazi,' Dan said, knowingly. 'It's them who invented the waltz.'

We all looked at him. 'How do you know?' Jamie said, not really believing him.

'I just know,' Dan said, brushing him off.

Tony pulled me around towards him. He clicked his heels like the Nazis on the television and said to me, 'Would you like to dance, Fräulein Slaven?' He put his hand around my waist.

'Yes, Herr Keenan,' I said, and we were waltzing at the corner of the bar, with Jamie and Dan laughing at the side of us. Some of the older people were pointing us out and we stopped, feeling everyone stare at us.

The dancing stopped and the man on the stage announced there was going to be a sing-song and they were looking for singers. I went to sit with Mum and Dad, and was happy to see that Kevin had joined them. He gave me a friendly pat on the head, but he was deep in conversation with Dad and they were debating something that I couldn't quite understand.

Mum and Mary were talking closely. Dad had had a lot to drink and he was trying to explain something to Kevin, who was also attempting to make his point.

'But Da,' Kevin said, 'I'm not saying you're a failure. But there is more you could have done. You have a good head on you. You could have made something of yourself.'

'I did! I did! I tried, Kevin! But every time I thought I was going somewhere it all fell through! All my dreams fell through . . . my whole life! No matter what I did, all I seemed to do was spit against the wind!' Dad's face was flushed and his eyes looked as though they were filled with tears.

'Well that's your answer. That's why I want out of here. There's another land, Da, another land with opportunity for someone like me. I'm going to take my chance. I'm not going to spit against the wind. But I want you to be behind me, Da, it's important to me. Give me your blessing, Da.' Kevin looked as though he was going to cry. They both looked at each other, their eyes filled with tears. Suddenly Dad shook Kevin's hand and threw his arm around his shoulder. They both hugged and Dad's eyes were closed as he squeezed Kevin tight. Mum suddenly stopped talking to Mary and they both looked at Dad and Kevin. Tears came to Mum's eyes.

After the break and the raffle, Father Flynn took to the stage again and shouted that he wanted everyone's attention. A chorus of 'sssh' went around the hall and finally there was silence.

'Now, ladies and gentlemen,' Father Flynn began. Kevin and I looked at each other, then at Tony, Jamie and Dan, who were all sitting at Mum and Dad's table.

'I want to take this opportunity to wish all the best on behalf of myself and the whole parish to these two fine young men, Kevin Slaven and Dessie O'Hanlon, who are off to a bright new land and, hopefully, a bright new future.' Everyone cheered.

Kevin and Dessie stood up and took a bow, shaking each other's hands. The priest continued.

'I am sure you will be a great success. And also, I have some ... er ... some news about myself that I want to impart,' he said, his voice faltering. We all looked at each other. Father Flynn seemed nervous suddenly. He had lost the kind of bullishness he'd shown earlier. I thought maybe he was scared inside that Kevin would stand up and tell everyone the truth. He wiped his forehead and continued. 'You see, I want to take this opportunity to ... er ... announce that I am leaving St John Bosco's.' A hush fell over the room, then the sound of mumbling, then silence. 'Y ... yes. The Bishop ... his Grace Bishop O'Toole has decided ... er ... in his wisdom that the talents and gifts the good Lord gave me would be better served teaching our brothers and sisters in the missions ... in Africa. Y ... yes ... I'm off to Africa.' There were more mutterings and then silence. 'So I want to say thank you for everything, from the bottom of my heart. My life has been here, and everyone has been kind and good. And ... er ... I want to say that if I've ever offended or annoyed anyone, then here and now I am truly sorry ...' Father Flynn's voice trailed off, shaking. Everyone was shocked. They'd all thought he was here for ever. Dan looked at me, then at Jamie and Tony, then at Kevin. We all smiled. Everybody was talking furiously about Father Flynn. But we were the only ones who knew the truth. We were well pleased. Dan looked jubilant, and laughed with the rest of us, but his eyes said that he was still troubled. He watched Father Flynn as he went around the tables, being hugged by old women and having his hand shaken by men who trusted him with their lives. If only they knew.

I thought about the poor black babies in Africa who would be too scared to tell if Flynn was doing anything to them.

As if their lives weren't bad enough without getting landed with him.

The old man with the accordion announced the first singer. It was Nellie McGarvie, a woman of about sixty who used to sing in all the pubs when she was young. She swayed a little as the man handed her the microphone, and Dad muttered something to Kevin about how Nellie had spent too much time in pubs in her day. Her voice was a bit shaky but she sang 'They Tried to Tell us We're Too Young' and everyone was joining in at the end. Next up was a man who sang 'Carrickfergus' and his voice was so powerful and pure that the whole hall sat in silence. I looked around me watching everyone enjoying themselves, except for Jake McCabe, who was standing at the bar, downing whisky and smoking fags like there was no tomorrow. He never applauded anyone, he just kept leering over at Mary, who was doing her best to ignore him. Dad was giving him the evil eye and I was beginning to get worried.

To our amazement, the old man announced that the next singer was going to be Kevin Slaven. We nearly died as Kevin got up, cigarette dangling from his lips, and strutted across the floor and on to the stage. Mum beamed with pride. I had only heard him singing in the bath, but I didn't think he would ever get up on a stage. He must be drunk, I thought. One of the boys with the band got on stage and spoke to Kevin, then started to play the guitar. Kevin began singing and a hush fell over the hall.

His voice was beautiful. He sang 'The Twelfth of Never', and the girls were all wide-eyed, watching as he sang, hoping he was singing for them. But he was only looking at one woman, Mum, and her eyes brimmed with tears as his voice filled the hall and carried out into the night. The hall exploded with applause when Kevin finished and two of the girls he'd come in with rushed forward and threw their arms around him. But he ignored them and sat back at the table with us. Dad went to the bar to get drinks and I went with him. He stood beside Jake McCabe, but didn't appear to be talking to him.

Next the old man shouted up for Mary McCabe and everyone cheered. We all knew what a great singer Mary was and everyone was clapping as she got to her feet, egged on by Mum. Mary looked nervous on stage, the lights making the shadows under her eyes even darker. But she had a confidence about her, thanks to the vodka she had been drinking. She cleared her throat and started to sing, her voice sweet and beautiful.

She sang, 'Born free, as free as the grass grows, as free as the wind blows, born free to follow our dream . . . Stay free . . .' I had never heard anyone sing so beautifully. I looked at Mary and thought of her face and her screams that night as Jake battered her on the street, and how she was crying on the steps. But here, up on the stage as she sang, it was as though nothing could touch her.

Jake McCabe stood staring into his drink, and Dad, standing near him at the bar, watched him with disgust all over his face. I looked from them to Mary, singing her heart out on the stage. Kevin was keeping an eye on everyone. Mary sang, '. . . As free as the roaring tide, 'cos there's no place to hide . . . Live free, life is for living, if you're born free.' The roar went up as soon as the song finished and Mary looked as if there were tears in her eyes.

Suddenly Dad turned to Jake McCabe and spat some words at him.

'Born free,' Dad said. 'That poor woman was only free until the day she met you, ya useless bastard! She's never been free in her life, tied to a fucker like you.' I couldn't believe my ears. I couldn't understand why he picked a moment like this to challenge McCabe after all this time. Maybe he was so emotional after talking to Kevin about how he felt his own life was such a let-down that he felt so sorry for Mary and decided to tell McCabe a few home truths. I knew there would be trouble. The words fell on Jake McCabe like a ton of bricks and it seemed to take a full minute before they registered. Then a rage rose in him that turned his face crimson from his neck to the roots of his hair. He smashed his glass down on the counter, breaking it and spilling whisky across the bar. He grabbed Dad by the collar and in one jerky movement stuck his head in his face before Dad even knew it was coming. Blood spouted from Dad's nose and he grabbed McCabe by the hair and punched his face. McCabe fell back against the wall then came back with fists flying. He knocked a table of drinks crashing to the floor and everyone at the bar jumped back.

'I'll kill you, Slaven! Ya bastard! I'll kill you!' He landed a punch full on Dad's face and he fell back on to a table. Two men got up and tried to have a go at McCabe. But before they got anywhere Kevin was in among it and had landed two swift fists into McCabe's face. As McCabe fell back, Kevin moved in on him, but suddenly someone jumped on his back. It was Eddie McCann, McCabe's only pal, another drunk who had served time for assault and robbery. He grabbed Kevin and tried to choke him. Dessie O'Hanlon jumped in from nowhere and started punching McCann. All hell had broken loose. The women were screaming and I was on the floor trying to see through all the bodies. There were people punching and kicking and glasses smashing. Mum had got hold of Dad and managed to calm him down. Mary McCabe was hysterical and crying in the corner. Kevin was punching Jake McCabe into oblivion. But he kept getting back up for more.

'All you're good for is hitting women, McCabe! You're a loser! C'mon, get up!' Kevin challenged him to get up for more punishment. Dessie O'Hanlon was fighting with Eddie McCann and at least four people were trying to break them up.

Suddenly everything stopped dead. Despite the mayhem, we all heard it at once. It sounded like it was gunshot. The whole place fell silent. Then a teenage boy from the village burst in the door.

'It's Barney Hagen! I think he's shot himself!' he said, and turned and ran.

Others followed him. I stood rooted to the spot, my stomach turning over. Barney Hagen had shot himself. The words rang in my ears. I knew how. I had seen his gun. He had always kept the bullets separate, so nobody would come in and shoot him, he told me. Now he had shot himself.

'It must have been that business with the police today,' I heard some woman say, but I felt dizzy suddenly. The hall was emptying and everyone was making for Barney Hagen's house. We could hear the ambulance siren blaring and in the distance I could make out the blue light as we approached Barney's house. I stopped suddenly, afraid to go any further. Dan, Tony and Jamie ran ahead. I felt sick. By the time I got to the gate I could hardly see for the crowd. Then as I peered through I could see the ambulancemen bringing an empty stretcher out. Two other men dressed in black came out carrying a zipped-up body on a stretcher. It must have been Barney. They put him in the back of a black van that looked a bit like a hearse. I felt as though I was going to choke. Maybe if I had not ignored him these past few weeks he wouldn't have felt so bad about all the gossip and rumours. Maybe he even thought I was one of the kids bad-mouthing him. Now he was dead, and I would never be able to tell him that I knew he was innocent. I know that would have meant so much to him. All the stories he told me about the war and his pain came flooding back to my head. I remembered him crying. I watched as the ambulance doors closed and the van pulled away with the blue light not flashing any more because there was no need to hurry. Barney was dead.

Chapter Sixteen

L ying in bed I watched the full moon make ghostly shadows on the wall. I closed my eyes, but sleep just wouldn't come. My mind raced over and over the events of the night, and no matter how I tried, every time I closed my eyes I could still see Barney's face. I prayed to God and asked him if it was partly my fault that Barney killed himself, because I had more or less abandoned him. I didn't think God was listening because nothing seemed clear any more. I saw Barney as a young man, his cap under his arm, going off to war. I could see him lying in the festering pond in the Jap prisoner-of-war camp. I tried to push the thoughts away and to concentrate on the rest of the night. It had been some night altogether. The punch-up was just like the movies, with men throwing fists and missing each other. Kevin hadn't come in yet, and I guessed he was off with his mates and the girls who were all congratulating him on beating up Jako McCabe. I wondered what happened to Mary when she went home. Jamie had walked home with her, but he was very apprehensive because his dad would no doubt be back to take out his anger on anyone who was an easy target.

Tony's mum and the Nazi seemed to be arguing by the time they left because she had been hanging around McCartney. In the middle of the fight the two of them seemed to disappear for a few moments and the Nazi went after them. In all the chaos we didn't bother to follow them, but by the look on his face, the Nazi had seen something he didn't like. Tony went home with them, but he looked worried.

I must have fallen asleep because it was the sound of a stone at my bedroom window that wakened me up. I opened my eyes and it was almost daylight. The moon had gone and the sky was pale. The stone hit the window again, and this time I could hear a loud whispering voice call my name.

'Kath! Kath!' I pulled back the covers and crept up to the window, wondering if I was having a dream and hoping it wasn't Barney Hagen's ghost come back for me. From my window I could see the figures of Tony and Jamie standing below, their heads upturned and their hands cupped over their mouths as they called my name again.

'Jesus,' I said, opening the window. 'What are you doing? What's wrong?'

'Open the door, Kath,' Tony said, stepping off the grass to the back door.

I pulled on my jeans and sweatshirt and tiptoed downstairs. I could hear snoring coming from my mum and dad's bedroom.

I opened the door and Tony and Jamie came slinking into the kitchen.

'What's the matter? God's sake, Tony, it's the middle of the night,' I said.

The kitchen was still quite dark, even though it was light outside.

'I know,' Tony said. 'Listen, Kath. We're running away. We haven't got a lot of time, so listen . . .'

Automatically, the three of us sat down softly at the table. Then I noticed that Tony had a cut with dried blood just above his eyebrow. My eyes darted from him to Jamie.

'What happened?' I put my hand out to touch his eyebrow but he drew back.

'Don't, Kath, it's sore. Listen.' His voice was urgent, commanding.

He told me that when they got back to the house, immediately they closed the front door, the Nazi grabbed his mother by the hair and started to slap her face. She fell down in the hallway and he kicked her in the stomach. Tony said she seemed to pass out and he jumped on the Nazi to stop him, but he just kept kicking. He had his arms around the Nazi's neck, but somehow the Nazi managed to grab him and drag him in front of him. He pushed Tony's face against the door, striking his eye against the handle. Tony said he didn't know what came over him, but suddenly he grabbed a candlestick and hit the Nazi over the head as hard as he could.

Tony's eyes were wide as he said, 'I couldn't believe it, Kath. He just kind of looked at me, then wobbled and fell on to the floor. I just stood there watching him. There was blood coming from the back of his head . . . I think I killed him!'

'Jesus,' was all I could say. Jamie sat quietly. He had obviously heard it already.

Tony told me that he wanted to hit the Nazi again and again, but he managed to stop. He said that suddenly he found himself in the Nazi's bedroom, and was dragging his money box out from its hiding place. As he told me, he pulled out a bag with wads of notes in it as well as the newspaper clippings about the Pole proving that he was really a Nazi soldier.

'I think I've killed him. But if I have, then I've got all this stuff here and I can tell the cops who he really is. Maybe they won't put me away for life. Jesus! They'll have to catch me first! I'm running away, Kath, me and Jamie. And we want you and Dan to come too! Are you coming?'

It was almost as though I didn't have any choice. He didn't tell me I must come with him or say that he would die if I wasn't with them. But I knew that even though my mum and dad would panic when they wakened up to find I wasn't in my bed, it didn't matter. I was going with Tony and Jamie, and it was as though I couldn't help myself.

187

'Yeah,' I said, getting to my feet. 'I'm coming.' Suddenly I was creeping upstairs and throwing a jumper and another pair of trousers into a bag. I felt fantastic. Like I was being powered by something I couldn't control. There was no stopping me. I tiptoed past my mum and dad's room and looked in. They were fast asleep in each other's arms. I loved seeing them like that and I closed my eyes to keep them there in case I never saw them again.

I went downstairs and grabbed some bread and cheese and two cans of beans and stuffed them into my bag. Tony and Jamie were on their feet and ready to go. Their eyes were shining in the thrill of this great new adventure. We were in our very own movie. We were the pioneers who took their wagons across the desert. We were the heroes who would win the war and free the world. Nothing would stand in our way.

'What about Dan?' Jamie asked. 'We'd better go and get him.' We nodded and made our way swiftly to Dan's house. His front door was open and we went silently inside and into his bedroom. I nudged him and Tony put his hand over his mouth in case he cried out. He opened his eyes and looked at all three of us.

'Are we running away?' Dan said, blinking away the sleep.

'Yeah,' Tony said. 'You coming?'

'You bet!' Dan said. He jumped from the bed and automatically put his hand between his legs. He looked surprised and pleased that he was dry. He half smiled and pulled his baggy trousers on over his pyjamas.

'C'mon, let's go,' Dan said.

I was amazed that Dan was coming with us, knowing how responsible he had felt for his mum and the other kids. But seeing his mum at the dance had made us all think that there might be a chance she would one day get over losing his dad and that maybe her life would get better. Maybe she would even get a new husband, because she seemed to be getting along with big Hennessy, the bookie.

You could have touched the excitement with your bare hands as we filed out of Dan's house and darted across the back gardens that took us out of the village and into the fields. We had no idea where we were going, we were just running away and that was all that mattered. We were off where nobody could touch us and we would run and run for as long as it took. We never even considered what lay ahead or what we had left behind. The world was ours for the taking.

All through the village nothing stirred in the houses. The curtains and blinds were all drawn and as we walked further and further to the edge of the village I glanced back at the deserted streets.

When we got into the field we stopped and looked straight ahead. There was an early morning mist hanging over the grass and the trees in the distance looked hazy in the moist morning air. There was no sound, save for the birds bringing in the dawn. We stood watching our breath coming out in steamy gasps in front of us. Suddenly it felt cold.

'Tell you what,' Tony said, his eyes scanning the horizon. 'We have to get a plan.'

We all nodded.

'What we should do is get out as far as we can to our hideout ... you know the one beyond the sewer pipe, right down the mineshaft, the one that nobody ever goes to any more. We should make that our hideout for a couple of days. Then we can decide where we want to go.'

'Do you think the cops will come looking for you?' Jamie said. 'I mean, if the Nazi is dead?'

'Sure,' Tony said. 'They'll be after me, no doubt about that. But all you guys' parents will get the cops once they know we're all missing. Everyone will be looking for us. But we'll be all right. We're sticking together. We'll make it on our own from now on.'

'Yeah,' Jamie said. 'On our own.' Dan and me nodded emphatically. But somewhere just at the back of my mind I could see my mum and dad wakening up and the shock when they realized I wasn't there. I pushed the thought away.

'C'mon then. Let's get moving. We'll need to cross the river to get to the hideout. We can't risk going by the roadway in case we get caught,' I said, remembering the route we took to the remote spot where we played last year. We all looked at each other. It was dangerous crossing the river, and we had never done it before. Any time we went to the hideout we had gone the long way, out of the woods and by road. This would be our first big test.

'We'll build a raft,' Dan said. 'I saw them doing it in *Robinson Crusoe*. You tie the logs together with branches and away you go.'

'Right,' Jamie said. 'That'll be easy.'

We walked off into the bright, fresh morning, our duffel bags slung over our shoulders, and we never as much as looked back.

Chapter Seventeen

We could feel the sun on our backs as we walked on and on through the fields, none of us talking much, each of us focused on the task ahead. We were glad of the shade in the woods to cool us off from the walk across the fields and over the hill, far enough away from the village. The woods were dark but we strode straight through, seeing ourselves in the jungle with no turning back. When we reached the end of the trees we were glad to see the light. The woods always made strange noises and if you stood still there was a branch cracking or a hissing noise somewhere around you making you feel uneasy and alone. Out of the woods, we stood looking down into the fast-flowing river. It looked massive to us, but it really wasn't that big because I had gone there once with Kevin and his mates and they were all swimming from one side to the other, despite the current raging against them. Kevin told me that on the other side of the river, if you walked for about thirty miles, you would get to the sea. I didn't know if it was true though, because I had only ever been to the seaside at Helensburgh on the blue train or on the bus to Ayr, and they were not on the same road. But if it was true, then maybe if we kept crossing the fields we could get to the ferry on the coast and I could cross to Donegal and see Ann Marie. I didn't want to tell the boys what I was thinking in case they said I was daft.

Tony looked at his watch.

'We've been walking for nearly two hours. I'm whacked.

Let's sit down and have some food.' We all sat at the edge of the hill and brought out the food from our bags. Nobody had actually taken any time to make anything. We had cans of beans, bread, cheese, water and juice. Tony had a pocket knife with all the bits on it. He set about cutting cheese and making sandwiches. We ate them hungrily, in silence, looking down at the river, all of us wondering what we had got ourselves into, but nobody daring to admit it.

'Once we cross the river, we'll walk for about another hour and that will take us to the mineshafts and the old workshop. We can stay there for the night,' Tony said.

'Maybe we should have brought a tent,' Dan said.

'We don't have a tent, Dan!' Jamie said, throwing a piece of bread at him.

'We could have borrowed one,' Dan insisted.

'Yeah. Like say to your next-door neighbour, "Can I borrow your tent? Me and my pals are going to run away."' Everybody laughed.

'First thing we've got to do is try and build a raft. We'll go down the hill and see if we can get enough bits of wood to make one,' Jamie said.

'Could we not swim across?' I said, thinking about Kevin and his pals. I knew we could all swim.

'Wouldn't like to risk it. There's undercurrents,' Tony said.

We all looked down at the river in silence. It rushed on relentlessly, foaming white torrents raging over rocks and pebbles, then on and on downhill and into the distance. It looked deep in parts, dark and scary.

We took ourselves down the hill and threw our bags off while we set about looking for wood.

'How are we going to chop logs?' Dan said. We all looked at each other. We hadn't really given it much thought. I was beginning to feel worried.

Jamie had gone off into the trees and suddenly we heard him shouting.

'Hey, guys, quick! I've found us a raft.' We rushed in and there he was, dragging what looked like an old home-made raft, built from railway sleepers. It looked as though it had been discarded ages ago, and the edges of it were damp through at one side where it had been buried beneath the undergrowth. We pulled all the leaves and dirt off it and kicked away the dozens of beetles, slaters and spiders that infested it. It was big, built from at least three thick sleepers that had been sawn in half and tied at the ends with rope. The rope was damp, but it held the sleepers together and we could see that it must have been used by older guys who played on the river at some time or another. It didn't seem like it was rotted and looked as though it might float. Tony found a long piece of branch twice his size.

'This looks as if it would do. It looks strong,' he said.

'I know they used to go down the river in rafts a couple of summers ago. My big cousin told me they used to race each other, so it must be safe.'

I wasn't so sure. But it did seem sturdy.

We dragged the raft along to the edge of the river.

To our amazement Tony pulled a piece of rope out of his bag and said: 'You see, I knew this would come in handy some time.'

'What were you going to do? Hang yourself?' Jamie laughed, as Tony tied the rope to the end of the raft.

'Watch this,' Tony said, as we pushed the raft on to the water and let the rope out gradually to see how it floated.

'Well, it floats,' Jamie said. 'But will it hold all of us?'

We watched the raft bobbing up and down in the water. It looked strong and the sleepers were thick so there was no water lapping over it. Tony dragged it back in.

'I'm going to give it a try first,' he said, and we looked at him, a bit worried.

'Maybe we should think about going by the road, Tony. Or just hiding up here somewhere,' I said.

'No, Kath. It'll be fine. We've got to try.' His face was serious.

He pulled the raft to the edge and crawled on to it. We held on to the rope as we gently pushed it back into the river. Tony looked scared, but determined. Dan's face was white. The raft was a few feet away from the river bank, but sure enough it floated.

We kept hold of the rope, but our raft was out there, floating on the river, and Tony was on his feet, proudly saluting us.

'Yahoo! We've got our own boat. C'mon, pull me back in.'

We dragged him back, carefully, and he clambered out.

'But will it take us all?' I said.

'I'm sure it will,' Jamie said. 'It looks really strong.'

We secured our duffel bags on to our shoulders and got ready for the journey. I looked across the river to the other side. It wasn't all that far, maybe about thirty yards, but at that moment it seemed like an ocean. The river swirled around in the middle and white waves drove it downstream. We all eased ourselves on to the raft one by one. Our faces were tight with concentration. Tony held the paddle and pushed us into the water. I swallowed hard, half expecting the raft to sink. But it didn't. It floated. There we were, the four of us, out in the open river. It was magic. Jamie hooted with excitement.

'Ya beauty! We're sailors! Yahoo!' He moved to kneel up but the raft bobbed around in the water and we all froze.

'Sit still, for God's sake,' Tony said, laughing as we all braced ourselves.

Tony put the paddle into the water. He said he could feel the bottom and pushed the raft so that we were now yards away from the side. We sat nervously as we slowly headed for the other side.

'This is brilliant!' Jamie said. 'I can't believe we've got our own boat! Maybe we'll go fishing tomorrow.'

I was beginning to feel more at ease. We were getting closer and closer to the other side and I could see the tall grass at the edge of the river bank. Everything would be fine.

It happened so quickly we didn't even see it coming. We were in the water before we knew what had hit us. Suddenly the boat just disintegrated. It didn't sink under our weight, it just broke apart, and by the time we were in the water all we could see were little bits of wood being carried away in the current. I was first to come up from under the water and I spat and gasped, looking around for the others. Jamie popped up beside me coughing and choking, then Tony, his face covered with a slimy reed.

'Where's Dan?' I screamed, treading water, but feeling the weight of my clothes dragging me down. I kicked and kicked with my legs, but I was getting further away from Tony and Jamie as the current carried me.

'Where's Dan?' I screamed, panicking, breathless.

'Oh shit!' Tony screamed, the current dragging him down towards me. 'Oh shit! Kath, where's Dan?'

Jamie swam towards the other side and we saw him grab the edge of the river bank and try to drag himself out. But the soft soil kept giving way under his hand and he was being dragged back into the river. Eventually he made it and pulled himself out. He was on his knees spitting and coughing. Then he suddenly looked out to the river and started screaming.

'Oh shit! Oh shit! Dan! Dan! Oh God! No! Dan!' Jamie was on his feet shouting into the river.

Suddenly we saw the figure being carried towards us. Face down. It was Dan. My legs stopped moving. They wouldn't move. I wanted to be sick.

'Oh Jesus, Kath!' Tony looked at me, his face white, soaking, his eyes red. He kicked himself up in the water and in one almost miraculous movement he grasped Dan's body just as it floated past him. I watched in terror, unable to move. Tony found strength from somewhere and suddenly he was swimming and dragging Dan's limp body on to rocks towards the edge of the river. He was out of the water and pulled Dan out, turning him on to his stomach. My legs moved and I started to kick wildly, punching and fighting against the torrent. I pushed and pushed, feeling my duffel bag slip off my arm and float downstream. I pushed and kicked and spluttered until I reached the side and dragged myself out.

'Oh God, no!' Tony was thumping Dan's back. 'Oh God, please don't let him die! Please, God! Please, God! Let me die! Not Dan! Come on, Dan! Come on!'

I stood over them, watching Dan's grey face in the mud, his lips a bluish colour.

'Oh Dan! Please don't die,' I could hear myself whisper through tears.

Jamie was clambering over rocks and mud to get to us.

'Oh Christ!' he said, as he threw himself on to his knees. 'Oh Dan!'

Suddenly Dan's eyes flickered, and he started to vomit water. He coughed and choked and Tony thumped his back. He was alive.

'Come on, that's it. Oh Dan, I knew you wouldn't die!' Jamie said, pushing Dan's hair back and rubbing his hands. Dan opened his eyes and started to cry. He sobbed and Tony pulled him towards him and hugged him tightly. I knelt down and threw up into the water. When I stopped being sick, I turned to them and couldn't stop my tears as I saw the three of them together, holding each other, and crying with the fright and relief of the whole thing. The sun was blazing above us and the river that had tried to swallow us up battered its way on.

We pulled ourselves up and staggered to the river bank. Then we sat down and stared into space. Nobody spoke.

We were stripped down to our underwear to let our clothes dry in the sun. But even though the heat was rising in waves, we were still shivering. Dan couldn't stop shaking.

'I read somewhere you have to take something sweet if you've had a fright,' Jamie said.

We looked at the contents of the two surviving duffel bags. I had lost my bag and Dan's had also been dragged away. Everything from Jamie and Tony's bags was emptied out on to the grass to dry. The bread was soggy and unrecognizable. But the cans were there and so were the cheese triangles and the bottles of juice. There were four Mars bars that were soaked, but still edible.

'We'll eat these,' Jamie said, picking one up.

'Not one each,' Tony said. 'We'll have to ration the food. Let's just have one between us.' He got his penknife out and quartered the chocolate bar and we stuffed it into our mouths. It tasted brilliant, sweet and wholesome, and we all eyed the other bars, desperate for more.

Tony was prising open the plastic box he had inside his duffel bag. It contained all the money and the newspaper clippings as well as a petrol cigarette lighter, and rolled-up inside some greaseproof paper were sliced sausages. Everything was bone dry.

'Mom had these boxes in the States. No air gets in. No water. Even if you're drowning, your lunch will stay dry.' He smiled, happy and relieved that we were not just still alive, but that we also had food.

'I think we should just make a kind of camp here tonight, Tony,' I said, feeling exhausted from the terror in the river.

Tony looked at me. He could see that I was tired and scared. He smiled.

'Yeah, maybe that's best. It's roasting anyway. We can sleep under the stars. We'll build a fire later and just lie here.'

We lay back with the sun warming our chilled faces, each of us recalling those terrifying moments in the river when we could all have died. It seemed unreal. I felt drowsy and my eyes began to close. I could feel Dan lying beside me, edging a little closer. I reached down and touched his hand and he clasped my fingers in his. Nothing stirred around us except for the cooing of a wood pigeon somewhere deep in the trees.

Exhausted, we fell into a deep sleep, none of us even knowing or caring for a moment what was to happen next.

I woke up shivering and for a split second couldn't work out where I was. Then I saw Dan lying beside me, his face peaceful. Tony and Jamie lay curled up next to each other. I shivered again. By the look of the sky it was early evening, still sunny, but in the distance I could see the horizon turn to red in the sinking sun.

I sat up and looked out into the distance. There was nothing but open fields and woodland, and the occasional tiny dot of a farm. I did not know for sure where I was, but I remembered Dad telling me that underneath the ground here for miles there were mine workings, and years ago the men used to travel on bogeys underground to get to the different parts of the pit.

I was feeling a pang of homesickness. I thought of how things would be in my house at this time of night. We would all be sitting after our dinner with cups of tea, watching the television. Dad would probably be asleep if he had been drinking, and Kevin might be dozing. It was always cosy, even if there were fights. I wondered what had happened when Mum and Dad woke up and discovered I wasn't in bed. They would wonder if I had got up early and gone to one of the boys' homes, and within ten minutes everybody would be at each other's doors asking where Tony, Jamie,

Dan and I were. They would all be panicking. I wondered if the Nazi was dead, or if he had killed Tony's mum. It didn't bear thinking about. I knew people would be looking for us. Deep down, part of me wanted them to find us, but I was worried that if Tony had killed the Nazi he would be taken to a boys' home. I knew we had to stick together.

'C'mon, are you guys going to sleep all day? There's work to be done. C'mon, get up.' I gently kicked each of them, stirring them from sleep.

'I'm starving,' Jamie said as soon as he sat up.

'You're always starving,' Tony said, getting to his feet and stretching. He shivered and put on his T-shirt that had been drying on the grass.

Dan sat up and didn't say anything. We all looked at each other.

'Howye feeling, Dan? All right?' I said, throwing him a shirt to put on.

'Yeah. OK, I think,' he said, rubbing his eyes. 'I dreamt I was dead. It was a crazy dream. I was floating somewhere, then ... then I saw my dad. He was smiling, you know the way he used to, and he was waving me towards him. But I couldn't get near him. Something was dragging me back. Jesus! Then he came towards me and put his arms around me and hugged me. Jesus! I could smell his hair! I could smell his hair!' His eyes filled with tears. 'Then ... he just seemed to disappear and I was left alone in this place ... I don't know where it was.'

None of us knew what to say. Dan wiped his eyes, then stood up, trying to pull himself out of the dream that had left him empty and sad.

'I read about stuff like that,' Jamie piped up. 'I read that if you are nearly dead, then you can have an experience that you actually see what there is after you die. Like heaven and that? Maybe that's what you got a glimpse of, Dan. Maybe you got a glimpse of heaven,' Jamie said, enthusiastically. I knew he was just trying to make Dan feel good, so I joined in.

'Yeah, that's right, Dan. Maybe you saw your da in heaven. It's good to know that, though, isn't it? That he's in heaven,' I said, with my own idea of what heaven was like up there among all the angels and saints and other people who never put a foot wrong while they were living. I wondered if Barney Hagen was up there. I couldn't see why not. He was decent and had never done anything wrong and ended up dead because people said bad things about him, just the same as Jesus, so I figured that he would be the kind of person God would let into heaven.

'We'd better get a fire going before night time comes,' Tony said, breaking the mood.

Jamie and Dan went off and started collecting bits of wood while Tony built a fire from pieces of stone set in a circle, the way the cowboys did. I gathered twigs and we knelt beside the stones, building the fire meticulously.

'You OK, Kath?' Tony said, as we knelt close together.

'Yeah,' I said, almost believing it.

'They'll come after us. I know they will. Especially if I've killed the Nazi,' Tony said. 'But you know what? I don't care if I've killed him. He had it coming.' Tony flicked the lighter and set fire to some twigs, both of us almost lying on the ground and blowing on the tiny glow in the middle of our makeshift hearth. It crackled and caught and in seconds there was a flame building up as we put bigger twigs and anything we could find on the fire. We sat and watched the smoke billow up.

'I got you a present, Kath,' Tony said, taking me by surprise. He went into his jeans pocket and pulled out something silver. 'It was wrapped in tissue paper, but it got wet.'

He handed me a silver bangle inside the soggy paper. It was the most beautiful bangle I had ever seen. I didn't know what to say. I felt my face go red.

'God, Tony! It's beautiful. Look at it. God! It must have

cost a fortune! Where did you get the money?' I said. But as soon as I said it I knew. He looked at me and laughed in the cocky way he did when he had won something.

'Where do you think?' he said, smiling. The firelight made his eyes shine but the dark shadows were still there.

'God, Tony. You shouldn't have,' I said, knowing that he had stolen the money from the Nazi. I knew it was wrong, but somehow the bangle seemed all the more important now that it had been bought by the Nazi's money. After all, he made Tony's life a misery every day. I slipped the bangle over my wrist and stroked it. There was a tiny blue stone in the centre of it that shone in the light. It was the best present I had ever had.

'Thanks Tony,' I said, and before I knew where I was I kissed him on the cheek. His face turned red and he smiled, slightly embarrassed.

'I'm starvin'!' We turned to face the shouts of Jamie coming over the brow of the hill with his arms full of firewood. Dan followed behind, the pile of wood covering his face.

Tony started opening tins of beans and cutting cheese.

'OK, I know you're starving. Dinner is about to be served.'

Chapter Eighteen

Later, in the darkness, we all sat by the fire, hypnotized by the flames. We had dined on beans and cheese, washed down with orange juice. For us it seemed like a feast and we sat back relaxing while the colours of the day grew into dusk.

'Do you think they're out looking for us right now?' Dan said, and you could hear the hope in his voice.

'I'd say so,' I said, hoping they were, yet dreading being caught.

'Even if they do find us,' Tony said, poking a branch into the fire and sending the flames higher, 'even if they find us, I'm going to keep on running. I've decided that no matter what, even if I haven't killed the Nazi, I'm not going home. I can't go back there. Even if they were to surround us right now, I wouldn't go with them!' He was determined.

My heart sank. Deep down I wanted to go home, and I hoped that if we did, we could all go back to being just the way we were. But it would never be the same now. Too much had happened in the last few weeks. I wondered how long we could last out here.

'What happens when we run out of food?' Jamie said.

'We'll take it in turns to sneak up to the farms. There's at least three of them not too far away. And we'll get eggs or something. Maybe milk. It'll be fresh, right from the cow,' Tony said, making the plan sound exciting.

'I'll go,' said Jamie. 'I'll just creep up there and before the hens know what's hit them, I'll be in there like a fox, raiding their nests. I might even steal a chicken.'

'What, to keep as a pet?' I asked. ''Cos who's going to wring its neck? Not me, that's for sure.'

'That's what I could go right now,' Dan said, his eyes widening. 'Chicken and chips, with loads of salt and two slices of bread.'

'No, I could go a Luigi's sausage supper. God, I can smell it,' Jamie said, his face agonized at the thought of it.

'Yeah,' I said, my mouth watering. 'Then a strawberry milk shake and a packet of Maltesers to eat on the way home.'

'Maybe if we survive the next couple of days, one of us can go to wherever the nearest village is and see if there's a chip shop and bring back fish suppers or something. We've got loads of money,' Tony said, knowing we were all dreaming of normal food.

'I'll go,' Jamie said, volunteering again.

'You'd probably eat them on the way home,' Dan said, diving on him, and the two of them wrestled on the ground.

Everything stopped when we heard the owl hooting. The silence was eerie as we all stayed quiet to listen. Darkness had come down suddenly, falling like a blanket, and beyond the fire there was nothing but blackness. You never saw it as dark as that back home because there were street lamps and lights from the houses. But this was just pitch black.

'What do you think they'll be doing back home?' I said, hoping they wouldn't think I was a wimp for thinking of home.

'My mum will be frantic,' Dan said, then quickly added, 'but I'm still staying on the run.' I knew he was trying to convince himself.

'I bet big Hennessy's up at my house,' he went on. 'I think he fancies my ma, but I don't want a steppie.'

'Your ma's not going to marry someone, Dan. It's only weeks since your daddy died. Don't be daft.'

'Yeah, I know. But big Hennessy's up quite a bit. I mean, he's all right. He's good to talk to and I think he cares about us. He brings sweets and sometimes brings a big box of food. But I don't know if you could have a laugh with him. Sometimes him and my ma sit in the kitchen drinking tea and she seems to cheer up a bit when he comes round. But she's still greetin' in her bed at night. I can hear her . . .' Dan's voice trailed off.

'He's got loads of money,' Jamie said. 'If he became your steppie he'd be able to take you to Blackpool and everything. Maybe even Spain. I'd have him as my steppie.'

There was a silence and I could nearly hear Dan's brain ticking over.

'Aye, but it wouldn't be the same, though. It wouldn't feel right.'

'Never mind home,' Jamie said. 'Let's forget about it. Think about something funny. Remember when Tommy Hanlon farted during the gymnastics at the Gang Show when he was jumping over the horse?' We all chuckled recalling the Scouts' extravaganza where all the local troops had met from across the county to have their own version of the Gang Show, like the one on the television every year.

'Aye,' chirped Dan. 'And remember Miss Grant's sticky fingers?'

We all smiled, remembering the day we saw Miss Grant shoplifting.

It was not long after we had seen her in Luigi's, the day she got stood up.

There was a shop down the road from Luigi's that sold everything from lightbulbs to table cloths and everyone from the villages nearby did their shopping there. Inside was a new photo machine contraption that would give you pictures of yourself in three minutes, and we were all fascinated by it. You put your money in and sat on the seat behind the curtain and the big flash would come and take you by surprise every time, giving you pictures that made you laugh. With the money Tony was stealing from the Nazi we had amassed a pile of pictures of Jamie and Dan with their fingers up their noses, and others of Tony and me pulling crazy faces. One time when we were outside waiting for the wet strip of pictures to come out of the slot, Dan nudged us to look down the aisle.

It was Miss Grant, and she was carrying a wire basket with a pie dish in it. We watched her closely as she seemed to browse at the haberdashery shelves. Then, to our amazement, she looked around her briefly and, with the quick hands of a magician, stuffed a measuring tape in her anorak pocket.

'Jesus,' Dan said. 'Did you see that?' Our mouths dropped open as she moved along the aisle a little and then lifted a handful of reels of thread. We watched in delight as she went to the check-out, handed over the pie dish and walked out of the door with the stolen goods in her pocket.

'Wow,' Tony said. 'Can you believe our teacher is shoplifting? Isn't it brilliant! No wonder her boyfriend stood her up. Maybe she was dipping his wallet.' We all laughed, remembering what a sight it had been.

The owl hooting once more brought us back to reality, and I could sense the unease in all of us.

'I wonder what goes on out there during the night,' Jamie said, his eyes wide, trying to focus on the direction where the woods were, but he could see nothing but the dark.

'That's when all the woods come alive,' Dan said, sidling closer to me. 'That's when the owls and the moles and all the other night-time animals and stuff come out to hunt for food. Badgers, rats, stoats, weasels . . . even snakes.'

'Yeah,' I said. 'I read that somewhere . . . that the jungle at night belongs to the animals. Er . . . do you think there's any wildcats here? Like the kind that come out at night ... great big things ... almost like a puma or something?' I was feeling spooked at the thought of not knowing what could jump out on us during the night.

'Maybe,' Tony said, looking around him. He stood up and pulled on a sweater.

'I think we'd better take it in turns to keep watch,' he said. 'Just in case something or someone tries to attack us.' His face was serious.

'And what are we going to do if something does jump out on us ... or someone?' Jamie said. 'It's not as if we've got a knife or a gun or anything.' He suddenly looked edgy.

Tony looked around the camp and picked up a solid piece of wood the size of a pickaxe handle.

'This will do,' he said, holding it up, then swishing it around in mid air as though he was thrashing the enemy. 'Whoever is on watch just sits with this and the first thing to come near us gets a smack on the head with it.' He swung the wood above his head.

None of us was convinced it was an ideal weapon and we all thought of ourselves trying to fight off a wildcat or a robber with a piece of wood. But nobody wanted to admit it. We all nodded and took turns to swing the weapon, with Jamie using it like a warrior, dancing around the campfire and thrashing the air

'Right ... I'll take the first watch,' Jamie said, standing to attention with the wood over his shoulder like a rifle. 'You can all get some sleep.'

We snuggled up to each other around the fire and lay back, me leaning on Tony and Dan curled up and huddled against my back. We didn't speak for a moment, just sat there staring at the flames. My eyes were heavy.

'Good night,' I said, trying to blot out thoughts of my mum, dad, Kevin and Ann Marie that kept coming back. I missed them and I wanted to go home to my own bed more than anything.

'Good night,' Dan said, his voice sleepy.

'Night,' Tony said, but I knew he was far from sleep.

I drifted off as I started to think of Tony, Jamie, Dan and me on the beach that day of the school trip, and how we laughed and ran around as if nothing in the world could ever bother us. I felt my face smiling as the dream carried me away.

I woke up staring wildly as soon as Jamie nudged me to tell me it was my turn to take watch. I felt as though I had only been sleeping for five minutes, but Jamie whispered that it was two in the morning. I yawned and eased myself away from Tony and Dan who were huddled up against me. I looked down at them and smiled to Jamie as we saw how deep they were sleeping.

'Tony looks happy,' Jamie said, turning to me. 'He hasn't looked happy for ages, Kath.'

'I know,' I said. 'It's all that stuff with the Nazi and his mum. He beats him up, you know,' I whispered.

'I guessed,' Jamie said. 'Tony was always a laugh when he first came here, but now . . . well, he's like sad all the time. It's not fair.'

Jamie sat down by the fire and stared straight ahead. I didn't speak, but watched his eyes fill with tears. They rolled down his cheeks, but he made no sound. I looked around at Tony and Dan, who were still fast asleep.

'What's wrong, Jamie?' I said, sitting closer to him.

He couldn't speak. Tears kept rolling out of his eyes and he wiped his face with his sleeve. His body shook as he tried to speak. Then his voice came out so softly that I could hardly hear him.

'The . . . the . . . cruelty people have been to see us . . . er . . . to the house,' he said, barely audible.

'Cruelty? What?' I said, not understanding, then a flash

of recognition came to me. He meant the people in charge of stopping parents being cruel to children. I didn't know what to say.

'They might be taking us away. Jesus, Kath, they might be taking us away from Mammy! Me and the weans. All because of that bastard! The woman came last week . . . some woman with a uniform on and a wee hat. She said she was from the cruelty . . .' He covered his face with his hands and his body shook in great heaving sobs.

'Sssh . . . sssh,' I said, putting my arm around his shoulder. 'They won't take you,' I said, not knowing the first thing about it. 'They only take people away when things are really bad,' I told him, desperately trying to reassure him.

'Aye, but it is bad, Kath. My da's been battering my ma and last week he started to hit our wee Nora. Christ, she's only four. He was slapping her on the legs and they were red raw. And when I tried to stop him he started on me . . . then Mammy got it as well.'

'Jesus,' I said.

'I don't know how these people got to know, but they came to the house and I heard the woman say to my ma that they would try and keep the children together, but they couldn't guarantee it because a lot of people don't want bigger kids like me. When she left, Ma was crying her eyes out and I had to put her into bed and give her a cup of tea.'

Jamie had stopped sobbing and his eyes were black from rubbing them with his dirty hands.

'Maybe if Jake left, things would get better,' I said, not really knowing what else to say.

'Yeah,' Jamie said. 'The woman said that if my da moved out they could try and help us, but as long as he was there then they said we might be in danger, because he's a bad, crazy bastard . . . I mean, my ma's even been taking Valium and stuff and half the time she's like a zombie, taking these pills to stop her crying, and something else to make her sleep. It's terrible, Kath. I hate it! I think I'll just stay away for ever like Tony. No matter where we end up it would be better than going back home!'

I couldn't argue with him, after what he had said. I couldn't blame him if he never went back home in his life again, as long as McCabe was there, making everyone's life a misery.

'You should get some sleep, Jamie,' I said. 'I'll do the watch now.' I took the stick from him and walked away from the fire. He crawled over and snuggled up beside Tony and Dan and within a minute he was fast asleep, his face still wet and streaked with tears and grime.

I walked around the campfire picking my steps carefully in case I wakened the boys. But I wished one of them would get up and join me. It was scary on my own, just the darkness and the night chill the minute you stepped away from the fire. I shivered when an owl hooted and jumped when I heard something scurry across the grass. I wished I was home sitting on the sofa next to my dad and resting my head on his chest as he slept off the afternoon's drink. I didn't like the smell, mixed with tobacco, but it was his smell and I longed for it on this dark, lonely night. I wished it was morning and looked across the black sky willing the horizon to turn red in the sunrise, but it didn't. I thought about Ann Marie and wondered if she was lying awake in her bed in Donegal feeling her stomach with the baby inside. I thought about the baby, how it was inside there and didn't even have a clue that when it came out it was going to be taken away from the person who had kept it warm and snug all these months. Then I thought, it didn't matter to the baby because it wouldn't know anything as long as it was getting fed and changed. But Ann Marie was different. She would come back after the baby was born and was supposed to get on with things as if nothing had happened. I thought about Kevin and how he was packing his bags and getting his life all organized for Australia and my heart sank at the thought that I might never see him again. I thought about Mum and how she had pretended to be strong for everyone over the last few months even though she was breaking up at the thought of losing Kevin, and I knew that deep down she knew it was wrong to send Ann Marie away to Donegal to give her baby away. She knew it was wrong, but she couldn't stand up and say it. She never complained. She just took it all. Nothing seemed fair any more.

When I sat down I couldn't keep my eyes open. Every time I shook my head and blinked, my eyes kept drooping shut and I couldn't control them. I got up and walked around a bit, but then sat back down again, feeling my eyes getting heavier and heavier. The light was changing. The blackness that had surrounded us was beginning to lift and the sky was changing colour. I was mesmerized. I blinked and kept my eyes open for as long as I could, looking across the fields that were now coming into focus as they became bathed in the light of daybreak. Then the sky grew more and more beautiful as a burning red sun began to peep up from nowhere and break through the horizon, making the whole world glow. I closed my eyes to take a picture of it, the way I always did. This was the most beautiful morning I had ever seen. I felt alone in the whole world and it was great. Yesterday we almost died and today we were alive, just the four of us with nobody to rely on except each other. I tried to stay awake to watch the colours change, but suddenly the dreams took me away and I drifted into a deep sleep, my last thought to convince myself that a wildcat would never attack us in broad daylight. We were safe.

'Some guard you are!' I could hear Dan's voice and opened one eye, blinking in the sunlight as he stood smiling over me. I sat bolt upright and looked at Dan and Tony, half wondering where I was. Then I remembered that I had fallen asleep during my watch.

'Jesus,' I said, standing up. 'God, I just fell asleep. I tried to keep my eyes open, but they just wouldn't. But it was daylight anyway,' I said, sheepishly.

'Never mind,' Tony laughed. 'Nobody attacked us anyway. Where's Jamie?'

'Jamie?' I said. 'He was here. I took over from him at two and he went to sleep. What do you mean? Was he not here when you woke up?' It flashed across my mind that he had run away because he was so upset, but I knew he would not go home and that he felt safer with us.

'He'll be around. Don't worry.'

'What if something's happened to him?' Dan said, always thinking the worst. 'I mean, what if he's been kidnapped or something?'

'Don't be daft,' Tony said. 'Who'd want to kidnap somebody who farts all night long? I mean, Jesus, did you not smell him?' Tony was laughing.

Dan shook his head and laughed. 'I thought it was the farm.'

'Farm animals don't smell that bad,' Tony laughed.

'Hey! Chicken shit!' We all turned when we heard the voice. It was Jamie, who appeared out of the trees with a great big smile on his face. He was running towards us and making a clucking noise like a chicken. When he got up to us he squatted down and started to cluck louder and louder with his face turning red. We all wondered what he was trying to do when suddenly he put his hand behind his backside and produced four eggs. We all fell about laughing.

'What the hell did you do?' Tony said. 'Dan thought you'd been kidnapped. Jesus, did you break into the henhouse?'

'Sure,' Jamie said, his face beaming. 'Told you I would. I got us eggs and I stole milk from the farm, but it's back there

In the trees because I couldn't carry it all. What do you think? We could live like this for ever.' He carried the eggs carefully over to the fire and set them down.

'Right. Somebody fill the bean cans with water and we'll have boiled eggs and bread. That'll do us, won't it?' Jamie was animated. He really believed that now that we had a source for food we could live here and he would never have to go back and face the pain of his home again.

Tony took the bean cans and went to the canal while Jamie and I went into the wood to retrieve the milk he had stolen. Dan stocked up the fire. We were ready for another day.

Chapter Nineteen

He seemed to come from nowhere, and for that first second we laid eyes on him we looked at him in sheer disbelief. It couldn't be him. But it was. The big, angry, hateful face just appeared from behind a tree and stopped us dead in our tracks.

It was the Nazi. He had a rifle over his shoulder, the one Tony said he used for shooting rabbits in the countryside. But to us, now that we knew what he really was, all that was missing was the SS uniform.

'Hallo, Tony,' he said, his hand caressing the butt of the rifle.

None of us could move. We stared at him, and I could feel my breath nearly stop. His thick lips stretched back in a sardonic smile. I swallowed hard, but there was nothing to swallow. The Nazi ran his hand over his chin and walked around, like he was on guard. Maybe he was reliving the old days.

'Well now . . . Well now . . . How's the camping trip? Hmm?' He took a step closer to Tony, who took a step back.

'You look surprised to see me, Tony. Did you think you'd killed me . . . you bastard?'

His big meaty arms reached out to grab Tony, who was frozen with fear.

Tony dodged his grasp. 'Fuck off! Leave me alone!' he said, walking backwards as the Nazi followed on. 'Fuck off! I know who you are! You're a stinking Nazi, and I'm gonna make sure you get jailed! You asshole! I've got all your papers! Ha! Ha!'

The Nazi's face was almost purple with rage. We edged closer to him but were terrified he would turn on us at any moment.

'Why do you think I've come here looking for you, Tony? Did you think for a minute I would let you get away with this, let you ruin my life after all I've worked for?' He put his hand out towards Tony.

'Now give me the papers and let's get back home, and we'll just forget all about this. C'mon now, Tony, your poor mother's worried sick. She's been walking the streets day and night searching for you.'

The Nazi's face almost softened and a tiny part of me was thinking that maybe he had turned over a new leaf and perhaps we should all trust him and go back home. I was tired and hungry and if there was a chance we could trust him, maybe we should go. But there was still that evil look in his eyes.

'What do you care about her anyway, you Nazi bastard!' Tony said. 'You make her life miserable. She hates the sight of you and so do I! We were fine until you came along and ruined everything.'

The Nazi sneered. 'You were a poor bastard child with no bottom to your trousers until I gave you everything . . . a roof over your head and food on the table. Now stop this nonsense and give me the papers.' He took the rifle off his shoulder. 'There is no other way, you know that. You're just a boy. There can only be one winner, and it won't be you, or any of your stupid little friends.' He lifted the rifle and pointed it in our direction. We all took a step back.

The Nazi licked his lips. He cocked the gun. I couldn't believe it. He was really going to kill Tony.

'The papers, Tony. Now! And my money. Now! You have five seconds.'

Then he swivelled around to us and pointed the gun. We took another step back, terrified.

We stood rooted to the spot. Dan put his hands in the air like he was in the movies. Jamie looked at him, then at me. He looked like he didn't know whether to laugh or cry. The Nazi turned back to Tony and started to count.

'Five . . . four . . .'

From the corner of my eye I could see Jamie bend down and lift the chunk of tree we had been swinging around earlier. He pulled it slowly upwards, then behind his back. I looked at him and shook my head. Dan kept his hands in the air. His face was white as a sheet. I felt sure we were all going to die. I closed my eyes and said a Hail Mary.

I stopped praying when I heard the thud. I opened my eyes to see the Nazi buckling at the knees. Blood was pouring from the back of his head as he fell to the ground. Jamie stood over him and smashed the wood on to the back of his skull. Tony jumped to his feet. Jamie raised the wood and was ready to hit the Nazi again when I leapt forward and stopped him.

'No, Jamie! You'll kill him! Christ! Let's go!' I pulled the wood from Jamie, who had a wild look in his eye just like his dad. I dragged him away.

Tony jumped in. 'Let's get the gun,' he said, and rushed forward to pull the gun from the Nazi's hand. As he did, he gave him a swift kick in the ribs and the Nazi made a gurgling sound. He was alive, but he wasn't going to touch us.

'Quick! Let's get out of here! Run!' Tony said, and we were off with our legs moving like pistons. In a minute, we were out of the woods and back to the camp. When we got there we threw ourselves on to the ground, breathless and sweating. I thought I was going to be sick again and tried to control the urge to throw up. Dan was ready to burst into tears, but Jamie and Tony were high as kites.

'Jesus,' Tony said. 'Did you see him go down? What a strike, Jamie! You saved my goddamn life!'

'Christ! Did you see him with that gun? I'm sure he'd have killed us. I mean, he's had plenty of practice. God, I nearly shat my pants there!' Jamie said.

'Right, let's get moving. We can't stay here,' Tony said, stuffing everything into his duffel bag.

'We'll go along to the sewer pipe. Nobody will ever find us there. Down by the viaduct. We'll hide out there,' I said. 'If the Nazi was able to find us, then that means they must be out looking for us.'

'How did he know where to look for us?' Dan said. 'I mean, he's not even from here.'

'Yeah, but he goes walks and stuff sometimes in the early morning to shoot rabbits. He knows a lot about around here. I guess he must have seen the smoke or something.'

When we got to a hill overlooking a deep clump of trees, Tony threw the rifle away. We listened as it tumbled through the thick blackness of the trees below.

'I'm starving,' Jamie said. 'Are you sure there's nothing else to eat, Tony?'

Tony emptied the duffel bag on to the ground. There was one piece of bread and a small chunk of red cheese.

'That's it,' he said, apologetically. 'We'll have to keep the bread until tomorrow morning, then one of us will have to sneak up to the farm and see what we can get.'

It was already getting dark and we huddled inside the sewer pipe, cold, tired and hungry. On top of that it was pouring with rain outside and all our attempts to light a fire kept failing. We were scared to light it inside the sewer pipe in case we got trapped, so we just sat there, our clothes damp and our bodies chilled even though it had been warm in the afternoon when the heavy shower of rain had started. We watched the drips gathering on the roof of the sewer pipe, then plopping on to the ground. All I wanted to do was go home, but I didn't dare mention it. Tony didn't feel the same. I knew that much. Since the Nazi had tried to kill him in the afternoon he knew there was no way back there and that was what made it all the harder for the rest of us. We couldn't leave him no matter what. And Jamie was determined he wasn't going back either, though he was worried about his brother and sister and his mum. Nobody was having fun any more. We were stuck and we had no idea what we were going to do.

'Tomorrow morning, first thing, I'll go up to the farm. I'll creep up even before they are out of bed and break into their house and take some stuff from the kitchen,' Jamie said, trying to convince us that all was not lost. 'I might even get some bacon.'

'God, I'd love a bacon roll right now, with some brown sauce on it,' Dan said, his eyes picturing the crispy bacon on a buttered roll.

'Don't think about,' I said. 'It will make you feel worse.' But my mouth was watering at the thought of it.

'Let's try and get some sleep,' Tony said, lying back and trying to make himself comfortable. 'Here, Kath,' he said, handing me his duffel bag. 'You lie your head on that.'

'Thanks,' I said, gratefully, worried that the damp sewer pipe would be crawling with all sorts of stuff in the night.

We lay down, huddled against each other, our arms all entwined. Nobody was sleeping, but we all closed our eyes and hoped that sleep would come. I prayed that we would wake up and it would all have been a bad dream, like all the other vivid, scary dreams I had nearly every night. The rain battered down outside and the night grew so dark we couldn't even see the light at the end of the sewer pipe. I felt my body jerk and shiver, but I was feeling hot all over.

'I'm sweating,' I said to nobody in particular.

'How can you be sweating? It's freezing,' Jamie said.

'Maybe you're sick,' Tony said.

I cuddled closer to them but couldn't stop myself shaking. My teeth were chattering, but there was sweat running down the back of my neck. I wondered if I was going to die and I pictured what it would be like walking in slow motion up to the gates of heaven to be met by St Peter in his big white flowing gown. I imagined him waving me in.

'This is a better place, my child,' he would say. And I would glide in there and see everyone who had ever died and gone to heaven. It would be packed.

I wondered if Barney Hagen was there, and Tommy Lafferty. Maybe Barney would nod to me to let me know that everything was all right and that he knew it wasn't me who spread the lies about him.

There were clouds and angels and then this great cool, happy feeling as I drifted off to sleep.

I felt something strange on my hand and I thought at first I was dreaming. I moved my fingers and it stopped, then I felt it again. It was something jaggy on my hand. My blood ran cold. I turned my head slowly and in the darkness tried desperately to focus. It was only the glint of the eye that I saw, but it stopped me breathing and I lay perfectly still. The rat looked up at me, twitched its nose and scurried away, climbing over Dan's feet. I turned my head around behind where Tony was lying next to me. There was another rat crawling around his head. I was terrified to scream because I had heard somewhere that a cornered rat would attack. I nudged Tony, who moved slightly and the rat scurried away. I nudged him again. He opened his eyes, immediately awake, sensing danger.

'Rats! Tony, there's rats everywhere!' I said, my voice trembling.

'Jesus!' He didn't even stop to look. He got to his knees in one swift motion and then kicked hard against the side of the sewer pipe.

'Piss off!' he bellowed, and Jamie and Dan were up like a shot.

'What the hell . . .'

'Rats! Quick! Let's get out of here!' Tony shouted.

'Oh fuck!' Jamie said, and he crawled out of the sewer pipe followed by Dan, Tony and me. We reached the end of the pipe and glanced back. It was beginning to get light and we could just catch a glimpse of the rats scurrying away back to wherever they came from, deep down the sewer pipe. There were dozens of them. I thought I was going to be sick.

'Oh Christ!' I said, feeling faint. 'Oh God! What if they had eaten us alive? It's just like Barney Hagen told me while he was a prisoner with the Japs. The rats came and ate soldiers' legs and hands away. Oh God! That could have been us.'

'Look, it's all right. Don't worry. They're gone now,' Tony reassured. 'Anyhow it was our fault for being in their home. Never mind, we'll just shelter under that tree.'

The darkness was fading and we picked our way across to a huge oak tree and sat down. We were stupefied from lack of sleep and shock. I was shivering again and I couldn't stop shaking. Tony wrapped his arms around me and held me tight.

Chapter Twenty

When I woke up, my head was pounding and my eyes were burning in their sockets. No matter which way I turned my eyes they were aching. My neck was stiff and even my skin was sore to touch. I could smell the fire and heard the crackling of twigs. My throat was like a furnace. I sat up and looked around me. Tony and Dan were sitting around the fire, their faces grimy.

'Thought you were going to sleep all day,' Dan said.

'Howya feeling, Kath?' Tony said, poking the fire and sending smoke billowing into the grey sky.

'Knackered,' I said. 'I'm all sore. I think I'm maybe sick or something.' It was an effort to say the whole sentence and I felt breathless. Something deep inside me told me I was going to die, and I shivered.

'Where's Jamie?' I asked.

'He's gone to the farm to steal some food. He's been away for over an hour now. He should have been back,' Tony said, looking at his watch. He stood up and walked away from the fire, straining his neck to see if there was any sign of Jamie in the distance.

I sat by the fire and the heat made me feel better. Dan gave me a tiny piece of bread and cheese and I ate it, wincing as I tried to swallow.

'God, my throat's killing me,' I said, rubbing my neck.

Dan threw another log on the fire and we sat on the damp grass waiting for Jamie.

I felt like sleeping again and could feel my eyes drowsing. We had been sitting around the fire for ages, but still there was no sign of Jamie.

'I think we should go and look for him,' Tony said. 'I mean, he should have been back by now. I ... I'm worried something's maybe happened to him.' He looked worried too.

'What if the Nazi's got him?' Dan said, getting to his feet.

'Jeez, I hope not,' Tony said. "Cos if he has, then I will kill him with my bare hands. Honest to God I will.'

I got to my feet unsteadily and felt my head pound. When I looked around, the trees were swaying a little and I had to blink to get my eyes into focus. My mouth felt dry and my hands were sweating.

'C'mon, let's go,' Tony said, and we followed him across the field.

We walked past the huge viaduct that dwarfed us with its size and strode across the field until we could see the farmhouse in the distance. There was smoke coming out of the chimney. Suddenly Tony stopped.

'Ssssh!' he said. 'I thought I heard something.'

We all stopped breathing, standing perfectly still, listening. Then we all looked at each other, our faces shocked and scared. It was the sound of whimpering. Jamie's whimpering. We strained our ears to see what direction it was coming from. We heard it again. First a slow, moaning wail, then a sob.

'Help me! Oh God! Somebody help me!'

'Christ,' Tony said, breaking into a run. Dan and I followed him.

'Over there,' I said, the pain and shivering suddenly vanishing as I ran towards the sound.

We ran and ran through the tall grass until the sound of Jamie's sobs became louder and louder. Then we stopped dead as we saw him.

He was lying on his side and his face was chalk white, his

eyes staring wildly as he pleaded with us. He didn't even look like Jamie, he seemed to be in so much agony. Tears ran off his face and his hair was wet with sweat. Then I saw the metal sticking through his leg.

'Oh shit!' Tony said, throwing himself down beside Jamie. 'It's an animal trap! Christ! He's caught in an animal trap! Oh Jamie! Jesus, Jamie!'

'Oh no!' Dan burst into tears. 'His leg's hanging off! Oh no!' he sobbed.

'Get me out of this! Please! Oh please, Tony! Oh, my leg! My leg! It's killing me! Stop the pain! Tony! Stop the pain! Please!' Jamie pleaded, water running out of his mouth as he slumped back on to the grass.

'Don't move,' Tony said. 'Don't move, pal. We'll get you out! You'll be all right! I promise.' There were tears in Tony's eyes.

We all knelt down beside Jamie and examined the metal. It looked like a jagged piece had snapped through his ankle and stuck right through the flesh to the other side. Blood oozed out of his ankle and through his shoes.

'Quick, Dan! Run to the farm. Tell the farmer he's got to come quick. Tell him a boy is trapped!' Tony said, and Dan was on his feet and running immediately.

It only seemed like a minute before the farmer and his wife came racing across the field. The farmer was carrying some kind of contraption that looked like giant wire-cutters. His wife was running with a basin and some cloths. They were shocked when they saw the state of Jamie.

'My God!' the farmer said, turning to his wife. 'Get an ambulance. This boy's badly hurt.'

Then he turned to us and said, 'What are you doing here anyway at this time of the morning?' We all stood quiet. Jamie was sobbing.

Then the farmer looked at his wife, and suddenly they seemed to know who we were. But they said nothing. She ran to the house while the farmer knelt down and tried to comfort Jamie.

'It's all right, son . . . you'll be all right. I'll get you out of there. Christ, I'm sorry, son. But the trap is for the foxes. They've been stealing my chickens every night. Jesus, son, it wasn't meant for a wee laddie.'

Jamie kept sobbing, his voice growing weaker. 'Please get me out of this, mister.'

The farmer's wife seemed to be taking ages, but eventually she came back. They both knelt down by Jamie and the farmer began slowly cutting the metal, carefully snipping each part to free Jamie's foot. When he cut it, he pulled the metal out of Jamie's foot and I thought Dan was going to faint at the sight of it. Jamie almost passed out with his head on the farmer's wife's lap.

'There now, there now,' the farmer said. 'That's the worst part over. Now let's see the damage.' Jamie was barely conscious as the farmer eased his sock off. We all stood over him as we saw the sock slip off and the gaping hole in his ankle. The farmer's wife soaked the cloths in the water that smelled of medical stuff and plastered them on to Jamie's foot. She held up his head and gave him a drink of orange juice which he gulped gratefully. The farmer looked around at the rest of us who were all standing eyeing Jamie drinking the juice. We were dying of thirst.

'Here, have this,' he said, and handed us a big bottle of juice.

We gulped it down, taking turns, pulling the bottle from each other's mouths. I couldn't get enough to drink if I had taken the whole bottle. I felt dizzy.

Jamie sat up and suddenly looked better, but his face was grey and grimy from tears.

'Jesus, Jamie,' Tony said. 'We thought we'd lost you. God, are you all right?'

'Yeah. I'll still beat you at running, even with a bad leg.' He smiled and the farmer breathed a sigh of relief.

The farmer looked at his wife and they both gazed across the field expecting the ambulance to appear at the farmyard.

'You'd better not walk,' the farmer said. 'Right, you guys lift him and I'll give him a piggy-back to the farm. The ambulance will be here any minute.'

'I'm all right now,' Jamie said, not wanting an ambulance because it would mean the game was up and he would have to go back home. But he knew he was so badly hurt he would have to go to hospital. We all knew it was over. We just looked at each other, and Tony's eyes filled with tears. He walked away from us.

'I'm not going back,' he said.

No sooner were the words out than the ambulance came screaming into the farmer's yard, followed by a police car. Then seconds later there were dozens of people walking across the fields towards us. As they came nearer I recognized some of them. Neighbours, relatives, the woman from the post office, Luigi's wife. I wondered what they were all doing and it didn't click for a full minute that the whole village had been out looking for us. My heart leapt and sank in an instant. Dan's eyes lit up.

I turned to Tony and he was walking backwards away from me. He was shaking his head.

'I can't, Kath, I can't go back there.' His eyes were full of tears.

'Tony, you have to. You can't run away.' I felt my voice shake. I was close to tears. 'There's nowhere else to go, Tony. Please,' I pleaded, but he was already walking away.

I ran after him and grabbed his arm, turning him towards me.

'Tony, it's hopeless. You're only eleven. You can't go any-where. Look what happened to us and there were four of us.

227

C'mon. You can't go away on your own.' I started to sob. I was desperate. Tony stopped and stood looking at me. The farmer turned towards us. Nobody moved. Tony looked at Jamie and Dan and shook his head. He started to sob too.

'I love you, Kath. I'll always love you,' he whispered as he walked away, tears running down his face. He started to run. The people from the village were walking faster and faster as they came towards us. I recognized my mum and dad, then I saw Kevin. I wanted to run to them, but I turned and went after Tony. Dan ran beside me, and then the farmer came after us, carrying Jamie on his back.

Tony ran and ran faster than any of us. We tried to keep up, but we were weak from hunger and I could hardly breathe.

We saw him go towards the viaduct and start to climb it. We stopped and looked at him.

He was like a monkey the way he scaled the wall, climbing higher and higher. Everyone from the village had almost caught up with us and we were all running towards Tony. He didn't even look back at us, he just kept climbing higher. We all stopped when we reached the foot of the viaduct.

'Oh God!' I turned to Dan. 'He's going to fall. It's slippery up there.'

'No, he won't fall. Tony's like Tarzan. He'll never fall,' Dan said, looking up anxiously at Tony, who was almost at the top ledge.

I was oblivious to the crowd who had caught up with us until my mum threw her arms around me.

'Oh Kath! Oh Kath! Thank God you're safe! God, we thought you were murdered, or kidnapped!' I burst into tears and squeezed her tight, but pushed her away almost instantly to look at Tony.

'What is he doing?' Kevin said, hugging me.

'He can't come back, Kev,' I rushed. 'The Nazi's been

battering him and he nearly killed him. The Nazi had a gun and he chased us.' I blurted it all out.

Kevin looked bewildered. 'Are you sick, pal? I think you're delirious.'

'No, it's true, Kev,' Dan said. 'Tony's got all the stuff. The Pole is really a Nazi. Tony's got the papers. We've all seen them.'

Dad looked at Kevin and Mum and then at me, his face screwed up, wondering what we were talking about.

Tony's mum rushed forward to the foot of the viaduct. She was screaming.

'My boy! My boy! Oh Tony! Oh Tony! Please come down! Oh God! Somebody get him down!'

Various men rushed forward and shouted to Tony.

'C'mon now, son. It's too dangerous up there. C'mon now. The game's over. Your mammy's frantic. Now c'mon down and everything will be fine.'

'No it won't.' We could barely hear Tony's voice through his sobs. 'It'll never be fine,' he sobbed.

I broke free of my mum and ran forward. 'Tony!' I shouted. 'Please, Tony. Come down. Everything's going to be fixed. Kevin will fix it, you know he will.'

Kevin rushed forward and shouted up to Tony. 'C'mon, son. Nobody's going to hurt you. Nobody's ever going to hurt you again.'

We all stared up at Tony. A hush fell over the crowd. Tony stood still. He had climbed on to the ledge near the top and was looking down, his face white. The silence seemed to go on for ages. He'll come down, I thought. It's over.

But it seemed to happen in slow motion. Tony had turned his body a little and looked as though he was about to start down the viaduct when suddenly he slipped. He was flying through the air. My mouth dropped open. I couldn't breathe. Tony was coming towards me. Everybody screamed when they heard the thud on the ground. But nobody screamed any louder than me. I screamed with a voice I didn't even recognize. I ran forward and threw myself on the ground on top of Tony. His body was still. His leg was buckled halfway up his back and blood poured from his ear. But his face was just Tony's face as if he was sleeping, like the way he was asleep the other night in the field when he looked happy.

'Tony! Tony!' I screamed into his face. 'Wake up! Open your eyes! Oh God! Oh no, Tony! Oh please don't die!' I sobbed on to his body. I could smell his clothes and feel the heat of his body and his shirt damp with sweat. I wanted to stay there for ever, to hold him until he woke up. But he would never wake up. Tony was dead.

I knelt up and turned around to see Dan fall to his knees and sob. Jamie was screaming, his head burrowed into the farmer's shoulder.

All sorts of people were pushing their way around Tony and I could hear them screaming that he was dead. But their voices were further and further in the distance and I could barely hear them. Everyone was spinning in circles and I tried to stand up, but I fell down, hardly hearing their voices. I could feel someone pick me up, but I didn't know if they were really lifting me or if I was floating in some kind of dream. I thought I could hear Kevin's voice telling me everything was fine. But I knew everything would never be fine again. I tried to speak but the words wouldn't come out. The pain in my chest was so bad I thought it would burst. The voices trailed away and I seemed to be sleeping, dreaming or dying. I had no idea. But I hoped I was dying.

Chapter Twenty-one

We were running along the beach, laughing and kicking sand, giggling as Dan stumbled and fell over. Tony ran faster than all of us and we chased him, shouting at him to slow down. Then he fell over and rolled on the sand laughing. Jamie, Dan and I all caught up with him and stood over him as he lay in the sand looking up at us, his face glowing and his eyes shining. Then his expression changed to fear and he opened his mouth to scream but nothing came out. I watched as rats came out of the sand all around us, climbing on to Tony's head and covering his face. We screamed. Dan and Jamie shook the rats off each other, screaming in terror. I fell down on to Tony, grabbing the rats off his face, but there were so many I couldn't catch them. I fell on to the sand, sobbing and screaming in desperation. Then I could hear the sea, lapping against the pebbles, hypnotizing me as it whispered back and forth. I opened my eyes and saw the four of us on a raft, laughing and shouting as we bobbed around on the water. I saw myself in the distance, then the raft disappeared and a cold, dark feeling ran over me.

I was sure I saw Kevin sitting on the edge of my bed, smiling at me. I tried to smile but my face wouldn't work. Then Kevin's face turned into the Nazi, then Father Flynn. The faces kept changing and I shrank back as all three faces leaned towards me. I could feel the bed shaking. My body was trembling. I felt rivers of sweat run down my stomach and down the back of my neck. I could hear somebody screaming. It sounded like me.

'Quick! Mum! Come in! Doctor!' I could hear the words in the distance, and when my eyes opened again there were three people standing at my bed. I felt my lips move. Who were they? Then I knew my mum, then Dr Morgan. My eyes strained but they were burning in my head. I saw the doctor shaking his head and sitting down on the bed.

'Kath? Kath?' I could hear him, far away, echoing in the trees. I heard the birds sing, but outside I could see it was dark.

'Kath?' the doctor said again. 'Kath? Can you hear me? Kath? Do you know who I am?'

I tried to speak but my tongue was stuck to the roof of my mouth.

'OK. Don't speak, Kath. Squeeze my hand if you know me,' I heard him say.

I felt his warm, fleshy hand in mine and my fingers wrapped themselves around his thumb. I saw everyone's faces change. Mum seemed to sigh and grabbed hold of Kevin's arm.

'Oh Kath!' She was by the bed now, rubbing my hand and pushing back my hair from my forehead. 'Oh Kath! We thought you were a goner.' Her eyes filled with tears. My chest felt heavy.

'Don't get her too excited now, Maggie. It's going to take a bit of time. She's been very sick. The pleurisy itself will take it out of her, never mind the shock. We're just going to have to let her take her own time. But I think she's getting out of the woods.'

I heard the doctor's words echo in my head. Never mind the shock. The shock? What shock? I could feel myself drifting away and the three of them began to fade before me. The shock. I was floating away.

The cold cloth on my head felt good and when I opened my eyes, shafts of sunlight streaming in the window made me close them again. My chest hurt when I breathed in. A sharp pain in my side made me catch my breath and I opened my eyes again, straining to see Kevin through the sunlight.

'Hi, tiger.' He smiled, squeezing the water from the cloth and placing the cold flannel on my head. 'Jeez, Kath, we thought you were going to sleep for ever.'

I tried to smile. Kevin looked beautiful, his hair gleaming in the sunshine.

'You've been out for nearly two days. The doctor and everything's been here day and night. You've been really sick, Kath.' He put his arm around my shoulder and gently pulled me forward as he puffed up my pillows. The effort nearly killed me. Every bone in my body ached and there was a sharp pain in my back, stabbing me every time I breathed.

I lay back, looking around the room, wondering where I had been. The nightmares. Terrible places, dark, horrible things flying around. And here I was in my bedroom, with its yellow walls and pictures of Mick Jagger that had been there since Ann Marie left. I felt warm and good, with Kevin sitting there talking to me. Then I remembered.

We ran away. It all came flooding back to me. There was a flashback to Tony flying through the air towards me. So fast. Then he was on the ground. I closed my eyes but I could still see him. Kevin put his arms around me and held me close to him.

'Tony's dead ... isn't he?' I murmured.

'Yes, Kath. Yes. He's gone,' Kevin said and stroked my hair. He smelled clean and fresh.

I felt the sob rising like a wave from deep inside me. My chest hurt and I was choking. I opened my mouth, gasping for air. Then the sobs came, in short bursts first, but soon my whole body was heaving and with every breath came the stabbing pain in my side.

'Oh Kevin! Oh Kevin! Tony's dead! I want him back! Oh Kevin! Don't make him be dead! It's not fair!'

'Sssh. There now ... sssh. You'll be all right, Kath ... I promise. I know it's hard ... I know, pal ... I know.' Kevin eased me back on to the pillows and I felt the tears run into my ears. He wiped them. His eyes were shining and he looked as if he was going to cry too.

'Try and relax, Kath. The doctor says it's important that you don't strain yourself. You've got pleurisy. It's a bad sickness in your lung. And you've got to be very careful. Try and relax,' Kevin said, looking away from me, tears in his eyes.

'I want to die,' I said, choking. If only I could die. If only the pain would go away and I could be with Tony, like the way we used to be. Like the very first day I saw him, when he was beautiful and funny and tougher than any boy I knew.

'Sssh,' Kevin said. 'Sleep for a while longer and we'll talk about it when you waken up.'

I felt myself drifting away again and I could hear Kevin's voice whispering in the hall to someone that sounded like my mum.

'Yeah. She knows now. She must have just remembered it. Poor wee soul. She's in a real state. I'm glad it's still four weeks until I go to Australia. I want to make sure she's on the mend before I go,' I heard Kevin say. Then the voices went away and I was sleeping again.

The rain was pouring down the day I put my feet on the floor. I stood up and felt wobbly as I walked to the window. Water dripped from the window sills and from the trees outside, making puddles, then little rivers running down the streets. Some kids were out splashing in the water, making boats from pieces of twigs and watching them as they floated down towards the drain. They kicked puddles of water on each other and one of them burst into tears. I felt my face smile. I sat back down on the bed and looked in the mirror. My face was white and thinner than I remembered it. My eyes looked watery and pale. I took a deep breath and there was no pain. I stood up and walked very slowly out of the room and steadily down the stairs to the hall.

I could smell bacon and eggs cooking and my stomach rumbled.

In the living room, Dad sat by the unlit fire reading the newspaper. I felt as if I hadn't seen him for ages.

'I'm starving,' I said, and he looked up, his face brightening into a big smile.

'Jesus, Mary and Joseph! Would you look who it is! Maggie! She's out of her bed.' He leapt from the chair and threw his arms around me.

'Oh my darlin'. God, you had us all round the bend with worry. Are you all right? I think you should be in bed. You were nearly dead!'

Mum rushed in from the kitchen, a tea towel over her shoulder.

'God almighty, Kath, I don't think you should be up. Quick . . . lie on the couch.'

'I'm all right, honest. I'm fine now. I'm starving,' I protested as she ushered me on to the couch.

I sat up, intoxicated with the smell of food, watching Dad trying to read the newspaper so that he wouldn't have to talk to me about Tony. I wished he would say something. He gave me a sideways glance like he could read my thoughts.

'You OK, Kath? You know, about Tony? God, it was the most awful thing. That wee boy . . .' Then he leaned over to me and whispered, 'I knew what he meant to you, Kath. I know it's a hard thing for you. Life sometimes does terrible things to you. But he'll always be in here for you.' He struck his chest with his hand. 'In your heart, Kath . . . in your heart.'

I felt tears in my eyes and I looked away. Mum shouted us into the kitchen. The table looked brilliant, with heaps of bread and steaming hot tea. She put a plate in front of me with crispy bacon, a fried egg and a sausage. My mouth watered.

I hadn't been this starving for ages. I stabbed the beautiful golden yolk and soaked a forkful of bread into it then wolfed it down, gulping a mouthful of piping hot tea.

Dad and Mum looked at each other and smiled.

'She's on the mend,' Mum said.

I managed to smile back.

While I sat with them in the afternoon, they told me all the news. Dad joined in the stories while he picked horses from the racing section of the newspaper and fiddled with the television aerial trying to get a good picture for the big race. Mum just shook her head. She knew if he won any money she would be the last to see it.

They told me that Jake McCabe had gone. He had walked out of the house the morning after Kevin's party. But not before he gave Mary McCabe a sore face. She had to have three stitches to her head. I told them about what Jamie had said about the cruelty people saying they would take the children away, but Mum assured me that she knew all about that, and now that Jake was gone, everyone was rallying to help Mary. But her face was still black and blue.

'I hope to Christ that useless bastard never sets foot in this village again. For if he does, someone will be done for murder. I only wish I had cracked his jaw years ago and maybe he wouldn't have kept on at her,' Dad piped up.

They told me that the Nazi had gone, that he had just disappeared off the face of the earth the day that Tony died and nobody could understand why. I decided not to tell them everything I knew until I had spoken to Kevin.

'When is Kevin going now?' I asked.

'Four weeks on Monday,' Mum said.

'What day is it now?' I had no idea how long I had been out of the world.

'Saturday,' Dad said, and we all laughed.

*   *   *

I was feeling stronger every day, and now that the sun was out I was determined to go outside and see Jamie and Dan. Mum nagged me all the way and had me wrapped up in a sweatshirt even though it was a warm afternoon. I protested, and as soon as I was out of sight I took it off and tied it around my waist.

Dan and Jamie were kicking a ball off the fence at the end of our street, and they turned around when I whistled. They smiled and came running towards me. For a minute I thought they were going to hug me, but they stopped just short of me and Dan gave me a playful punch.

'Christ, Kath, you look skinny,' Dan said, looking me up and down.

'Yeah. Like half starved. You all right?' Jamie said.

'Yeah, fine. I had pleurisy. It's some disease in your lungs. Jesus, I couldn't breathe or nothing,' I said, quite proud that I had been sicker than they had ever been.

'Aye,' Dan said. 'We heard you nearly died.'

'I did,' I said, slightly pleased at the attention.

Automatically we walked out towards the edge of the village and sat on the grass where the old railway track used to be. Dan lay back in the long grass and closed his eyes. Jamie stood over him, tickling his face with a piece of dry grass until he got up and grabbed him. The two of them rolled around the ground, Jamie getting the better of Dan, sitting astride him and holding his arms up with his knees, then tickling under his arms until Dan screamed for mercy. Nothing had changed, it seemed. But it had.

After a while they stopped and we sat on the grass staring at the cars on the road below.

'You miss him, don't you, Kath? Even more than us,' Jamie said. I nodded, holding back tears.

'It's not fair,' Dan said. 'How is it that somebody like Tony dies and other people, people like Father Flynn, get to live? Why does God do that?'

'My mum says God's got a funny way of working,' Jamie said.

'Yeah . . . I don't know why it happened,' I said. 'I mean, it shouldn't have happened. Can you remember? Tony was going to come down. He was going to be all right . . . then he slipped. Jesus, it was terrible. I keep seeing it.' I closed my eyes, seeing Tony's face as he lay on the ground.

'Aye,' Jamie said, staring into middle distance. 'It was terrible. I keep having nightmares.'

'Me too,' Dan said.

'Do you know my da's away?' Jamie asked, looking pleased.

I told him my mum had told me and that I knew about his mum's face. He said he blamed himself for running away and that if he had been there he might have been able to protect her. But he might have got hit as well.

'Did you hear about the Nazi?' Dan said. I nodded.

'He ran away the very day Tony died. When Tony's mum got home from the hospital, he was gone. All his clothes and everything,' Jamie said.

'What about the money? And the passport and stuff?' I said.

'Your Kevin gave it to Tony's mum and told her everything. He told us she said good riddance to him and she's got all the money. I think there's thousands. It was in Tony's bag and Kevin took it after he fell,' Jamie said.

'Did you hear about Miss Grant?' he added.

'No . . . What about her?' It had seemed such a long time ago since Miss Grant was in my life.

'They took her away,' Dan said. 'She's away to the mental ward.'

'What? You're kidding.' I couldn't believe it.

'Yeah! It's true, Kath. Remember when we saw her stealing in the shop? Well, the cops caught her a few weeks later and it turned out she'd been doing it for ages. My ma said she's had

238

a breakdown. When they took her away she was singing hymns at the top of her voice. She's off her rocker.' Jamie almost whispered the last words, conscious that his own mother had been so close to breaking point.

'My God!' I said, trying to imagine Miss Grant being carted off to the mental ward. But I didn't feel sorry for her. There was a slight pang of guilt when I recalled how distraught she looked that day we stole her clothes, and how sad she seemed the day she got stood up. Then I remembered the look on Tony's face the day she beat him up in front of the whole class. To hell with her, I thought, then immediately asked God to forgive me.

We sat for a while in silence, all of us remembering those days when we ran away. Our great adventure. I wished we hadn't gone, then Tony would still be alive. I tried not to think about it.

'I'm going home,' I said. 'I feel tired . . . The doctor says I've got to rest.' I didn't want to be around them any more. I just wanted to go home and close my eyes and remember Tony.

On the way back I stood outside his house, looking up at the window, hoping to see some sign of life, some sign that this was Tony's house where we used to sit together and watch television on rainy afternoons and his mum would bring us orange squash and biscuits. But now there was nothing. The house looked dark from the outside and the grass was overgrown and neglected. I was about to walk away when I saw the face at the window. It was Tony's mum. She stood looking at me, hesitant at first, then she came right to the front of the window so I could see her. She waved me in. I stood for a moment wondering if I should just walk away, but my feet made me go up the path and the door opened as I climbed the steps.

Inside the house was dark and silent, eerie. Tony's mum stood in the hall before me, her face older now somehow and tired. Dark shadows smudged under her eyes and her neck looked scrawny. She tried to smile, but her face was sad.

'Hello, Kath.' Her voice sounded strangled. 'How are you? I heard you were far through.'

'I ... I'm OK now, thanks ... I'm fine really. Er ... how are you?' I didn't know what to say. I wanted to go home. I wanted to run upstairs just to make sure Tony wasn't in his bedroom.

She turned her back to me and opened the fridge, pouring a glass of milk. Then she took some biscuits out of the tin and put them on a plate. She walked past me in the hallway.

'Come on in. Have a glass of milk and a biscuit. You like that, don't you?' she said, as I walked behind her into the living room.

The room that had been filled with our laughter as we fought over games and played football while she wasn't in now seemed desolate. I sat on a chair by the window, with my feet dangling below me. She put the milk and biscuits down beside me and I smiled a thank you. I wasn't hungry, but I took a biscuit and nibbled it half-heartedly. The clock on the sideboard ticked. I had never noticed it before, but in the awkward silence it ticked and ticked like some kind of constant background throb to the aching sadness. She sat down on the chair by the fire and crossed her long legs. I thought about her with Slippy Tits McCartney and I felt sorry for her.

I couldn't bear the silence. Finally she spoke. Her eyes were warm and soft and full of understanding.

'You miss him, don't you?' she whispered.

I nodded. It was all I could do. I felt tears coming to my eyes and I swallowed hard.

'Me too,' she said, biting her lip.

We sat there in the darkness of the sad room, the clock ticking on. I felt tears spill out of my eyes and run down my cheeks. She looked up at me through tears, sniffing them back. She shook her head and the tears just flowed. There were no words.

I wiped my face with my hands and sniffed. She was sobbing. I didn't know what to say or do. I wanted out of this awful, lonely house to run a million miles away and be some place where you didn't always feel sad. To be some place where everybody you loved stayed with you for ever and nobody went away and left you crying on your own.

She was sobbing and I couldn't stop her. I got off the chair and slipped out of the room, leaving her behind with her sorrow, and angry and sad that I couldn't help her. I closed the front door softly and wiped my eyes as I walked into the bright afternoon sunshine.

Chapter Twenty-two

The morning finally came. I had been dreading it every day and counting the hours. But now, as I lay in bed, it was really happening. Kevin was leaving us. I could hear him buzzing around his bedroom, singing and moving his bags. The radio was blaring downstairs. I cheered myself up with the thought that after we saw Kevin off at the train station, we were going straight to meet Ann Marie. She was coming back from Donegal and it was going to be brilliant to see her. But I wondered what she would be like. I wondered how she would be feeling, having had to give her baby away, then coming back home and trying to pretend that everything was going to be fine. I had spent the last two days getting everything ready in her room to welcome her back home. I hoped she wouldn't be too sad.

I dragged myself out of bed and got dressed. I passed Kevin in the hallway, and he smiled at me.

'Hiya ... This is it, the big day,' he said, ruffling my hair.

'I know,' I said, trying to smile. I walked off downstairs.

Mum's eyes were red from crying half the night. I had lain awake listening to her sobbing and hearing Dad's soothing words as he tried to comfort her.

We all sat around the table for breakfast, Kevin wolfing down his food like it was the last he would ever see.

'You'll need to work eighteen hours a day to feed yourself,

the way you eat,' Dad said, just beating Kevin to the last piece of bread.

'I'm a growing boy,' Kevin said, finishing off his tea and getting up from the table.

Mum and Dad looked at each other, then away. They both looked at me.

'I wish he wasn't going,' I said, suddenly, surprised that I wasn't able to stop myself.

'Sure it'll be fine,' Mum said. 'Anyway, Ann Marie will be home today so the house won't be empty. We'll all be together. It won't be so bad, you'll see.'

'I wish he wasn't going too, Kath,' Dad said. Mum looked at him, surprised. 'But I know deep down that it's for the best. He's a great laddie, our Kevin. And he'll make something of himself. Not like me. We'll be proud of him, Kath, and you'll even go and visit him some day.' Dad said it as if he meant it. He had been different towards Kevin after they had the big fight in the house, and the night of his party I had never seen them so close.

There was a knock at the door and I could hear Brendan O'Hanlon's voice shouting.

'G'day, Bruce,' he said in an Australian accent.

He walked into the kitchen, smiling, with Dessie at his back.

'How're you all doing? All set?' Brendan said, looking around. Dessie lifted a biscuit from the table.

'As ready as we'll ever be,' Mum said, getting up and clearing the dishes away.

Kevin and Dessie dragged his bags out to the van and stuffed them in the back. The two of them were laughing and slapping each other on the shoulder. They were excited and happy and I wished I could be like them, but I was miserable as we all prepared to walk out of the house. Kevin came back in, walked into the living room and took one last look around. He stood, nodded his head and smiled.

'Yeah . . . I'll miss it. I know that much. Part of me misses it already.' He threw his arms around Mum and squeezed her tightly. Dad put his hand on Kevin's shoulder.

'Come on,' he said. 'Don't get all sloppy.'

Kevin had his arm around Mum's shoulder as they walked down the path. She was sniffing, but laughing at the same time.

We all piled into the car and I remembered the morning we took Ann Marie to the bus stop. Why did it have to be like this? Why couldn't everything just be as it was before?

At the train station in Sunnyside, people milled around, saying goodbyes and pushing bags on to the carriage. I watched a boy and girl kiss for ages and wondered when they would come up for air.

This was the train that would take Kevin and Dessie to Glasgow, then another train to London for the special flight to Australia that would be filled with people with great high hopes.

A whistle blew and a voice shouted, 'All aboard.' We all looked at each other. It was really happening. Kevin put his arms around me and hugged me so hard I thought I would faint.

'Watch my pleurisy,' I said, through tears.

He laughed, but his eyes were filled with tears too.

'I'll see your beautiful face every day in my head, Kath. Your crazy curls and your big questioning eyes. I'll see them every day. And one day . . . one day . . . you'll just be there right in front of me. I promise.' Tears sprang out of his eyes.

Mum was already sobbing on Dad's shoulder. Kevin put his arms around them both. Dad's eyes were full of tears.

'I'm sorry, son,' he said to Kevin, his lip trembling. 'I'm sorry for that night. And for all the nights and days I let you down. And I'm proud of you, pal. I always have been. I . . . I just don't know how to say it, that's all.' Tears rolled down Dad's face.

'Aw, Da. Don't ... I am what you made me. You'll be proud ... honest. One day. Thanks, Da ... Thanks for everything.' They hugged. Dad stroked Kevin's hair as they held each other.

Kevin turned to Mum. 'I'll change my pants every day,' he laughed. 'And I'll miss you,' he said. 'More than you know. More than you'll ever know.' Mum dissolved into tears. 'And if I ever meet a woman like you, Ma ... I'll marry her straight away.' He laughed and wiped the tears from his cheeks.

'C'mon,' Dessie O'Hanlon said. His dad stood biting his lip. He was on his own now. His wife had died three years ago and now there was nobody.

Kevin ruffled my hair one last time and stepped off the platform and on to the train. The doors clunked shut one by one on every carriage and Kevin opened the window and stuck his head out. The train's whistle blasted and the metal wheels screeched and started turning. The train slowly pulled away, and with it the picture I would carry with me for the rest of my life. Kevin's eyes full of hope and excitement for this brave new world, yet his face wet with tears as he waved and waved until he was only a dot in the distance, still waving as he disappeared from view.

We walked out of the station and got into Brendan's van. Nobody spoke a word.

'Just let us out here,' Mum said. 'We'll walk up the hill to the bus station and meet Ann Marie. She should be here any minute.'

Mum, Dad and I got out of the car and waved Brendan off. We hurried along the road towards the foot of the hill and I slipped my hand into my dad's as we walked. He squeezed it and smiled down at me. I wondered if I would ever feel happy again, the way I used to, before Tony and before today.

Then somewhere on the brow of the hill I saw her. But it

couldn't be. We all saw her at the same time and we stopped in our tracks. We shaded our eyes from the sun with our hands to make sure that the figure coming into view was really her. There was no mistake. It was Ann Marie. And she was pushing a pram. I thought my heart was going to come right up and out of my mouth. Mum's eyes were wide with shock. Dad's mouth was half open. Ann Marie was waving furiously. She stopped at the top of the hill and waved both hands, just in case we weren't sure if it was her. I broke free of my dad's hand and ran towards her.

You can buy any of these other **Review** titles from your bookshop or *direct from the publisher*.

FREE P&P AND UK DELIVERY
(Overseas and Ireland £3.50 per book)

A History of Forgetting	Caroline Adderson	£6.99
The Catastrophist	Ronan Bennett	£6.99
The Mariner's Star	Candida Clark	£6.99
Hallam Foe	Peter Jinks	£6.99
The Gingerbread Woman	Jennifer Johnston	£6.99
The Song of Names	Norman Lebrecht	£6.99
In Cuba I was a German Shepherd	Ana Menéndez	£6.99
The Secret Life of Bees	Sue Monk Kidd	£6.99
My Lover's Lover	Maggie O'Farrell	£6.99
Early One Morning	Robert Ryan	£6.99
Missing	Mary Stanley	£6.99
The Long Afternoon	Giles Waterfield	£6.99

TO ORDER SIMPLY CALL THIS NUMBER

01235 400 414

or visit our website: www.madaboutbooks.com

Prices and availability subject to change without notice.